BAD MEDICINE

Rules of Magic, volume 1

Lance Horsman

Yamabushi Publishing

ISBN: 978-0-7961-2555-2 (Print)
ISBN: 978-0-7961-2556-9 (e-book)

Chapter 1: The rules of magic
Ghent, Belgium, not so long ago

Eddie burst through the open door as a rush of fire filled the passageway.

Instead of squinting back into the sudden inferno, he gripped the totem around his neck and channelled more bear. His skin tingled with power. He grew ever so slightly wider, and taller, and, after a few seconds, let out a soft, deep growl. Then he charged forward and dived through the cheap drywalling into the next room.

An oversized part-man, part-bear crashing through a wall like a juggernaut, knocking the table, chairs, and wall hangings through the air like a tornado in Kansas, was not what anyone expected. Let alone Chance, the infamous Louisiana Rat.

Chance yelped, backpedalled, and cast a leaping spell. As if shot out of a cannon, he flew through the doorway and out of the room. Eddie gave chase. Endowed with the strength of a bear, he could jump further and run faster, and – sadly for Chance – that meant he barrelled through the doorway, not too far behind.

Far enough, however, that Chance could pull some knives out of his backpack and start hurling them at the chasing mage. Three knives flew towards Eddie with dangerous precision, faster and more accurate than they had any right to be. Chance had cast The Gooseknife, an old spell, rarely used as the modern versions were quicker and required less power. Still, it was a beautiful spell, and Chance cast it well.

The deflection charm on Eddie's wrist hummed as it kicked out energy and two knives whistled past him. One knife still hit, slicing into the side of his arm – thankfully, a minor inconvenience to a man who had a hide as tough as a bear's.

Chance turned and ran again, slipping down an old, wooden, spiralling stairway lined with rich carpets. It looked like he was heading for the ground floor, fixing to make his escape into the road.

The fires behind him were beginning to die down, there were two daggers buried deep into a nearby wall, and in the room at the top of the stairway behind him, a drywall had been utterly destroyed. Thus far, Eddie mused, it was an interesting start to the morning.

He called after the fleeing wizard, "Chance, I just want to talk!"

Chance's breathless voice echoed up from the bottom of the stairwell, "That's what your mother said!"

Eddie shook his head. Everybody thought they were a fucking comedian. He bounded down the stairs in pursuit of the small, pale wizard from Louisiana, jumping four stairs at a time. Chance ran as fast as he could, but Eddie was gaining ground. The rat-like wizard dropped a smoke spell. Eddie had seen him use it before, and it was the go-to that Chance used for quick escapes. Eddie hit the small landing just above the ground floor, before the wood- and carpet-covered stairway dropped down to the rooms below. His khaki overcoat, with the bottom two buttons torn off, flew behind him as he leaped and landed, a bit like a light brown cape. He grinned at the thought – Captain Beige.

As soon as his feet hit the marble floor, Eddie carried on running, charging through the smoke Chance had dropped.

He made out the fleeing wizard faintly through the smoke. Chance was making for the front door, and then, presumably, out into the street.

Chance ran like a man who never ran. He was not athletic, or fit, or co-ordinated in any way. However, he was sneaky, and he was desperate. Also, he was a wizard with some power.

Eddie was gaining on Chance, for sure, but it looked like Eddie wouldn't be able to catch him before he got outside, and once there, escape options increased. Outside was good for Chance, but poor for anyone on his tail.

With his heart pounding, his breathing ragged and desperately sucking in buckets of air, Chance, streaming sweat, ran across the entrance hall, only feet away from the thick, dark, wooden front door.

Eddie hit the reception area and, with a single hand, ripped the fire extinguisher off an elegantly wallpapered wall. He threw it violently and powerfully at a fleeing Chance. To say that the fire extinguisher flew like a rocket would have been wrong. A rocket flies smoothly, and in a clear, beautiful trajectory. The extinguisher flew more like a plague-ridden corpse that had been flung through the air by a ballista, accelerating violently and crashing through the air with absolutely no consideration for grace or aerodynamics.

Spinning like an out-of-control, high-speed, car crash, the fire extinguisher thundered into Chance. It hit his back and broke his ribs, smashing him forward off his feet, launching him face-first into the front door, so hard that when he hit it his nose broke with a sound like a dog crunching a chicken bone.

Chance lay on the floor, suddenly unable to breathe through his nose, battling to get air into his lungs, his eyes watering, and his head ringing. It felt, for the fleeting seconds before he passed out, like everything was in pain.

*

Chance woke up.

He had never been a good-looking man. Pale and balding, with an ever-growing forehead and round, pouty lips, he increasingly reminded Eddie of a sex offender on a police most-wanted list. His perpetual state of sweatiness and nervous, rat-like disposition didn't help much. Now, he looked even worse than normal. With his broken nose, his eyes were ringed with a fantastic set of dark bruises, making him look like a scrawny raccoon. It was not a good look for him.

Eddie had duct-taped him to a chair. A salt

ring had been set around him, and Chance's hands had been placed in a rune-covered, velvet bag. Eddie had sprinkled enchanted silver dust on the Louisiana magician, and all in all, he had bought himself a few minutes at best.

None of the measures were significant enough to stop a caster like Chance permanently, and it was only a matter of time before he would be able to cast again. Eddie had no time to waste – in all honesty, he had never thought it would go down like this.

Chance had always been a reasonable guy. Questionable, yes, but reasonable. It wasn't like most of the magical community didn't surf a fine line between what was legal and outright criminality, but there were rules you just didn't break: the rules of magic.

Eddie pulled up a chair to face the Louisiana magus. "Chance, look at me."

Chance looked up.

"What the hell happened?" Eddie asked, his hands opening in an enquiring gesture.

Chance stayed silent.

"You need to speak to me, Chance. Let's figure this out together. Come on! You were casting unsunk magic. Big unsunk magic! Talk to me."

Eddie was fighting against his rising frustration. "You know that casting without a sink breaks shit and if you did it enough, we would have to stop you. You knew that exactly this was going to happen, but you did it anyway. You left us no choice."

Chance sat there, still silent.

Eddie – who was never that patient even at the best of times, and with residue of bear still running through his veins – was growing increasingly irate at Chance's silence.

Bear began to rise, unbidden, inside of him. Not just bear – like the kind in YouTube videos eating sandwiches at park benches at camping grounds, but Bear – the spirit that underpinned who and what the animal was. The archetype of what a bear was in the human psyche – strong, vicious, unrelenting, dangerous, powerful. One of the original dark forces that went bump in the night and gave our ancestors pause to leave their campfire.

The thing that rose up inside Eddie was one of the reasons we tell our children cautionary fairy tales at bedtime. Chance looked at Eddie and felt infinitely less safe. Eddie hadn't moved, but the space between them suddenly seemed crowded, teeming with tension and danger.

Even though Eddie's breathing hadn't changed, Chance felt suddenly warmed by the hot, near breath of a predator. On his intake of breath, Chance smelt something like wet fur. The damp of an ancient cave. The smell of old bones.

Eddie sat in the same chair, in the same position as a few scant seconds ago. The difference was that only an instant ago he had been a man, relaxed and in control, and now there seemed to be something else in his chair – something primal and wild, and entirely unpredictable.

Chance knew Eddie, and some others in the family too. Eddie was a tough guy, but basically a good guy. The family were like that. They did the right thing and kept their noses clean. To be fair, they helped others out if they slipped up because they knew what it meant to be a magic user – but he had never seen Eddie like this. The Bear this big and out of control. This was dangerous, and very scary.

But it still wasn't as dangerous or as scary as talking.

"Eddie," Chance spoke through a cracked and parched throat. Nervous tension pulled his neck taut and he shifted uncomfortably in his bonds. "Eddie," Chance began again. "You don't know what these guys are like. You don't know what you are asking me... what they'll do."

"Well, if you told me what I am asking, or maybe what these guys are like, we could do something. We're pretty tight with some powers. We could get you safe..."

"What do you mean, 'safe'? These guys own everything. They are everywhere..."

"Not in the Elven Kingdom, they aren't. If that isn't safe enough, I know some places in Mexico. Sko is the best tech mage in the world. We can keep you safe."

"Arguably."

"What?"

"Sko is *arguably* the best tech mage in the world."

Eddie felt the Bear begin to subside. Chance was talking, at least; this was a good sign.

"If I come, how would you get me out? They own this city."

"Eric Deschamps, the head of the Ghent coven. He and his team are on their way already. They'll cover your tracks, leak your death out to the press. We'll keep you enchanted until we drive across the border, then get a plane out of somewhere they'll never expect. What's more..." Eddie held up a black, passport-sized book. "I have one of these for you. They'll never know which plane you're on or under which name you flew, how it was paid, or which airport. These things are perfect and untraceable."

Chance exhaled, then inhaled. He seemed to be visibly calming himself down, like some sort of breathing exercise. He spoke again. "Okay, so maybe we can do this. Maybe you can get me out of here and get me in hiding. I suppose if anyone could do it, it's you guys. If half the stories are true, then, yeah, maybe. But what then? What happens when you get me to wherever I am going? How long do I stay there?"

Eddie held up his hands. "Calm down, Chance. We'll figure it out, we really will. I promise. Let's first just get you out of here with Eric's people – then we'll work out which plane and airport. One step at a time. We don't need to rush; we have some time..."

A floorboard creaked outside.

"It's them!" Chance screamed through his hoarse throat. "Get me out of this shit!" He frantically struggled against the tape, and the chair fell over, his head and neck landing outside the circle of salt.

Eddie felt a breeze whisper past him.

They had no more time.

A tall, lean gentleman stepped into the doorway. His face was all angles and bone, his jaw a lesson in acute geometry. He wore a tan leather fedora with a bright red feather in the brim. For most eccentric dressers, that would have been enough, but the mysterious stranger took it several large steps further. He wore a pair of black jeans, ripped enough to make any teenager proud, with a silk, turquoise shirt, and a pair of yellow braces. In his left hand, completing his look as a Disney villain, he held a magnificently polished walking stick. The head was a silver hand, holding a silver needle. Draped across his arm was a dark overcoat, damp from the light snow outside.

Eddie growled out words through gritted teeth: "And who the fuck are you?"

"I am the Stitchmaker... Of Ghent, obviously." He waved his walking stick around, as though that were a show of his claim to the city. He had a genteel, accented voice. "And you are?"

Eddie opened his mouth to answer, and he heard Chance kicking and squirming behind him. He turned to see a heavy-set man – equally outrageously dressed – blinking in and out of visibility, with his hands around Chance's neck. As Eddie turned, the Stitchmaker raised his walking stick, and brought it down swiftly towards Eddie's head. The walking stick glowed blue, and hummed with potency.

Sometimes, sadly, life is unfair. Sometimes our

best laid plans devolve into cheap halls and queues of followers handing out Kool-Aid in small South American countries. Today, life's great lesson turned out to be that swinging a magically powered walking stick at the head of Eddie Burma was an exceptionally bad idea.

Eddie dropped to the floor as the walking stick rushed at his head, and the Stitchmaker lurched unsteadily forward as the anticipated contact didn't come. Eddie launched himself from all fours into the body of his lean attacker, the power of the Great Bear instantly returned.

Eddie gripped the tall man's neck in his left hand, and his crotch in his right, and squeezed them both in a grip that could hoist well over a thousand pounds. He lifted, roaring, and pulped them as hard as he could.

A windpipe crushed and throat tendons ripped and tore beneath his hand. Testicles burst and Eddie leapt forward, in a movement reminiscent of a giant ape, and threw the strangely dressed gentleman – the Stitchmaker – through the door, his head and legs catching the doorframe on the way out. If he hadn't already been unconscious and soon to be dead, it would have hurt immensely.

A scream went out behind him – the gut-wrenching, soul-raking scream of someone who had just lost everything. The beefy man wearing an open leather biker's jacket and a hot pink vest charged forward, his eyes scrunched in tearful fury and his mouth snarling beneath a thick, black moustache.

As the raging, bereft man charged towards Eddie,

he suddenly disappeared, and a tug of wind gusted past Eddie, who turned to track the wind and got a meaty fist slamming into his face as Moustache reappeared behind him.

Again, sadly for the henchman, Eddie was as strong as an 800-pound grizzly bear. The punch, as impressive as it was, had the effect one might expect on a grizzly bear: it simply irritated him further.

Eddie responded with a slap that hit Moustache hard across the jaw. His head snapped to the side, and he slumped to the floor. Immediately, Eddie ran over to Chance, but the small man was dying. Ragged breaths were trying to come, but they could not. His eyes bulged, imploring Eddie to give him air, get some oxygen into his lungs. But by the time Eddie had crossed the room, it was too late. It had been too late the moment Moustache had gotten his garrotte around Chance's neck.

Chance clutched Eddie by the arm and, with his last vestige of breath, uttered his final, dying words: "Oddly... dressed..."

His head slumped onto the floor, and Chance Belaflor, the Louisiana Rat, was no more.

Eddie dialled Eric Deschamps and his clean-up crew, still not believing that he had to ask them to clean up Chance, as well as Stitchmaker and Moustache... for sure, two oddly dressed gentlemen.

Chapter 2: *No good deed goes unpunished*
Washington, then Colorado, USA

"Passport?"

Eddie handed his passport over the counter. The bored-looking lady on the other end – pretty, in a tight-bunned, naughty librarian kind of way – typed into her terminal, and after a cursory glance, stamped his passport and gave it back to him.

"Welcome home, Mr. Valdez. Safe travels back to Colorado."

Eddie nodded, took his passport back, and walked off to get his luggage.

Patently, he was not Enrique Valdez, but what was the point of being able to twist the fabric of space and time if you didn't have a magical passport that could get you in anywhere, through any official? Whomever the official was, you always looked as if you were exactly where you needed to be, with all the right details.

Eddie had a similar credit card, which he used from time to time: the black card – it worked at any bank in any country, in any currency, and there was no limit.

It sat in his wallet, alongside his gold card that he used in his business. He now used the gold card to buy a water and a handful of Snickers bars – because a man couldn't be too healthy. He ate a Snickers, pocketed the rest, and moved smoothly through baggage collection, then made his way to the gate for his connecting flight to Denver International.

Eddie slumped his meaty frame into an empty seat in the waiting area and flipped out his cellphone to check messages. He stashed his beanie and scarf in his jacket pocket, running his hand along a thick head of brown hair, thinning at the crown and at the temples – Stage 3 on the Norwood scale of male pattern baldness, apparently. Or so Maggie said.

Messages pinged through on his phone – a handful. Two from Maggie about a horse that needed to be seen to right away. He needed to call her the moment he landed at Denver.

Five messages from Wayne:

"Call me"

"Call me now"

"Burma!!!!"

"What the fuck"

"Seriously???"

Then a voice note:

"Eddie, where the fuck are you? Get your hand out of some horse's ass. There's some shit going down here, some old friends of ours."

And another:

"I'm not fucking kidding, Eddie. Shit is getting real! Call me, you non-call-returning fuck. I may not be around to take the call if shit carries on escalating like this!"

Eddie dropped his phone into his lap and hung his head in his hands. He sighed, breathing slowly, for a moment's peace.

He had just travelled halfway around the world to see the death of a mage, who – although he wasn't a friend – fell squarely into the acquaintance zone. It looked like he'd arrived home to a horse that probably needed a magical cure (that's why they came to him). Best horse man south of Denver, so it was said.

Then Wayne, a bar owner in Alamosa, source of information and occasional friend, was having some troubles – clearly. He was a panicky sort of guy, but the last time Eddie got messages like this, it was pretty bad. Particularly ominous was the phrase "our friends". A local witch group, *los Alamosa Brujos*, had stirred up some pretty bad local nasties before, and Eddie had put them down. If they were back to their business again, somehow… things would not be good.

They were big, and had their hands into all sorts – drugs, prostitution… rumoured connections to South American cartels. That was just what he didn't need right now.

Eddie's phone made one more ding.

He looked down warily – it was a message from Sko, Eddie's best friend, mage extraordinaire, and the nominal head of the informal group of mages who lived in the Southwestern United States.

"Hey, Eddie – I hope you're okay after things in Belgium? Let me know. I have some news for you – I think you'll like it. Give me a call when you hit the ranch. Adios!"

Oh well, at least not all of the messages were shit. Eddie settled in for a quick nap before his flight was called.

*

The long-stay parking at Denver International was always overpriced, and Eddie always paid, because sometimes you just needed to be the bigger guy – besides, at some level, money was meaningless to him. He could always make more using magic, or barter with some other user for what he wanted. There was always a way. Put it like this: there was no mage alive worth their oats who went hungry at night, unless they wanted to.

Eddie, beanie and scarf back on (because it was late November in Colorado – the sun hadn't set yet and it was already below zero), still had a four-hour drive back to his ranch outside Fort Garland. It was going to be a cold one tonight, and if it snowed hard, it could be a tough drive back home.

He approached his 1976 Ford F100, white with a thick, cherry-red stripe along the side and a small advert in oval on the side of the front door: "Fort Garland Vet", the phone number and a website.

He tossed his bag onto the passenger seat. She started perfectly, and on the first click, her massive, 5.9-

litre V8 turned over and she started to rumble. Eddie smiled and patted the dash gently.

"That's my girl," he said, and drove off into the late afternoon sun, hoping to get home before 8pm.

En route, he made some calls. The first was to Margret – Maggie. She ran the front desk at the Vet and helped him on the occasional field call.

She picked up on the second ring.

"Hey, Mags."

"Hey, Eddie. How was the flight?" Eddie could hear the concern in Maggie's voice – she was 5 foot 4, with a heart 8 foot tall and 10 foot wide. Maggie was the nicest person Eddie had ever met, and he was glad she was in his life. Professional life, that is.

"It was alright," he replied. "Glad to be back."

"Everything okay in Europe? Are the equine of the royal houses behaving?"

Eddie grinned wryly at the lie he'd had to tell her. "Ahh, all good," he prevaricated. "Just want to get home. So, tell me: sounds like we have a mare in distress?"

"Glad you got the message. Yup, Eric Johnson over at the Y-O Bar had his old mare jump at something on a ride in the creek at the back of his place. She came down hard, and if you ask me, she's broken a back leg. But he won't see it. He's adamant that Doc Ed can perform a miracle cure, the way he done with the pups."

There was disbelief in her voice, but some desperation there too. Ed could smell it a mile off. Eric

Johnson was well loved in the area, and his mare Sheila Run was loved by loads of the local kids as she'd been the first horse that many of them had ridden. Eric would break hard if she died. If he went to almost any other vet, she probably would.

"Okay, Maggie. You call Eric, tell him I'll be there in four hours. He's to keep her warm and comfortable and, obviously, off the leg."

"Righto, boss."

"Then you go to the office and get my green box that sits near the back door."

"The big plastic one, heavy and smells funny?"

Eddie laughed. "That's right. It's full of old Indian herbs, so it doesn't smell great. Anyway, load that in your car, and meet me at Eric's place near 8pm. Make sure you got a big coffee on hand–"

"...and a Snickers in reserve, to keep you going."

"You evil woman!"

"That's me, evil to the core," she giggled. "Thanks, chief. If you can do something... well, even if you can't, I'm sure that Eric will be glad to know you're on the way."

"Righto. See you in four hours."

The next call was to Sko.

"Hey, Sko. I got your message."

"Good. How are you holding up, my friend?"

"Mmm... well, Europe was... tough. I can't

believe Chance was killed and we didn't even get anything. And also, those weird guys who came, all maged up, but not expecting to meet me. Clearly, there's a shitload here that we don't know."

"I'm sorry," Sko commiserated. "I really am – I never meant for it to end that way. I never in a thousand years thought he'd do anything so serious that they'd send guys after him. He was too petty, you know? He's just never been the type."

"I know," Eddie continued, all business. "Eric from the coven got Chance's body and took photos of the other two guys... you got the pics?"

"I have. We'll figure them out and get to the bottom of this. Don't worry about that for now though, Ed. This mystery will hold – we can still tackle it tomorrow, or the next day, or next week, or whenever. But Eddie, listen: I need you to know that we did the right thing in chasing Chance down. This was his choice, not yours, okay? He was deep into something bad, and we're the guys who stop that sort of thing. Right now, I'm more concerned about you. How are you really doing?"

Eddie shrugged to himself. "Okay, I guess. Maybe I haven't really processed... I don't know. You know me and feelings. I take my time, right? Look, I'm not feeling too bad. I mean, he was definitely into something rotten. Who knows where it could have ended up?"

"Damn right. You did the right thing, Ed. Now, why I messaged..."

"Listen, Sko, I can't take anything big on right

now. It's looking like I'm going to be walking into some shit with the Alamosa coven again."

"Ed, don't get involved in this – if it's crime, it's not our bag. They have the police for this. We only step in if they're breaking magic."

"Well, I don't know what it is, Sko. I need to have look at least. Wayne called me, as panicked as a hen in a foxhouse. But I give you my promise: if it's local crime stuff, I'll leave it to the Sheriff's Department."

"Good. Then make sure you get to the bus stop in Fort Garland tomorrow at 3. You need to pick up your new apprentice."

Eddie paused.

His hand slid into his jacket pocket. He pulled out a Snickers and bit the wrapper off before putting half the Snickers in his mouth.

"Jesus, Sko!" Eddie mumbled through half a bar of nougat and nut. "You can't just drop this shit on me. The answer's no. Why the fuck me?"

"We all get them, Ed. I've had two – and besides, she looks to be an animal mage like you..."

"She?"

"That's right. Her name is Mathilda. I'll send you a pic and her details. Be nice."

"But..."

Sko put the phone down.

"Jesus, fuck," Eddie exclaimed to the empty car. "I should've stayed in Belgium!"

He threw his phone onto the seat next to him, and shoved the rest of the Snickers in his mouth.

Chapter 3 : A change in time
Montgisard, Kingdom of Jerusalem, 1177

The sound of battle grew dim. The riot of men screaming, the clash of weapons and the thunder of hooves, the vain struggles of desperate warriors – all receded into the background. His vision grew narrow until his eyes were thin slits straining up against the blue sky. His breathing became shallow and, despite the sun, he was cold. He couldn't feel his legs. A thought pulled at him from a long distance away... he was dying. He sighed. And then his eyes closed.

The darkness was soft.

Suddenly, bright, intense light, and an intake of breath! His lungs seemed to explode at the taste of air, glorious and sweet. After a moment, his vision shifted and normalised. The ringing in his head stilled, and gradually, his senses returned.

Mathieu was still on the field of battle. He lay on a mound of grass, staring up at the sky, except where it was blocked by the silhouette of a man – a priest. It was old Thesibides, the Greek. He nodded gently and took his hand off the knight's chest.

Smiling through an exhausted mask of dark, wrinkled skin and a pointed white beard, the old priest raised his hand, and pointed into the distance. Mathieu marvelled at the thin, papery texture of the old man's hand. The bend of his yellowing fingernails, and the flecks of dried blood on his skin. He wondered if he would ever live long enough for his skin to get that thin, and for his knuckles to get that gnarled and bent.

He grimaced, steeling himself, then breathed in deeply, and sat up. Surprise registered on his face because the grimace had been unnecessary. There was no more pain in his chest. There was no more pain anywhere, not even in his bad hip, or the knuckle he had broken as a child, hitting the baker's boy because he made soft words with Melody. Melody of the big blue eyes and long blonde plait the colour of wheat. He had not thought about her in years – maybe it was the battle, or his proximity to death. This time had been his closest – the old Greek priest did not tend to you unless it was dire. If he died today, would he see her, pale and beautiful as she was the day he had seen her last? A small cough of blood on her lip, skin pale, her big blue eyes closed for good. Would she be there to meet him, he wondered? He hoped so.

Mathieu reached for his mace and shield, and made his way towards the centre of battle.

*

A running boy, surely not much older than 16, died with his face mashed in by Mathieu's bloody mace. He had been fleeing from the battle so fast, he hadn't even realised that he had been going in the wrong direction. By the time he saw the large knight, it was a split-second before the mace cracked his skull in. Dazed, and not yet dead, he fell to his knees and dropped his short spear, which, in truth, he had been clutching out of reflex more than anything else. Mathieu's second strike caved in the side of his head and face, and from there, the boy fell to the floor and bled out, thankfully unconscious as he died.

Mathieu's next kill was a large, bearded qaraghulam rolling on the floor in mortal struggle with a young, leather-clad Frank. He, too, never saw the blow that killed him, but Mathieu hit him several times, because he kept on stumbling away, as if trying to escape by some unconscious instinct, like a chicken without its head.

The Frank – Jules was his name – decided that behind Mathieu was the safest place to be, and so he fell in behind the advancing knight. Mathieu was grateful to have someone covering his back.

A short while later, they entered the main battleground. The rough hillside, littered with clumps of long, yellow grass and brown rocks, sloped gently down to a small river churned into dark mud on either side. The slopes were strewn with corpses and those not quite yet corpses. Broken spears, rendered shields, and riven armour. The smell of blood was thick in the air. It was quiet near the top of the hill, with the occasional moan from some poor unfortunate not yet dead, but as they made their way closer to the river, the fighting had been heavier, and more recent, and so men were clamouring for help. Some groaned unintelligibly, like an animal that keens as the abattoir knife whets on the stone. Some crawled through the mud, dragging their body, or their limbs, out of the river towards dryer and higher ground, as if it were their salvation.

Already, some of the Turkish skirmishers had begun to loot the dead and dying – Jules swore at a pair of ragged spearmen who were tugging the armour off a man, who clung to it, whilst he moaned in protest. They pulled anyway, ignoring the moans of the injured man, as well as Jules. Jules tugged at Mathieu's sleeve. "But if he survives, he will need it."

"If," said Mathieu, who looked down and focused on his footing through the river.

He paused, in the middle of the stream, the water just over his knees. The water was cool, and he liked the way it brushed against his boots. Further up the hill ahead, the Crusader forces were converging on a rocky outcropping where the fighting was fiercest.

At this stage of the battle, many of the Frankish knights were unhorsed, fighting alongside the infantry. Mathieu could make out the banner of Eudes de Amand amongst the rolling mass of steel-encased men and battling Mamluk soldiers. He saw none of the other leaders, but Eudes would do fine. Around him, would be the bulk of his men – the men of the Knights Templar. Mathieu's brothers in arms.

He pointed towards the hub of the battle with his mace.

"Jules? See Eudes and the Templars battling that knot of qaraghulams in front of the Mamluk askar?"

"Oui!"

"Our destination."

*

The tide had turned – the day was almost won. Like a bulwark against the onrushing sea, the small force of Templars had broken every single attack of the Mamluks. Eudes – Odo to his friends – master of the Templars, stood over the battlefield like Ares. His tabard was ripped, armour blackened, and pot helm dented and bent. The red cross still stood out proudly on his black kite shield, and a morning star hung loosely in his right hand, its heavy, flanged head resting on the ground. Shield strapped to his arm, he raised his visor, and took a view over the field of battle. Blood ran down his forearm as he raised and lowered it again. Every muscle ached, his breathing was ragged, and his shield felt heavy. In truth, no tale of a priest's most prolific torment from hell could compare with what lay around him: a field of broken bodies seemingly disgorged by a distempered earth, and all of it wrought by the hand of man. On the battlefield of Montgisard, thousands of bodies lay broken, cut, ripped, beaten, and dying. Men bled silently, hoping to close their eyes and fade away. Others protested all the way to their maker, screaming on their way out of this world, just as they had screamed coming in. Most suffered in some way, because the deaths visited upon them on a battlefield were not easy ones. Silently or screaming, they all died, one way or another.

War was hell but, as it turned out, hell was his business.

The day had started well. Saladin, as wily a Saracen as had ever walked God's green earth, had chased all before him as his Mamluk legions had swept along the coast, towards Jerusalem, the great prize.

Philip of Alsace – a strutting ponce of a man, unfortunately, born into wealth and power – had taken the bulk of the Christian forces to Syria, leaving the Kingdom of Jerusalem woefully undermanned, with less than 500 horses, and only 80 Templars. Saladin planned to take full advantage of the error. The Ayyub army had spent two weeks chasing shadows as the mobile and grossly outnumbered Christian army had danced before them, enticing them deeper into the hills and swamps. Looting and pillaging the cities of the coast, the Ayyubs had become slow, and, given the river crossings, swampland, and hills between Jaffa and Jerusalem, increasingly spread out. What this ultimately meant was that an unsuspecting, stretched-thin, ill-prepared Mamluk army would get caught between the anvil of infidel ill-discipline and the hammer of the most powerful heavy cavalry in the world.

The day had begun as intended, with a momentous cavalry charge of knights breaking the Ayyub centre. The Saracens had broken, and the Christian infantry had poured into the breach. The infidel had fallen like Philistines at Samson's feet, but the Christians were too few, and the Ayyub too many. Despite corpses piling up high, friend falling upon friend, ghulams tripping over the bodies of their brothers, the day was not yet over. On the strength of sheer numbers, the Ayyub had rallied behind Ahmed Ad Din in what was a brave charge, inspired, and worthy of a Christian. It was this charge that had bunched the Mamluk cavalry and heavy spearmen up against the remaining knights of Jerusalem atop a small hillock just off Montgisard. Despite the slaughter – it may have been for naught. A vainglorious bloody day out in the sun.

Unless they could end it.

The grand master felt his age. He let his shield drop to the ground and pulled his visor down. Now the final act would begin. He sunk to his knees and began to summon potency. The world receded into the background, as it always did when he drew on the power at his disposal. He felt the familiar rush of dynamism, of spark, of life directly from God that coursed through his veins. Once, in the north of Castile, he had stood under a waterfall as warm as the queen's bath. He had never forgotten that feeling, because it was the closest thing he could use to describe how his power felt as it surged through him. His armour glowed as it sunk the time off his casting. What was the use of being a grand master if you couldn't use magical armour?

As he drew in power, his armour began to warm. Sweat dripped down his forehead, his skin tingled, and he found himself clenching his teeth, to help hold it all from seeping out. Standing, the old warrior glowed, red light pushing through his armour. He shone like the afternoon sun.

A qaraghulam broke through the steel cordon of tightly pressed Frankish warriors and chased to the commander standing on his own. It was a brave and valorous deed, but unfortunately one that could only ever end poorly. Odo de Amand ran forward four quick steps to meet his would-be attacker, his morning star dragging furrows behind him through the dense brown dirt. Suddenly, he whipped his weapon up into the face of his assailant, the tall and lean captain of the Mamluk guard. The captain brought his thick-bladed falchion smashing down toward the neck of the grand master. The flanged, dirt- and gore-covered steel head of the morning star hit the chest of the onrushing veteran. The impact was colossal. The morning star exploded through the air and tore up the torso of the unfortunate Mamluk, throwing him upward and backward. From a particular perspective, one might have said it was as graceful as it was unexpected. The captain's body rose through the air, curved backwards in a long, reaching arc – not unlike a crescent moon – and collapsed into the dirt in a messy, bloody pile. Once the back of his head had slammed into the ground, his chest and body piled on top of it and his legs came toppling over. All in all, it was a spectacular strike, but over in little more than a second.

Odo advanced towards the hard-pressed line of Frankish steel. Blows were raining down upon them. Shields locked; axes and spear tips fell. It was an almighty tussle. Odo de Amand was about to end the stalemate. He hoped.

The grand master ran towards the line, leapt onto a rock and then atop a waist-high pile of the dead, and used that to springboard up and over the front press of bodies. He sailed through the air, morning star whipped up over his head and spinning in a circle as he fell to the earth. As he landed, with his momentum, his magical power, and all his might, he slammed the morning star into the ground with both hands, casting the one spell he knew, that he had never cast before.

"*Invictus!*" he shouted, casting it with all that he had.

The impact of the flail sent a magically inspired shockwave rippling through the surrounding soldiers, propelling them backwards in an explosion of heavenly energy. Men flew in all directions as the circle of force expanded, surging to a radius of almost 25 feet.

It was not enough to defeat the enemy. But it was enough to open a hole in their shield wall and let in his army of trained warriors... and that was enough to defeat the enemy.

Aglow in red, the grand master of the Templars

stood up, and called on his troops to follow.

*

Mathieu, with Jules behind him, charged into the gap. The grand master had been magnificent. He had torn the enemy apart and opened up their formation in a formidable display of might, then he had set upon them with the strength and endurance of a much younger man. Mathieu was proud of what his grand master had done.

Mathieu ran into the fray and met a thrown spear with upraised shield. He charged deeper in towards the centre of the battle and hooked a scything war hammer out of the air with his mace, before returning his weapon's direction and landing a glancing blow on his opponent. Not enough to harm, but enough for him to scramble out of the way so another could step into his space. A spear thrust out from behind Mathieu and caught the next incoming warrior in his arm, and Mathieu took his knee. The man fell and Mathieu gave him a heftier dose of fury before he stepped on to the next one, letting Jules finish him off with another spear strike. And so the afternoon went.

As the sun threatened to set, dousing the sky flame red, the battle was well and truly won. Ahmed Ad Din, son of Saladin's nephew, fought bravely. His strength would not flag; his courage would not fail him. It was not his life that he feared losing, but that his general would fail. His life was a gift to give in the service of God.

As his men charged to his defence, they were cut down by heavily armoured Templar knights. Spearmen harried their flanks, and the hated Crusaders still harassed their fringes – on tired horses with weary bow arms, but still deadly. Their time would come soon. Every man among them knew it. They would die today; that was a certainty. But tonight, they would dine in paradise.

A tall knight in the hated tabard of the Templars hacked his way through a line of men, long axe smashing through raised shields, steel-clad fist pumping furiously into arms and faces. His long axe rose and fell, again, and yet again. Every time it fell, another brother died. Ahmed stepped up to face the long-limbed adversary. Spear against long axe – this fight would not last long. Ahmed shoved his spear tip towards the join at the top of the knight's leg, but it was knocked away with the butt of the axe. Ahmed rapidly drew his spear back and shot its tip in the direction of the knight's throat.

The knight was a veteran and was faster in his heavy armour than one might have thought. He shifted to the right and the back of his axe head caught the spear tip and knocked it away, and before Ahmed could pull it back, he stepped forward, in reach of the Ayyub commander. Ahmed scrambled backwards, his heel catching on an upraised root, and he fell heavily to the ground.

In the end, his life was worth an upraised root. He shifted and squirmed, but the downstrike of the long axe caught his chest. He rolled away, but the next strikes caught his leg, and then his back. He fumbled at the dirt, trying to pull himself to safety, but the last strike hit him in the side of the neck. It was a strange thing to smell his own blood leaking out of his throat.

Ahmed Ad Din closed his eyes, never to open them again.

Frederic of Köln stood up straight. His back was killing him. That last fight had tweaked something. It had been a long day of killing, and he would be glad of having it behind him. He didn't see the sword that caught him in the rerebrace, slamming into him just below the shoulder, sliding down his arm, biting sharply into his left elbow. He winced and stumbled, turning to see the face of his attacker change from victory to dismay, as a spear caught him in the side. Frederic saw a young Frankish soldier leaning into the spear, driving the Saracen two steps away and into the ground. As he pulled the spear out, a short, powerful Templar stepped in and batted aside the attacker's upraised arm with the tip of his kite shield, and followed it up with a deadly mace strike, caving in the man's head. There was only one knight he knew that could handle a mace like that.

"Mathieu!" Frederic raised his good arm in thanks.

"*Mon frere!*" Mathieu tapped his mace to his helm in salute.

"Look!" Jules pointed his spear, and they turned to see at what.

Saladin was racing from the Kingdom of Jerusalem on a camel, bobbing along in its ungraceful gait. His entourage swarmed around him, seeking to protect him from the barbs of any Crusader troops in range. Behind them, a group of horses was giving chase. Raynard, cousin to the king, was in the vanguard of the pursuers, his hatred for Saladin burning hot, despite a long day of fighting in the sun.

Mathieu moved to stand alongside Frederic, who

was still clutching his injured elbow. Jules approached and stood with them and, shortly afterwards – the fighting now done – came Eudes de Amand, the black-armoured grand master. Some others joined them. All eyes were on the race in the distance – horse and camel, tracking across the sands towards Jaffa.

Visors were raised, and hands lifted to shield eyes against the afternoon sun. Men watched the chase unfold in silence.

To the east, a lone figure on horseback crested a ridge that put him within 200 paces of the fleeing Ayyub leader, albeit almost a quarter of that up off the desert floor. The figure could never get there in time, but he had time for a shot with his bow at least.

From this distance, Odo knew him.

"It's Mustafa-Oglu Emin – Emin, the son of Mustafa," Odo told his comrades. "He's a captain in the skirmishers and one of the surest hands I have seen with a bow. I think he has a chance of making this!" Surprise registered in his voice – he had thought that Saladin was all but gone. The grand master did not believe that Saladin would be captured by the king's cousin – the Ayyub leader had too great a lead. But now, with Emin dropping off his horse and planning a shot at the fleeing, richly armoured foe, Odo thought they may have a chance.

"Say," Jules piped up from behind Mathieu. "A silver penny says our man doesn't make the shot!"

Odo turned briefly to regard the boy with his stern and grizzled visage. "Our Lord cast out the moneylenders from the temple, if I recall, boy?"

Jules visibly shrank.

"But a fair wager amongst Christian men of

honour should not be turned from lightly, either." A smile tugged at the corners of the grand master's mouth. They had, after all, recorded a famous victory today. "If Emin makes the shot, I'll take your penny, boy. If he misses, I'll pay you twice that!"

Cheers went up from the surrounding men. Not one to miss out on the action, Frederic chimed in: "I will take a piece of that! Same odds as the grand master. You have the pennies, boy?"

"*Oui*! Of course! After today's victory, every soldier has the pennies!"

Mathieu burst out laughing and clapped Jules on the back. "True that! Just don't gamble it all away before you get to spend it!"

"Come, friends!" Frederic called them to focus. "Let us see our man take on this task, worthy of Roland himself!" They stood alongside each other in silence.

It was a surreal scene. Around them, the dead and the dying made oddly shaped mounds across the plains, hills, and swamps of the Kingdom of Jerusalem. Over 20 000 men lay spread out in a map of carnage, a gruesome artwork painted in blood and broken bone by these standing knights gathered, who were surely master painters.

The setting sun glowed red and the sky faded orange through pink and blue. A dust trail in the distance betrayed the fleeing Ayyub leader and what was left of his retinue. The small hill that gave them their vantage point became still.

On the eastern hill, Emin, son of Mustafa, had braced his feet, bow in one hand and arrow in the other. With the light fading rapidly, and the speed of the escaping riders, he would only have time for one shot. In the distance, the fleeing Saladin changed his escape angle to evade the pursuing Crusader cavalry. Emin adjusted his feet. He looked up into the sky, and felt the wind gently flap the torn edges of his robes. He looked down again, nocked his arrow, and raised his bow. The short skirmisher bow would be at the edge of its effective range. It could still kill.

He drew back, a solitary form on the hillside as evening's shadows crept ever closer in. An out-breath. He loosed his arrow.

At first, it looked like he had shot too high, and sighs from the watching knights gave away their disappointment. But the arrow lost some of its power as it climbed. It slowed, and its barbed tip began to describe a graceful, downward course that looked like it would meet up directly with the galloping Ayyub party. Hope raised in the Christian onlookers once more.

The arrow plummeted with the speed of a peregrine falcon, and just as deadly for any in its approach. The arrow tracked on a path that looked like it may hit the fleeing Saracen general. As it neared, on a flight arc that seemed to take forever, confidence in its success shifted from uncertainty to hopeful conviction, to absolute surety that it could not miss. With mere feet until impact, the arrow had no way left for it *not* to hit.

It was travelling so fast, and in the dark, and the dust, and the panic of retreat, Saladin had not even seen the arrow. It seemed that the first time he would be aware of it, would be when it pierced his lungs and took his life.

But time is not what we think it is. Nor is reality. These can be playthings – like putty in the wet hands of a craftsman, or clay in the hands of a ceramicist – if you knew how to bend such forces.

Time stopped. And in that instant – that one brief, shining instant – the arrow shifted to the right by a hair's breadth.

Time continued again, and the rider next to the great Saladin flew back out of his saddle as the arrow, unseen as a ghost in the night, took him in the neck.

In an instant, the flow of history had changed. The course of time had shifted, and things were now what they should never have been.

Odo muttered under his breath with a heavily furrowed brow. They had won for today. Their victory was resolute and undeniable. Bells would proclaim their success across every church in Christendom. But something had just happened, and he wasn't exactly sure what it was. With Raynard and the other knights giving chase, it was time he got back to the king. The day would need some celebration.

He turned to leave, and gave a gentle punch to Frederic on his chest plate. "Pay the boy, will you?" He motioned to Jules. Then the grand master of the Knights Templar walked back to where he had left his horse, across a field that was more charnel house than grassy plain.

"Well, then," Frederic was still clutching his arm, a wide grin across his friendly face despite the discomfort. "It seems I owe you some silver, *Monsieur*?"

Jules bowed. "Jules Montclerc, at your service."

"Right, Jules. I have a fire on at my campsite, and I have the most gorgeous, tanned Persian woman in the world, who cooks with spices like you have never tasted, roasting a lamb with such mastery it would make your heart weep to taste it only once. What say you to you and Mathieu coming over and giving me a chance to dice my silver back?"

"Aye!" Mathieu stepped in between the two men. "Of course he accepts, doesn't he, Jules?"

"Yes," said Jules. "Of course!"

Chapter 4: *The reason for the name*
Southern Colorado

Driving down from Colorado City and turning off the highway at Walsenburg, travellers hit the R160 – a road that morphs from a single to a double lane and back to a single again as it stretches across the great state of Colorado. The R160 swoops beneath Silver Mountain, under Slide Mountain, eases on past Mount Lindsey, and finally bows low at the feet of the towering Blanca Peak, the tallest summit in the Sangre de Cristo range.

The Navajo call the mountain *Sis Naajin.* The locals say it means "white coat", because of the white covering the mountain gets over winter. In truth, they don't know the real reason, because it scared them too much as children. It scared them so much that they couldn't repeat it to their own children, and would rather forget it altogether. Not that it would make the reason go away, but most people would rather *feel* safe, than actually be safe. The locals can forget the reason, but the reason might not forget the locals.

Driving on past Blanca Peak, past Fort Garland and on towards Alamosa, there is a biker bar; a small, dingy building with two gas pumps off to the side and a beer barrel over the front door bedecked in fairy lights. A dirty sign – The Beer Keg – painted in white on a dull, red background was mounted on the rough, grey wooden facade.

Given the swooping and sliding of the road, the gorgeous rolling hills, mountainous vistas, and blue sky so tall it pushes the heavens back, the R160 was a popular ride for groups of bikers out for the weekend, and this weekend was no exception.

"Hello, Sheriff Barnes. Can you hear me? It's me, Annie, from the Keg... No... Sheriff? Goddamn door... Lemme just..."

Annie dropped the phone onto the table and walked over to the door leading into the bar and slammed it shut with her hip. It stuck, still partially open, and she got it good on her second swing. The door screeched as wood scraped on wood, and slid home into the door frame.

The office suddenly became a lot quieter, the noise from the bar muffled. Annie would have a time getting the door open again, but at least now she could speak. She picked up the phone again, sliding it beneath her bob of shocking red hair, and placed it against her ear.

"Hello, Sheriff Barnes?"

"Hey, Annie, how's the beer at the Keg tonight?"

"Fine," said Annie – she always began this way. "It's just that there's some mighty mean-looking fellas in tonight – those Diablo guys from New Mexico. And with it being month-end... I just, well... you said if ever I was worried, I should call?" She shrugged, even though she was on the phone.

"Thanks, Annie... Geez, the line's bad... Yeah, Annie, I appreciate the call. You got some Diablos

Cuchillos in the bar tonight? They're bad *hombres*. I'll send some deputies around. Tell Tom to rein his neck in and not get rough with them. I know he's tough, but these are bad guys – you understand? I'll send a car around now, okay?"

Annie nodded. "Okay, Sheriff." She put the phone down and struggled with the door, opening it again after some tugging and scraping. The music from the jukebox, the click of pool balls, and patrons shouting across the bar settled on her like the arm of an old friend as she walked out. Best to let Tom know that the sheriff had a car on the way. He was tough as leather, old Tom, and she'd seen him in a scrap or two over his years at the door, but these Diablos were bad men and she wouldn't like to see anything happen to Tom. Not after all these years.

Annie walked out from behind the bar, past Suzie, Matt, and Debs serving up drinks, and surfed through the waves of bodies out for a Friday night post-payday drink. As she did, she saw the three Diablos Cuchillos at a pool table, one sitting on a stool, the other two passing a stick back and forth with some ranch boys.

Her grandma used to say that folks like that had bad air around them. She felt the bad air, as if wherever they stood there were just too many shadows.

The one on the stool looked at her – directly at her. He knew she had been watching him, and, with a smile, silver teeth showing through thin, split lips, he winked at her and nodded his head. A lone, long lock of black hair fell around the front of his face, and for a moment she felt a chill. Lazily, he turned his head back towards his friends around the pool table, but Annie couldn't hear what he said. She carried on over to Tom at the door who, despite his years, and that cut across his forehead, still looked good with that tight, black tee stretched across his chest and arms.

He propped his tanned, muscled bulk against the doorframe. Standing next to him, speaking closely, was a girl young enough to be his daughter. Perks of the job, Annie supposed, because the pay was shit and the hours were long. Didn't apply to her, though. Her perks were getting to call the sheriff and dealing with criminal bike gangs. Life was not fair sometimes.

"Tom!" she shouted, but he didn't hear her over the music. She put a hand on his arm, and he looked at her, whispered some sweet nothing into the white miniskirt's ear, and bent down to Annie's level.

"Hey, Annie." His voice gruff and manly, he tilted his face towards her and he smelt of horse and sweat and beer. Annie could have hit that miniskirt skank with a bottle. Damn, Tom smelt fine.

"What's up?"

Annie leant in and placed her forehead against Tom's temple, her lips almost touching his ear. She suddenly became acutely aware of how close she was to him. If she stuck her tongue out, just a bit, she could get it in his ear. Just a taste.

"Annie!" Tom's voice seemed to call her through a fog. "What's up? You fine?"

"Sure, sure," Annie blurted. "The sheriff 's

sending a car around just in case. He says you stay away from the Diablos."

He nodded, eyes glancing over to the white miniskirt. "Sure, Annie. Whatever." Tom clearly had other ambitions for the night.

Annie turned around to head back behind the bar, and paused – her way was blocked by three men walking out. Three bad men. In the centre, the long, dark-haired leader of the Diablos Cuchillos, with a henchman on either side.

He was long and lean, with silver in his teeth, lanky, dark hair that fell to his chest, and tattoos showing on his neck and hands. He wore a heavy, black leather biker's jacket and boots over black jeans. The others were dressed to the same theme, adorned with over-large, silver belt buckles and heavily ringed fingers.

The patch on the frontman's jacket said, "*El Capitan*", above a stylised picture of a red Satan with horns, hooves, and a pointed tail, brandishing a knife. The devil's knives. *Los Diablos Cuchillos*.

Annie scrambled out of the way and they walked past her, past Tom, and out into the parking lot to their bikes.

It was cold out, but not snowing yet, even if there was still some snow on the ground from earlier in the day. Annie was relieved when the throaty growl of their bikes started up, and they headed off into the cold night.

*

A narrow promontory of land that headed out over Acre's Canyon started out flat, and rose up to a point, giving it the look of an old Navajo tent at the end of a stretch of land. Some people called it the Tepee, or Tepee Rock. Those less inclined to speak softly in front of children or old women called the rock the Teat. And still those who remember what their grandparents had called it and knew what it had been called back then – they called it the Witch's Teat.

Three motorcycles, growling against the still of the night, headlights yellow beams through the dark, curved off the R160 and took the short, winding road. All in all, just over 100 yards from the road to the beginning of the promontory.

They stilled their engines just at the point where the promontory left the land, reaching out into the canyon, a brown finger of rock just over ten yards wide, tapering to a point where it rose up in a triangular spire, sharp and dark – like the teat of a witch.

Leo, captain of the Diablos, got off his bike, swinging his leg over the seat in a smooth and practiced action. He reached into his saddlebag and pulled out a heavy, sawn-off shotgun. He checked in his jacket pocket for his brass knuckles, and in his boot for his knife. He looked at his men – they were doing the same.

"Carlito," he waved at the man to his left. "Go up onto those rocks over there, near where Padrino goes to piss, and take the rifle with you. I want some eyes from above."

"*Si, patron.*" Carlito hopped off his bike, pretty nimble for a guy carrying all that weight, and walked up a narrow path to his left that led to a small overlook, some twelve yards up. He had an old Mannlicher hunting rifle. Old, but accurate. Carlito had shot in the army, and he could put cans down across a football pitch. Leo felt happier that Carlito was watching over.

"Colin," Leo called the other Diablo over. He was the youngest of the three, newer to the gang, but already a made member, fully patched. He carried a pair of six-shooters that he was now belting on, like some fucking cowboy from the movies. He was fast with them though, and he was accurate.

Leo closed one nostril and shot a wad of snot out of his nose onto the ground, then wiped his nose with the back of his hand.

Being fast against paper targets is one thing. Being fast against some *pendejo* shooting the fuck out of you was another.

"Bring the bags, put them here in front of the bikes."

Colin nodded and pulled a pair of dirty canvas saddlebags off his bike, then pulled another one off Carlito's bike and another from Leo's.

Four bags in all. Three had drugs, one other had herbs and medicines from Mexico.

"Careful with that bag," Leo motioned with his

shotgun. "That one's worth more than all the others put together."

"Fucking joke, *esé*. We deal more blow and weapons than anybody in this county and we're worried about a bag of old Mexicans herbs."

"Joke's on you, *pendejo*." Leo was dismissive of the younger biker, with his six-guns and education. Thought he knew something, but he knew nothing. "These fuckers are *brujo*. Not like when your aunty reads a palm, but real *brujo*. Evil shit. You'd learn a good thing if you learnt some respect."

Colin bowed his head, but snorted, to show he heard, but kept his own thoughts.

That's the problem with the newer members coming into the gang, Leo thought. Too many clever ideas, not enough room in their heads for old ideas and old ways. Everything had to be new. New education, latest iPhones, electronic bikes, new drugs... One day, when that little shit met the boss, El Jefe... Leo grinned evilly to himself. That would scare the modern right out of his ass. The boss would set him straight.

In the distance, he heard the sound of a car engine, and tyres on the gravel. Then the high beams of a car's headlamps shone through against the rocky hills that framed the curved road from the R160 to where the Diablos were parked, at the base of the Witch's Teat.

A dark van, exact colour difficult to say in the dark, turned the final bend and drove slowly towards the parked bikes.

The passenger door opened and a small figure

stood up, got out. He walked forward with an exaggerated swagger, like he watched too many rap videos, and that was how drug deals went down.

"That's close enough," said Leo, loudly and firmly. "You Rydel?"

"That's right, bitch. You Leo?"

Leo nodded.

"Hey bitch, who you calling bitch?" Colin piped up from alongside Leo, who, surprisingly, was still calm. He'd ridden this rodeo before.

"Hey, Ben!" Leo raised a hand to the figure in the driver's seat of the van. "That you?"

Ben stuck his head out the window. "Yeah, it's me, Leo – you all good?"

Leo grinned. "I will be when these pups quit their pissing contest."

"Yeah. They still got shit to figure out, I suppose. Hey, you! Rydel! Go give Leo the cash and pick up the bags. My balls are getting cold sitting here."

Rydel glared back at Ben, then glared at Leo and then at Colin. Colin pulled his coat back to show his six-guns. Leo just smiled. Hell, these young bucks were full of shit – he hoped he hadn't been that bad coming up, but probably, he was. That's how it goes, he supposed.

And he stopped supposing.

He held his breath.

The entire area around the exchange suddenly felt like death.

All at once, the area felt colder. Tendrils of fog began to whip up from the ground. The men in the space stopped comparing ball size, and shrunk into themselves as if trying to make themselves as small a target as possible. The inherent fear that lives in all of us – from when our ancestors were stalked by predators bigger and faster and stronger than we were – that fear, primordial and unanswerable, rose from the belly of each man.

Rydel buckled over and started to puke. Colin tried his damnedest not to piss himself. Leo and Ben had been around the block a bit, and knew the smell of death. Not of dead bodies, but the essence of death itself. Some Diablos and Brujos knew about these things.

A feeling insinuated itself into the space, like that of flapping wings. Big, silent wings.

Leo had the instinct to check on his man who was alone, up on the rocks.

"Carlito?" he called again. There was no response.

He walked over to the canvas bags and threw them at Rydel.

"Here, man, take your shit. Give me the cash."

Ben got out of the van, pistol out of his belt and in his hand, and went around to the back of the van to get the bags of money.

Leo turned around, looked up to where Carlito was hiding. "Carlito! Stop fucking around, man. Come down."

Ben disappeared behind the van. The others waited.

There was the sound of wings.

Ben didn't return.

Rydel backed up to Leo and Colin, eyes not leaving the van.

He began babbling incoherently. "What was that, man? What shit is this? What the fuck, who the fuck, how the fuck, don't fuck with me I'm a *hombre*, you fuck, I'll nail you bitch ass…"

Leo kept his shotgun in his left hand, and placed his right on the young Brujo's shoulder.

"It's okay, kid. We'll be good. Let's just stick together." Leo looked over towards Colin. "Come in here, *amigo*."

"I don't like this, man."

"I know, brother. Let's just keep fucking steady, and stick together. Now, we're all brothers here. No Diablo gets left behind – and us and the Brujos go back some time. So, all three of us are going to walk to the back of the truck to check on Ben, right? He couldn't just disappear into thin air. Then we're going to walk up that path behind us and we're going to check on Carlito. If anything or anyone comes at us, we open up and fill them with holes. Let's show these fuckers what men can do."

Buoyed by Leo's calm and experience, the gangsters settled down a little, and slowly started to edge towards the back of the van. Within three short steps, the tendrils of white fog had become a blanket across the ground. In a few more cautious seconds, they had almost reached the back of the van, and the fog was thigh-high now, and thick. The sound of their feet on the gravel was muffled.

They reached the back of the van, and Ben was nowhere to be seen.

Rydel almost broke and ran.

"It's okay," said Leo. "He's probably down on the floor, covered by the fog. Let's just walk around a bit and if he's here, we'll find him." Soon afterwards, they did, as their feet nudged into his still body, lying on the floor, obscured by the dense fog.

"Colin, I'll keep watch." Leo pointed downwards into the fog at his feet. "Over here, feel down for a pulse."

At this stage, Colin knew not to argue. He knelt down and felt for Ben's body.

He screamed and jumped up, his hand covered in blood.

"Fuck, man! His heart is ripped out his chest – I put my fucking hand inside him! He's covered in blood! Who could do this? How could they do it so fast? Where'd they go? Why..."

He stopped and pointed towards the entrance of the roadway in. They all stopped and stared.

A figure seemed to glide slowly towards them. A woman, pale-skinned, with long, dark hair and a white coat draping her slender form, down from her shoulders. As she neared, they could see it was a coat of feathers.

"Hey, you!" Leo called out. She drifted in towards them, silently. "Fuck this shit!" Leo cocked his shotgun. "Let's see if she can float through lead!"

He opened up with his shotgun. In an instant, Colin had his six-guns out and he was pouring bullets into the floating woman. He was fast. Rydel pulled his pistol out from the small of his back, and was shooting as quickly as he could. Abruptly, the woman stopped floating and sunk to the floor, all trace of her covered by the fog.

"We get her?" Colin asked. "She went down. We must've got her?"

"I know I popped that bitch." Rydel walked forward tentatively with some confidence after the number of bullets they had just unloaded.

"Make sure you reload," said Leo. "Just in case."

Rydel pulled another mag from his pants pocket and suddenly was pulled to the ground, his gun and mag flying up in separate directions.

"Fuuuuck..." he screamed, then fell silent.

Colin was solidly reloading, and Leo dropped a shell and pulled some more from inside his jacket. Then he slowly reached down and pulled his knife out of his boot.

"This is some crazy demon shit going down here, *amigo*. I've seen stuff like this before with the chief. He's into this sort of shit. He's crazy. Let's just fuck all of this, get our bikes and get out of here. I don't care what kind of feathers she's got on her, she won't fly as fast our hogs can take us, that's for sure."

"With you, boss." Colin had started sidling towards the bikes.

Something pulled him beneath the mist, and he went down shooting. At least four shots he got off. The kid was good with six-guns.

"Kid?" There was no response.

And then there was one. The lady rose up from the fog between Leo and the bikes. Now that he could see her better, Leo could see she was tall and thin – probably a foot taller than a woman should be. Her face was angular. Broad cheekbones. Wide, flat lips. If she wasn't so pale, he would say she was from one of the tribes.

From beneath her coat of white feathers, she raised a hand. Her fingers looked pointed, like bird talons, and they were covered in blood. Dark, arterial blood. She pointed at Leo, and her mouth split into a tooth-filled grin.

"One more," she said, softly.

Leo started pumping shells, but all he heard was the rustling of feathers and all he saw was a white coat descend on him through the night and the fog.

Chapter 5: Things begin

Eddie woke up bone tired. It was 9 in the morning, and Maggie was at the front door. He looked sideways at Odelia, the plump bulldog who was asleep next to him, snoring on her back, jowls flopping down like mudflaps.

"Some watchdog you are."

Odelia opened an eye just to show him that she actually had woken up – she was just ignoring him. Effort expended, she closed her eye and went back to sleep.

He wandered through to the front room of his cabin, and let Maggie in.

"Hey, Maggie-may."

"Hey, sleepy old man. How you feeling this morning?" She handed him a coffee in a takeaway cup. "Here's a coffee."

"Thanks."

Eddie took it and sat down at his breakfast nook, not looking his finest in a pair of fading, blue boxer shorts, stretched-out T-shirt, and furry, brown slippers.

Eddie sipped the coffee in silence, slowly, just surfacing for the morning – Maggie knew his routine; knew how the big man worked. He'd do anything to save an animal. His methods were crazy, but worked. Nobody – literally nobody – could pull off the stuff he did with animals.

Last night he'd saved Sheila Run's life for certain. Eric Johnson, proud southern cowboy from a family of ranchers going back over a hundred years, was in tears when Eddie told him Sheila would be okay.

Eddie deserved some rest after his heroics last night – on top of just landing from a flight out of Europe and driving four hours straight home. She sighed. He had appointments today, first one at 10.

"Eddie, your first appointment's at 10, then you've got five more over the day."

Eddie grimaced and rubbed his eyes.

"Mmm..." he mumbled. "I need to pick up someone at the bus stop at 3. An old friend's daughter is thinking of doing something in animals, so they sent her out to me."

"What's she like?"

"Don't really know. You know teenagers nowadays, they're different people every day. But she's probably a handful."

Eddie stood up and began shuffling through his kitchen for a pan and some eggs.

At the sound of movement in the kitchen, Odelia the English bulldog dragged herself off Eddie's bed and scuffled her paws along the floor until she reached the doorframe.

"Odelia, you lazy girl!" Maggie leant down to scratch behind her ear. Odelia let her. After letting

Maggie coo over her a bit, and receiving some wrinkle squishes and a couple of kisses on her soft, furry head, Odelia waddled into the kitchen and sat on the floor, looking up at Eddie. Breakfast was on.

"Anyway," Eddie continued. "I was thinking that if Mathilda is half okay, she can help out at the Vet for a bit."

"Her name's Mathilda."

"Yup." Eddie carried on in the kitchen, beating some butter and eggs. "Odelia and I will be down at the office at 10. After I get Mathilda at 3, I want to take a drive out to Alamosa and see Wayne."

"The snake guy?"

"That's the one. He called me for some help and I said I'd pop around."

"I don't like him. Him and his bar – they're into some seedy stuff down there. I don't know why you hang out with him."

"Yes, Mom!" Eddie flashed her a sarcastic grin. "Besides, we go back some ways. History counts."

*

Traffic was light around the bus stop – clearly there weren't many passengers expected. From what Eddie could tell, there were only two other cars waiting for the bus.

He pulled up nearby and switched the Ford off. Odelia got up off the seat and placed her front paws on the dash, and looked around. She sniffed her wrinkled nose.

Then she turned to Eddie.

"Somethings smells wrong." Her voice pinged in his head.

Eddie nodded – being an animal mage meant you got to speak with animals you bonded with. Well, in your head, at any rate.

"I feel it too, girl. Any ideas?"

The bulldog tilted her head, thinking a bit. "It's like there's something else in town now. Something new that's changing the air. Like when they were dumping that stuff in the Wilsons' river and it was making the fish sick?"

"Pollution?"

"Yes, it's like that, but in the personality."

"You mean the spirit."

The bulldog looked over her shoulder at him. She knew what she meant and didn't like being corrected.

Odelia was more than she seemed. Way more. She was a bulldog that had been abandoned and ended up at Eddie's vet. He'd taken her home for a bit while he figured out what to do with her, and that was about the time that he was helping a local wolf pack with a malevolent Ute werespirit that was chasing down members of their pack and savaging local livestock.

Dangerous for the livestock, the ranchers, and also bad for the wolves.

With the help of the pack, Eddie had set up an ambush on his land for the werespirit, when it turned into a giant, red-eyed, fanged and clawed version of a wolf, more than doubling in size. Things didn't go according to plan and the werewolf and Eddie got down, toe-to-toe. Eddie was wrestling it using his bear strength (animal mage perk) and every other creature backed away from the destructive tussle of two creatures that could each lift over a thousand pounds rolling in the dirt. The werewolf pinned Eddie and was about to take a snap at his unguarded face with fangs the length of steak knives, when who should come charging across the ground but a 50-pound bulldog, less than a foot high, all wrinkles, short fangs, and sheer obstinance.

Growling and yapping, Odelia charged into the fray and threw her entire tiny body at the back leg of the werewolf, which gave Eddie the time to break free and put the werewolf down – but not before Odelia took a bite to the head.

The result was that Odelia had the ability to become a weredog, and with a small magical charm on her collar that Eddie charged from time to time, she could control her werenature.

If she had a stubborn streak before, imagine how much attitude a bulldog got when she could become – literally – the biggest dog in town by over 400 pounds.

From time to time, at the right time of night, one might have the privilege of seeing a 500-pound bulldog racing across the long, grassy hills of the Golden Bear Ranch with a wolf pack, frolicking like a puppy. That was a sight one didn't forget.

Eddie smiled as the bus pulled away. A group of passengers dispersed, leaving a lone girl standing at the station.

She looked about 15 or 16. Teenager, definitely. She had pale blue hair, oxblood Doc Martens, black tights with the obligatory holes, a flared, yellow and black tartan school skirt, and an oversized black hoody. She reached to her mouth with multicoloured fingernails and played with her gum.

"What you think, Odelia?"

The bulldog peered towards the girl and sniffed the air.

"Smells nice. Like a lonely puppy."

"Right. Let's see if we can make this puppy less lonely."

*

Mathilda had recognised Eddie from a picture that Sko had sent her, and had come over to the pickup. Soon, they had said their "hi's", she was in the front seat, and they were on their way.

Eddie put on the radio, which was playing some country – something he'd never gotten used to, so he flipped through his playlist, looking for something that would sound good, but also would make him seem at least a little cool.

Metallica. Surely, Metallica was still cool. For kids with black stockings and Doc Martens, it had to be.

After a few minutes, Mathilda reached out and turned the volume down.

"So, you're this big animal mage?"

Eddie nodded.

"You don't look like much to me – just a tall, overweight guy that smells of horse."

Odelia lay with her head on Mathilda's lap, fast asleep. The teen had her hand on Odelia's head, idly stroking a wrinkle.

"Well, what did you expect – a long beard, a cloak, and a wand? Hagrid maybe? Dumbledore?"

"I'm impressed. You can read."

"I saw the movies… Anyway, the point is that I spend my life trying to *not* look like a wizard. As far as the people of Fort Garland know, I'm a vet, and a good one. That way I get to use my power for good, and I get to pay my taxes and be a citizen."

"That sounds boring as fuck," Mathilda replied with teen certainty. "What's the point of being able to cast spells if you spend a normal life doing normal things, paying normal taxes? Why aren't you travelling the world? Why are you stuck in this backwater town? When I'm maged up, you won't see me for dust. Bye-bye, settling down. I'm going to travel the world."

"Of course you are," said Eddie. "Every mage finds their own way to deal with their powers – and all of us have travelled, or had the choice of being rich or living in a skyscraper or a penthouse apartment. Everyone gets to choose. Magic gives you the one thing that most regular people dream of – and that's the power to choose."

"Aah, I get it." Mathilda nodded. "This is the Spiderman speech – with great power comes great responsibility. Don't worry, I won't be turning fuckers into frogs or anything."

"No," said Eddie. "You won't." Damn teenagers. Eddie eyed Mathilda. She looked like she could use a good meal.

"You hungry?"

"Sure." Noncommittal as ever.

"Great. I know a place. Best fries ever."

Eddie turned off the main drag, towards Minty's Diner, home of – literally – the best fries ever.

*

As it turned out, the burgers were pretty good too. But Eddie was right, the fries were truly out of this world. Crispy outside, soft inside, sprinkled with a dash of oregano and salt.

Mathilda took the vegan burger and the loaded fries. Eddie took a double burger with cheese and bacon.

Minty's dipped their bacon in maple syrup after frying, but before they put it on the burger, and that just gave it something special.

Eddie and Mathilda sat in a booth with worn, orange seats, Odelia next to Mathilda, who was already feeding every second chip to the fat bulldog.

"So," Eddie opened, between bites of food. "Sko found you?"

"Yup."

"And he reckoned you're an animal mage?"

"Yup."

"Why is that?"

"Sometimes I hear voices in my head. I feel like it's birds or critters trying to speak to me, you know?"

Eddie nodded. He knew. "Anything else?"

"I..." There was a small pause of uncertainty. Mathilda exhaled before continuing. "I healed some animals."

Eddie nodded again. He lowered his voice, like trying to soothe a skittish colt, or calm a nervous dog. "Well done," he said. "That's awesome." He ate a handful of fries. "You know you're not crazy, right?"

"Sko told me, but I'm not convinced yet."

"And how long have you been feeling like you can hear animals? When did you first heal one?"

She shrugged. "A year ago? Maybe more?"

"And?"

"Well, then I started getting sick. The doctors said I had allergies."

Eddie nodded again.

"And then Sko found me out of the blue, showed me some crazy stuff."

"The Dancing Phone?"

She grinned. "Yeah. And he told me about the guy who never misses a shot and the girl who can look like whatever she wants to, and the guy that turns into animals. Turns out, that's you."

"That is me. But I can do a lot more than just that."

Eddie pulled a small necklace out of his pocket: a brown, leather thong threaded through a wooden stick only a few inches in length, not much thicker than a fat pen. Runes – circles, odd shapes and lines – were carved into the stick, and there was a small, polished grey stone that looked glued to the top with some kind of resin.

Somewhat awkwardly, Eddie handed it across to Mathilda. "This is for you. Put it on."

Mathilda took it and held it in her hand, then raised it up to get a better look at it. "Thank you. Nice thought... but it's not really my scene... I'm more of a goth look, you may have noticed. This is a bit... native American? You know what I mean?"

"It's not that kind of jewellery. It's a spell sink. If you're going to be a magus, you're going to need one."

"What?"

"It's magical. I'll explain more later, but for now, you need to put it on, so any side effects of you using your magic won't impact on you – or the world around you. It'll be absorbed by that necklace and keep you and everyone safe."

"Oh."

"Don't worry, over time you'll learn to make them, and maybe even buy some ones that look how you want. That was one of the first I ever made, and it saved my ass quite a bit. It's more powerful than it looks."

She put it over her neck and slid it beneath her top. On, but out of sight. Fair enough, Eddie supposed.

Mathilda opened her mouth, about to say something, and stopped. She shivered, blinked, and shook her shoulders. "What the hell! What just happened to me?"

"Nothing. Don't worry. It's just the sink connecting with you. Now, next time you hear voices, you can try and focus on them, worry-free. You'll see."

"Wait, what?"

Eddie put up his hand for her to pause while he thought.

"Alright. I want you to focus on Odelia. We're going for a drive to go see a guy I know who needs my help. For the next while, I want you to just watch the bulldog. Try to absorb her movements, gestures, and the sounds that she makes, by using that part of you that you feel when you do magic. That part that lit up when you healed those animals, or the part that tingles when you hear voices."

"Aah, okay... Why?"

"Because that's how the spell works that lets you talk to animals. Odelia here," he pointed at the bulldog, who turned and gave Mathilda a pointed look , "will be your guide. Now eat up. We got places to go and people to see before we get you to your new home."

*

The High and Perky Titty Bar on the corner of Hadida and San Palima Boulevard was typical of a stripper bar in a small city in a remote part of the country: nobody ever claimed to go there, but it was always busy.

From the girl who was going to swing her tits all the way out of the small town and into the big city, to the college kids hitting the strip joint on Friday evening, to the regulars who stuffed small bills down loose thongs almost nightly, all the way down to the sassy barmaids and seedy owner with a past, the High and Perky was in every respect what one could expect from a small-city strip bar.

It was closed now – every Sunday evening and every Monday – but Ed knew that Wayne spent Monday afternoon in the bar, catching up on paperwork.

"Some education you're giving me," Mathilda commented. "Right off the bus and straight to a strip joint. Classy guy. Way to set an example for the troubled teen."

"It's not that way, Tilda." (She had asked to be called Tilda, but not Tilly – that was too old fashioned.) "The owner has some magical problems and around here, I'm the guy they call for that sort of thing. Consider it a practical lesson." Eddie looked down at Odelia waddling along beside Tilda as they crossed the road. "Odelia, I think it's about time. You should tell her..."

Odelia looked up at Tilda. "He isn't here to mate these bitches," she said in matter-of-fact way.

Mathilda stopped dead in the road. "How...?" She shook her head.

Odelia looked up at her with a stare out the side of her head, raising one eyebrow and ear, as if to say "really?".

Eddie tapped his chest, mirroring where the spell sink sat on Mathilda's chest. "What can I say... welcome to your first lesson? You're clearly an animal mage and have been hearing them for some time anyway – you just didn't know what you were hearing. Odelia is... enhanced, so it's a bit easier than with other animals, but it's a great place to start."

Shock still in her eyes, Mathilda asked, "Enhanced? What do you mean? How?"

"Well, you know about werewolves? Well, Odelia is a weredog. That allows her to talk more easily to me, and other animal mages."

"What, weredog? Wait, what does that mean?" For the first time since she'd arrived in Fort Garland, Tilda showed real interest in something other than her phone. "So, if I can hear her, then I really am an animal mage, right?"

Eddie put up his hand for silence and walked to the bar entrance.

Wayne's car was outside, parked in the main road, but the bar was locked up. Again, nothing out of the ordinary.

Eddie dialled Wayne and put his phone to his ear.

Wayne picked up, sounding breathless. "Eddie! Geez man, bad timing! Where the hell you been?"

"I've been away. I'm back now. I'm standing outside the bar. Let me in, so we can talk about the messages you keep sending me."

"Shit, yeah, sorry about that, but I got some pretty bad threats from the Brujos – wait a sec, give me ten minutes. I'll open up now."

Wayne killed the call.

Eddie put his phone back in his pocket.

Tilda looked at him. "And now?"

Eddie leant against the wall next to the door. "Yes, you are definitely an animal mage. Over time, you will learn to interpret the gestures, movements, and sounds of different animal types, and as your spell becomes more powerful, you'll be able to basically speak with just about any animal – if they want to, that is.

It's easier with Odelia because she has a higher intrinsic level of magic. She seems to like you, so maybe you guys can talk bit more. See how it goes."

Ten minutes later, Eddie heard the rattle of a chain and the click of a padlock before Wayne (still breathless) opened the bar door, swinging it inwards.

Wayne peered out the door, looking left and right before pulling his head back in again. "Come in, quick. They're watching me. I can't see them, but I can feel them – I know they're watching. Damn Brujos."

Eddie and Tilda entered hastily. Odelia stopped to sniff at the doorway. She didn't like Wayne.

Eddie looked around the High and Perky. Booths ran down the left wall, black Naugahyde and buttons all a-glisten, but not so much in the light of day, where the cigarette singes and alcohol spills were more easily seen. Running along the right wall was the bar, behind which there was a door to the storerooms, and also a set of steel stairs that led to an upper level that ran above the bar, that held three offices. Mounted on the back wall of the bar were two large, glass enclosures, each holding a snake. Ball pythons, to be precise. A fat, rotund python, almost 6 feet long, and a slightly shorter yellow and white albino one. Slim and shady. The reasons Eddie knew Wayne in the first place. Eddie waved to the snakes.

Opposite the entrance, dark red velvet curtains draped the wall, except in the centre, where a long stage reached out to the middle of the floor. There was a circular platform at the end of the stage, with a silver dancing pole proudly jutting up out of its centre.

Normally, tables and chairs would fill the space on the floor around the stage, near the booths and bar, but they had all been stacked at the back, up against the curtains leading backstage, so the floors could be swept.

This was the High and Perky – the sad daytime shell of a nighttime of sexy pleasure. Having seen it in full cry on her busy nights, Eddie felt like it represented the strippers who plied their trade there: when they were dressed up on stage, they were sexy, powerful, tantalising… yet when they were back home, they were regular moms, sisters, students covering fees.

In the daytime, ready for the cleaners, the High and Perky was just a building along San Palima Boulevard. At night, she was the place where teen dreams came true.

And standing in front of him, shirt dishevelled, massive silver Desert Eagle tucked into his waistband, bright pink lipstick smeared on his cheek, and thinning hair tousled, stood Wayne Munston, the man who made the dreams come true.

Behind Wayne stood a girl – clearly (to Eddie's eyes) not as young as she would like folk to think, but still in really good shape – reapplying bright pink lipstick to her lips, and as they came in, shoving the makeup back into her small clutch purse, and straightening her black miniskirt.

Eddie didn't need to be a genius to see that Wayne had been busy, but not with the books.

Wayne eyed Eddie, then gave Tilda an appraisal that made her feel distinctly sleazy, and finally he cocked an eye at Odelia.

"You brought your fucking dog?" He raised an eyebrow at Eddie, who ignored him. Odelia waddled past Wayne, slowly, to make him wait for her before he closed the door. "Come in," he ordered. "I think they're watching."

Odelia trudged in, and Wayne shut the door, then ran a chain through the handle and padlocked it shut. Then, as if only feeling safe when the door was finally locked, he let out a long sigh, and ran his hand through his hair.

They made introductions – the girl's name was Candy, and she had started working the club recently – and a bit more, by the looks of it.

They pulled up a set of barstools while Wayne poured them all a drink.

He served Candy first, then Tilda, then Eddie, talking while he put their drinks together. "So, it goes like this: remember La Jolla, the captain of *los Alamosa Brujos*?"

Eddie nodded. "Yup." La Jolla was a drug-running, woman-beating, violent, car-thieving criminal, all-American piece of shit who had been caught in the club dealing some blow and it had been the lead into the Alamosa Brujos that the local police had needed. Eddie had gotten involved (unbeknownst to the cops) by lifting wards and witch blessings on the Brujos' soldiers that allowed the police to blow open their operation. At least, in Alamosa.

Wayne, unlikely enough, was a sensitive – one of

those few people who are able to feel the ebb and flow of magic – and he knew that Eddie had somehow been involved and was good to have around.

The way Wayne described it, he had a good gut instinct about people. Eddie knew that Wayne was a sensitive and, given some training, might even be able to pull off a low-level spell or two. But there's no way he'd be having that conversation with him anytime soon.

"So, La Jolla got out of prison," Wayne told them. "How the hell he managed that, I don't know. But guess the first place he heads to?" He shrugged. "You guessed it. He had a beef with me, cos I sang to the cops, and so he heads out to the Perky for some revenge. Except Mike at the door spots him coming and tells him he can't come in and he lets me know, and I call the cops.

"A squad car pulls up, and La Jolla disappears fast, and a few days later I get a lot of guys in here who turn out to be Brujo foot soldiers. The whisperings I hear is that something big is going to go down, but I'm not too sure what it's going to be. For all I know, La Jolla is planning to blow the Perky to Kingdom Come because I helped fuck up his Alamosa operation, or he's planning a hit on me. Basically, I have no idea. But my girls hear snippets here and there.

"So, already, at this point, my back is up. I start carrying Monique here," he pats the Desert Eagle at his waist, "and I start to get this gut feel that somehow, these fuckers are watching me."

Eddie raised a hand. "Hold on. Isn't Monique your wife's name?"

Wayne gave a pointed look at Candy. "Yes, but we're separated, don't forget. Besides, she's the meanest bitch in all 51 states, except for maybe Hillary Clinton, but... well, maybe she's worse... anyway, where was I?" He took a good sip of whiskey to recharge the constitution. "Ahh, yes. So I'm on edge, because every time I go outside I feel a tingle down my back, like somebody's watching me, but I just can't see them. I tell the cops, but they can't do anything more than sending out a car to investigate. So anyway, three nights ago I'm in the club, minding my own business, when I come down onto the floor – it's a quiet night – and I walk past a booth and hear some guys talking. I hear mention of Brujos and coming back. So I go and grab Tracy, the waitress who'd served them, and she told me that they'd been bragging about how the Brujos had some big mojo and someone called Uvehe would give them the power they needed, and that they were coming back into Alamosa and this time, no one could stop them.

"So I told her to keep quiet and just keep serving drinks, and Tracy's good like that. But it seems that one of the Brujos didn't like the way she was listening and started roughing her up, accusing her of spying on them, and so I stepped in and pulled Monique on him, and then Mike and the boys from security stepped in, and we got them out with the threat of the police. But not before me and that fucking punk had some choice words, and he told me to watch my back because they were coming back to level some scores, and I would be first on the list."

Wayne took another slug of his whiskey, and poured himself more. "I know it's probably just a punk mouthing off," he admitted. "I told the cops. But I can't help feeling in my gut – deep in my gut – that something about this whole thing is messed up. There's more going on than meets the eye, I can sense it. Just like last time. I don't know what it is, but I do know that the Alamosa Brujos have no reason to like me or the Perky, and after two threats in three days, I'm feeling nervous as a choir boy alone with the limp-handed bishop, you know what I mean?

"Also, I can't shake this feeling, like an itch between my shoulder blades, like I'm dead square in someone's sights, but I can't see them. I can't prove anything, but I know it deep down. Like that feeling when you walk in a room and everyone stops talking, because they were talking about you – you can't prove it, but you know they were. It's like that. Something is rotten, I can smell it. But I can't say where it's coming from.

"And there's this new boss, Uvehe. Who the hell is that? I mean, how did they get a 15-year stint for La Jolla dropped after six months? Naah..." He downed the rest of his glass. "Something isn't right here, Eddie. And I know you deal with things that ain't right in this sort of way. We got history, right? So what do we do next?"

Eddie nodded and sat for a while, hand on his chin, rubbing a four-day-old growth of beard.

"We leave town," Candy piped up. "Let's just get out of here for a while – let the police handle this, and then, when La Jolla is back behind bars, we come back. In the meanwhile, Stacy can run the Perky..."

"No fucking ways!" Wayne slammed his whiskey

glass onto the counter. "No way I'm letting them run me out my own place!"

"Hold on," Eddie interrupted. "Maybe you guys getting out the way for a short while isn't such a bad idea. I can handle the police, and also, there's some people I can speak to about this Uvehe. I have some connections. Maybe while we try figure out what the Brujos are up to, you and Candy take a nice romantic trip – just a couple of days, a week at most…"

"I ain't running–"

"You're not running, Munston, you stubborn mule! You're getting out of the way so I can understand what the hell these guys are up to. They are bad guys, and you don't know the half of it. I can't dig into their new mojo, their new boss, La Jolla's release, and their new big plans, AND watch your back at the same time. There's only one of me. So you need to get out of town while I figure out what it is that we do next."

At this point, Tilda left the bar and sat in a darkened booth on the side of the stage while Eddie and Candy argued with Wayne. Odelia came with her, and they snuggled wholesomely together in a booth – not the sort of snuggling it was normally used for, she was pretty sure.

With the bulldog firmly tucked up against her side, and her bag as a pillow, she lay in the booth with her Walkman in hand, an old, worn cassette playing through her earphones.

Yeah, Walkmans were so 80s, but she was an animal witch (in training) and could do magic and she was snuggling with a werebulldog that could talk and she was with her new magic teacher and he was talking about taking down a drug cartel with a stripper and a titty bar owner. Basically, she was cool as hell, so what the fuck, she'd do whatever the hell she wanted, thank you very much.

Tilda realised how tired she was as she lay down and, even with the 90s rap charging through her earpieces, she found herself drifting in and out of sleep. The last few days had been pretty crazy for her. Outside the booth, across at the bar, they seem to be arguing back and forth, Eddie wanting Wayne and Candy to get out of town while he figured out what to do, Wayne not wanting to leave the bar... it was his life's work, he had all his money tied up, blah blah blah... she missed some stuff because she fell asleep. When she woke up again, Candy was reassuring Wayne that he'd always have her. It was painful, and sounded soppy amidst the drama (Tilda figured out that Wayne enjoyed the drama) and it seemed as if Wayne was coming over to Eddie's perspective and liked the sound of that place in Red River Creek... She lay back down again and closed her eyes, Snoop Dogg playing on her Walkman, easing her to sleep.

*

Everything went black. Not like when the internal lights go out, but there's still some light streaming in from outside. Not even like a really dark night in the countryside, when the clouds are covering the stars.

More like being down a mineshaft a mile underground and your batteries run out. And you're blindfolded.

It was so intensely dark that Mathilda could feel the darkness slither on her skin like oil. She could smell it in the air like ozone and dirty garbage cans, and she could feel it sliding its way into her nose and mouth, forcing its way behind her tongue and then down her throat, making her breathe it, invading her being. It was a dirty, toxic darkness that made her feel nauseous and violated.

Across the bar, Mathilda heard Candy retching violently. Wayne screamed out against the darkness, his voice shrill: "Fuck you, fuckers! Come for me in my own joint, I'll fuck you up!" Suddenly, his pistol barked out a flame into the darkness. "Come at me, *amigos*! Let's see if you got bags big enough to take Munston!"

Mathilda felt Eddie nearby. "Listen to me, Tilda!" he whispered harshly. "Stay down, low to the floor, don't get up, don't try any magic, no matter how much you might want to. You don't need these fuckers to know you can cast." He tossed something small and hard over the edge of the booth. She heard it clatter on the table.

"Take that – it's a taser. Feel for the button. It has a plus on it. It'll tase them worse than a normal taser, it's magic. Only use it if you know it's one of them. You got this! Odelia, you get the entrance!"

A quick bark back, and Eddie knew she was on it. Trying to get her off the couch was typically a titanic struggle. Getting her to do anything that she didn't want to was an almighty nightmare, stubborn werebulldog that she was. But given the chance to sink her teeth into a pack of bandits, she was like a missile, homing in to cause fanged destruction. He almost felt sorry for them.

Being an animal mage didn't mean that Eddie could only do animal magic. That's just what he was best at, and he could control the sink of that magic better than other types. He activated his jade totem necklace; it would allow him to pull on a range of animal-based powers.

Eddie called on the bat, and suddenly the darkness lit up in his sight, each sound echoing in a cacophony of colours. Then he called on the jaguar, and he felt power and speed course through his veins. Claws tore out through his fingertips. Eddie dropped to all fours, his senses of smell, sound, and sight ringing with sensations beyond the range of his human sense.

Each of the Brujos in the club had their own unique smell. There were seven of them, a full hit squad – a two-Cadillac crew.

He knew by their breathing where each one of them was. He knew by their smell where each one of them was.

As they came into the club, the Brujos spread out from the door, weapons already. Eddie risked a look in the spirit – if they had any charms or magic on them, he would see them, but if they had any skilled users amongst them – real *brujos*, not just thugs, or magic sensitives – it would be like setting off a flare if their *brujo* was looking. Eddie hoped and went for it, preparing to run, just in case.

He opened his spirit sight. The Brujos looked like thugs, but they were charmed. Each of them wore markings on his face that clearly allowed them to see in the darkness. They had charms around their necks as well that looked like old Navajo warrior charms he had seen before. They made their skin tough – able to take light knife cuts, glancing bullet shots even – depending on the power of the *brujo* who had cast it And this one looked like he had some bad medicine.

On the floor, not too far from the entrance, lay a stone, covered in markings and wrapped in skins. That was the source of the darkness, and with one glance at it, Eddie could tell the *brujo* was bad news.

Whoever had sent these guys was no Sunday caster. He was packing serious magical heat, and if it came to a straight-up duel, Eddie wasn't convinced that he could take him. Good thing he had sent these cowboys, and hopefully they didn't suspect him to be who he was. The Brujos knew that he had some skills. But not just as many as he did.

Wayne let off a few more shots, shooting wildly into the air. It made the Brujos duck, but it also showed them where Wayne was. Silently, they changed direction and started stalking off towards the office where Wayne was hiding, where he'd pulled Candy along with him.

Eddie felt Odelia change. The air rippled, like someone had fanned it, and it rolled across him with a scent of wet dog and blood and rich soil, along with the idea of running through the woods at night. It was exhilarating. And suddenly, there was a scream as 500 pounds of bulldog crushed a Brujo head in her jaws, and she flung his body aside.

"What the shit!"

Odelia was wagging her tail as four other Brujos near her turned to face the giant bulldog.

Eddie leapt and ripped out the throat of one as he landed, instantly pouncing and grabbing the gun arm of a second, who had a moment to scream as he was pulled off balance, before Eddie tore his head off with jaguar claws and strength.

Odelia charged at another, who squeezed off a shot before the bulldog knocked him flying, and then silenced him for good. Eddie tracked the fifth, who was running towards the offices where the other two had gone. The Brujo squeezed off some wild shots, and one hit Eddie hard. It was a good thing that Eddie's bullet charms were working.

He carried two on him, in the form of bracelets. One was made by his friend, Tod. Tod was an accuracy mage – this particular charm that he'd crafted for Eddie made attacks against him less accurate. It meant he got hit a lot less than he should. The other was a pretty pricey piece of gear that effectively made him bulletproof. To disperse that much kinetic energy often required quite a sink, but Eddie had that covered. He had a 40-acre ranch, wired for totems and mage sinks. As long as he could keep the charm powered, Eddie could catch bullets all day long.

Of course, the bullets still hit with some sort of impact, and it hurt. Eddie rolled on through the darkness to get to the cursed stone that was its source. Eddie reached into his jacket pocket and pulled out a large, steel knitting needle. He stabbed through the skin covering, hitting the rock, and he sent a surge of power down into it.

In retrospect, he probably should have been more careful. Maybe it was the jaguar running through him, or adrenaline. Seeing how easily they'd taken out the Alamosa Brujos soldiers, maybe he hadn't been expecting the spell to have a trap embedded.

There was a sudden bang. All the lights came on, but Eddie was flat on his back, ears ringing, head pounding, face speckled with blood. His entire body had taken a full kinetic blast strong enough to level a wall. Eddie's bullet charm was ripped to shreds, overloaded with more power than it was ever designed to handle. His deflection charm was also torn apart, but it had channelled massive amounts of power around him. That must have been something to see – the effect of full grenade going off in his face, and somehow, most of it missing! But enough hit to blast Eddie off the floor, and onto his back. The immediate area around the stone was blackened, and thankfully, Odelia had been at the back of the room – away from the direct blast, but still, close enough to be stunned by the sound and shockwaves.

The last three Alamosa Brujos ran out from the passageway that led to Munston's offices. They took pause at the light, the blast damage, the bodies lying across the floor, and the giant bulldog growling and shaking its head across the room from them.

A short, Mexican-looking thug with a villainous scar down his left cheek from temple to chin and a sawn-off shotgun in his hands, ran out first.

"*Vamos, amigos*! It's time to fly!" he shouted. "There some real shit going down here."

"But Pedro, that fucker Munston..."

"We'll get him another time – we got four men down and a giant fucking dog the size of a pony eating our people – looks like he's got a *brujo* of his own. We need to get back to let Betty know."

The remaining Brujos raced to the door, but as they entered the room, Odelia saw them and, enraged, charged. They raised their guns to pour her full of lead.

Through the haze in his head and half-closed eyes, Eddie, lying on the floor, saw the Brujos run into the room, guns raised.

Eddie's head pounded like a grenade had just gone off in his face, which was basically what had happened, but he knew he had to do something. He couldn't let them pour bullets into the room – not at Odelia, and certainly not at Tilda, who he was hoping like crazy was ducked behind a wall somewhere.

He couldn't rely on hitting his target. He couldn't aim. He could barely lift his head to see, and if he could, his head was ringing so hard, he couldn't see straight anyway.

Time was running out.

The Brujos charged into the room, spreading out, two lifting guns up towards Odelia, one scanning nervously behind, his head suddenly swivelling at movement on the far side of the room – Tilda, in the cubicle.

Eddie racked his brain… He only had one choice. He summoned his power, hoped that the sink on his totem necklace could take the dump, and cast his spell.

"Hita Málmur!" Eddie mumbled the words, but the spell took, and he felt the power leave his body, like somebody had pulled plug out of a bath, and all the water suddenly fled. And then he passed out.

*

"Eddie? Eddie, you okay? You there?"

Eddie's eyes opened. They felt like sandpaper and, in waking, he realised how much his head hurt. It felt like a jackhammer was drilling on the inside of his head.

Odelia sat next to his head, back down to normal size again, panting. She leant over and licked him on the face.

Eddie reached a hand out to her.

"Yes, girl, I'm glad you're okay too." Then he realised that her entire front half was splattered in blood. But she was sitting looking at him with a self-satisfied smirk on her face, panting happily. Clearly, she was fine.

Candy had his head in her lap (apparently, she

had been studying as a nurse), and Mathilda knelt next to him, alongside Odelia.

Behind him, pacing around with a shiny, silver Desert Eagle in his hand, and a machete tucked in his waistband, Wayne was trying to make call on his cellphone, but seemed to be having problems.

"Eddie," Mathilda asked again. "Are you okay?"

"Mmm..." Eddie nodded, but it hurt his head. "Painkillers..." He dropped his head to the floor and closed his eyes. A few moments later, Candy and Mathilda were helping him up, and they gave him a glass of water and some tablets, which he swallowed. Eddie closed his eyes, and slept.

Eddie woke again. This time, the throbbing in his head had largely gone, and his body felt comfortably numb. He was propped up against an office wall, overlooking the main bar area, which looked like a killing ground. Whilst he had been out, Wayne – assisted by the clearly disturbed, but still compliant, Candy – had stacked the bodies up against the wall near the front door. There were mostly seven – Odelia had been busy.

"Jesus, Eddie!" said Mathilda. "I don't know what the hell you cast, but I felt the power coming off you like a substation! I've never felt anything like that – your spell gave me a bigger headache than the explosion! What the hell was that? And how the hell is Odelia a fucking werewolf... dog... thing? I know you told me she was a weredog. But to see it!" She was worried, and freaked out, but in her voice, Eddie heard one thing beneath it all – Tilda was excited.

Eddie grinned a bit. "Okay, so what happened after I passed out?"

"Everything! Keys melted, the stairs glowed red hot – everything metal instantly became hot as lava – super hot! The guns in the Brujos' hands exploded and parts of them melted in their hands! It was crazy! One fell to the floor instantly with half his hand blown off, the other two were around but battling, the one screaming because his gun had melted into his hand! Wayne popped him with his big phallic silver gun – weird that the spell didn't affect him – and the last Brujo got pounced on by Odelia, who picked his whole fucking body up in her mouth and shook him like a dead snake. I think I actually heard his spine snap! What the hell was that spell?"

Eddie, tired and with a head that felt like it was stuffed with wool, smiled a bit more. Her excitement – particularly in the face of violence and gory deaths – showed one thing: the kid had moxy.

"The spell was Heat Metal, a particularly nasty Finnish version used by ancient arctic explorers and, later, by Viking blacksmiths."

"Can you teach me?"

"Sure. Let's see what you take to, huh?"

Eddie turned as Wayne and Candy came across from the far side of the bar.

"Hey man," shouted Wayne. "I knew you were some sort of friggin' heavy hitter, but I never knew you were *that* heavy! You and that psycho of the Baskervilles over there!" He motioned his head towards Odelia, who

– covered in blood – was licking her foot complacently. "Alright," Wayne conceded. "I'll leave town for a bit, go up to that place in Red Rock Creek you were telling me about. Lie low for a while so you can find out about these *pendejos* coming for me. I know enough to know that we got lucky this time – and they always send more, and you can't always see them coming." He turned to Candy. "Pack your bags, baby. We're going on a holiday!"

Between Candy's squeals of delight, and her totally nonchalant stacking of *bandito* bodies up against the wall after they were savaged by a giant weredog or destroyed by a series of spells, Eddie wondered what her exact mental state was – but it was too much thinking for his tired head. With Tilda assisting, he stood up, and after a moment of the world spinning around him, his head settled and he slid his feet across the bar, over to the bodies. Something wasn't sitting right with him. He felt uneasy. Not the kind of uneasy one would would expect after melting some men to death – sadly, magic was a tough game, and by the time you reached your big, bad mage Noddy badge, you've seen enough gory stuff to make an average teen horror movie look tame.

Eddie felt uneasy because beneath the fatigue of his power discharge, beneath his aching body and head and beneath the drug fog that numbed his face, he felt like he was missing something. He had a sense – born of magic, born of instinct, and born of years of good, old-fashioned self-preservation in a world where very little was what it seemed – that he was missing something.

He walked over to the bodies and began to search through their pockets, gingerly extending a sense out to them, looking for some sort of artefact or item or miasma of power. They had finished these guys quickly, but that darkness stone was some tough magic to pull off, and the power it set off was enough to kill him. Besides, no mage sent out that many soldiers armed with magical artefacts and charms like they were, without having something to see what was going on – some link to the action. Unless, of course, these guys were so low in the ranks that the caster didn't even care about them and there were hundreds more where they came from. Scary thought.

After some searching, Eddie found it. He knew it the moment he touched it, and he also knew it was a grave mistake.

On the inside jacket pocket of the thug that he could only assume must have been the leader – but was now a dog-chewed corpse with a gun melted into his hand – he found a small, leather pouch. The outside was covered in symbols – that familiar light brown colour of old blood. The drawstring was wrapped in feathers and tied and sealed with wax. Eddie placed it gingerly on the bar counter, and summoned up some power, directing the sink through his totem necklace, like he normally did.

Immediately, he felt the drain, and he realised how much that blast had taken out of him. But he wasn't trying anything powerful – he just wanted to see, to look at the pouch, give it the once-over in a range of spiritual spectrums. There had to be some link on this thing back to the mage who had cast all this magic.

It was as if he'd slid on a pair of sunglasses, changing his view of the world. Eddie wasn't the best at power shielding, but he was far from the worst – he was a damn powerful mage, overlooked by others who saw him as a "Dr Dolittle". Those who knew him best knew that he was far more than that.

He found it. As he flicked between spells that hid evidence of power in different ways, he tried an old Ute spell, taught to him by a shaman who had died in the Sangre de Cristo Mountains years ago. He used beams of daylight as a screen, stretched and pulled across the lines of power, leaving little to no trace of them being there. But Eddie knew the signature – the shape and feel of the spell.

"*Po-Ib Neh-shoo-mu Ts-Shee*," he incanted the words of the spell in the ancient Ute language, and suddenly the pouch shone with power. Through the leather pouch, glowing like a torch, an eyeball – still bloody, and marked with symbols of arcane power – peered at Eddie. The mage who had cast all of these spells, who had seen Eddie and Odelia destroy this hit team, had been watching all along.

Eddie smelt the mage's power. It was strong. It literally reeked off the pouch, and it smelt like death. Old, ancient, and dead. And now it knew Eddie had seen him.

Eddie turned off his spirit sight, but he was badly shaken up. If he came within a city block of that mage, Eddie would recognise his magical signature instantly. He was powerful, and really old, and he felt, to Eddie, as though he were dead. Or near to death. These feelings could be vague, and it was an art, after all, not an exact science. Nevertheless, Eddie had the sinking feeling that there was more to the Alamosa Brujos now than there had ever been before, and he would have his work cut out for him.

It was a bad time to have an apprentice.

Chapter 6: Continuation
Chateau de Brie, Provence, 1187

The winds blew through the fields of wheat like a mother's hand running her fingers through the ruffled hair of her favourite child. It was a gorgeous day. Rich, golden stalks of wheat swayed gently. The sky was the kind of blue that brought back the great, carefree days of childhood. A good day to be alive, when life treated you tenderly.

And riding beneath it, on a sedate chestnut mare, was Mathieu. Older, wiser, greyer. Lord of Chateau de Brie, knight of the crown and the Comte de Gardanne des Alfons. Time had been kind to the brash young boy from the south of Avignon.

Wistfully, he surmised that his life could be summed up as a series of rides: he started out hoping to hitch a ride on a passing merchant's wagon, progressed to riding warhorses in the far-away, burnt deserts of the Holy Land, and now he rode well-trained, gentle mares through meadows of green, lush, and fecund lands. Lord of all he surveyed. There was nothing quite like a summer's day in Provence for reminiscing about a life well spent.

He was far older now – the glory days of his youth behind him, spent on God's demands and the glory of King Philippe Auguste, first king of all France. The world had changed. Mathieu no longer lived in

Frankia, but in France. The throne of England no longer ruled the northern coasts of his country, and soon they would be evicted for good. He had fought with Eudes de Saint Amand, grand master of the Knights Templar, and even, for a short while, with the greatest knight of the age, Guillaume de Marshall, called William by his countrymen. He had loved a woman, singularly and with all his heart, and she had never strayed from his side in anything, nor failed in any endeavour she undertook – bar the absence of an heir.

The only thing that still eluded him in life, the only success still not in his grasp, was an heir. He and Miriam, still all these years without child. She claimed it was her, but he refused to believe it. She had begged him to move on and find a younger wife, a fat Gascon girl who would squeeze out babies like butter from a churn, but he refused. He loved Miriam with the entirety of his being, and he always would. She was his wife before God and, if that was what the good Lord had seen fit to award him in his life, then he was pleased with his lot.

Mathieu still remembered when he knew that Miriam would be his...

It was two short weeks after the victorious battle of Montgisard. The Kingdom of Jerusalem was ebullient, the mood of King Baldwin was abundant, and all of Christendom rejoiced at their miraculous victory. Almost half their force had died, but those left alive were covered in glory and riches – not many could claim to have so decisively beaten Saladin, and with so few.

If the victors of the battle were the crown of all Christendom, then the jewel in that crown was the 60-

odd Knights Templar who had survived. Tales of their valour and prowess spread like wildfire, and the white and red tabard of the order was a badge of honour and an instant pass to fear, respect, and riches.

Of course, the knights of the order were devoted to God, penitent, chaste, and committed to a penniless life. But the order took the riches due the knights, and invested them. When they left – if they left – they would take a large sum with them. Heads turned the other way when women moved in and out of the rooms at night, heavily robed, fragrant, and sometimes giggling. The knights were not perfect; they had never claimed to be. But they were always devoted. Yes, the odd early morning mass was a case of endurance trumping devotion, as some knights were in no sober state to get out of bed, let alone praise the Lord with solemnity and devotion. The will was there, but the flesh, as they said, was weak.

Mathieu smiled at the memory of attending an early morning mass with only one sock, the other left on a bedroom floor beneath the dress of some maiden still passed out from the night before. Those had been glorious, heady days.

Frederic had been in ill health since the battle. His left arm had still not returned to full strength, and even though there seemed no sign of infection, his infirmity lingered, and he tired easily on the training ground. He was to leave the order and return home, to the wife he had left in in Köln to claim plunder and glory.

Frederic's quarters were not as austere as a

Knight Templar's quarters should be, but Frederic, most truthfully, was not a man who suited austerity. His sitting chambers were luxuriously decorated with carpets on the walls and floors, fabrics thrown across furniture, purple, red, and gold running through much of the decoration.

The smell of cumin and lamb and spices as exotic and luxurious as the furnishings, filled the air. Mathieu and Jules – a friendship that was gaining momentum as done does after sharing tumultuous times – walked in together, and grinned at their friend, who turned from the window as they entered. Frederic had thinned and greyed considerably over the last few days. He was, physically, a shadow of the man he had been before his injury, even though his eyes twinkled with that same mirth. He was still a joyful and an unruly spirit, if ever there was one.

They sat down for supper and wine, talking of times past and future plans, and as his Persian slave woman brought the platter of food in, Mathieu saw her.

Now, obviously, he had seen her dozens of times before when visiting Frederic, but for the first time, as she entered with a platter of hot, fragrant meat, he *saw* her.

Their gazes locked, and for a split-second, he was lost. Her eyes were dark, almond-shaped pools that he wanted to swim in forever. Hair that was black and long, a hint of a smile at her red lips, and skin the colour of the sky over the desert beneath the setting sun – a soft caramel brown that spoke of warmth and closeness.

She, shyly, smiled at him – seemingly only at him – and placed the platter on the table, before turning to go.

Suddenly needing to remain in the same room as her, Mathieu reached out and grabbed her arm as she turned.

He didn't know why he did it; he just knew that he had to.

"Erm..." Frederic and Jules looked at him. She looked at him with a quizzical smile, the corners of her red lips slightly upturned as she was the only one in on the joke, her eyes, ageless in that young face, as sweet as an angel's.

Mathieu stammered, "To the cook!" He raised her hand, and his cup. "For meats divine, and for caring after our beloved friend!"

They all cheered, but letting her hand go – warm in his, her fingers fitting in his palm as though they were designed to do so – was the hardest thing he had ever done.

It was a glorious night with Frederic, who was a dear friend that they would surely miss. Although she was on the periphery, Mathieu's eyes craved only a sight of Miriam... that was her name, and that night was the first time he had heard Frederic utter it. Frederic had much to look forward to – he was the eldest son of a wealthy lord, returning in glory with even more riches and a reputation of valour to add to the family name.

Looking back, it was their last goodbye.

Days later, Frederic had succumbed to his illness and his bright blue eyes shut one final time.

Miriam was free, and the day after Frederic's death, there was a knock on his dormitory room door. He did not have a room near the palace like Frederic, the son of a powerful lord. Mathieu opened the door to find Miriam looking up at him.

She stepped in without a word, and kissed him. It was a kiss that lasted years.

Miriam was gorgeous, with curved hips, a straight back, and well-formed limbs, her skin so sun-kissed that he was jealous of the sun's lips. Her deep brown eyes still held him captive, after all these years.

They came home to Frankia, she professed her belief in the one true Lord, and they were wed.

The years had been kind to her, her body not fattening nor widening as many women were wont, and no grey showing in her hair. To his eyes, the eyes of an adoring husband doting on a younger wife, she hadn't aged a day and was as beautiful as the day he had first laid eyes on her. The day he first really saw her.

Rounding the bend to home, Mathieu urged the mare a bit faster down towards their castle, where his wife awaited.

Artists from all over Europe came to Provence because the sunlight – as it stumbled, thick like syrup, through dappled green trees – was the best in the world. So they said. Mathieu believed them. He'd had time to appreciate it now, and as his life had eased into the soft routines of a lord, he had taken more time to smell the flowers and appreciate the nature that surrounded him.

Mathieu was a man who had achieved much over a glorious and successful life. His crowning achievement was the document now in his bag. Sealed by the hand of the king himself, signed by Pope Innocent the Third and Philip of Swabia, king of the German empire.

As he entered the castle courtyard – to much fanfare by his servants – his adoring wife, beautiful as ever in a simple emerald silk dress (she loved the colour) was waiting for him, eyes aglow.

"And?" she asked.

He leapt off the horse like a much younger man, and swept her up in his arms. Then, theatrically, he pulled the scroll in its leather case out of his saddle bag.

"I have it! We have done it!"

She kissed her husband deeply and then took the leather case from him.

"Come, my husband," she said, walking away, purposely swaying her hips, then looking back over her shoulder. "I have made lamb with cumin, like I did in the early days in Jerusalem! Tonight, we feast!"

*

The night had been uneventful, and Eddie had woken up to see Mathilda taking in the sunrise in one of his shirts that she had pulled out of the washing basket.

At least the coffee was on. She walked in from the porch and poured him a cup, Odelia waddling behind her like a puppy. He eyed her out as if to say "traitor", but Odelia just gave little snort, and carried on waddling behind Mathilda.

Clearly, he was old news, and Odelia had moved on.

Mathilda handed Eddie a coffee. "Can we talk?"

"Sure. I think we need to."

"Well," she shrugged her shoulders, lifting his shirt disturbingly high up her thighs. It looked like she was only in her underwear. "It's everything. Magic, talking dogs, exploding drug assassins – I mean, I thought you were this, like, veterinarian guy – and you sort of are, but also you aren't, and why am I so unfreaked out about melting humans getting eaten by giant weredogs? I mean, don't people faint or freak out or something? How long do I live here with you? Do you like your coffee black? What do we do next? What did you see in the pouch you pulled off the dead guy? Also…"

Eddie held up his hand.

"Jesus. Whoa, whoa! It's too early for a million questions. So, let's put on some eggs. I've got sausages in the fridge we can warm up. You put on another pot of coffee, and get a notepad and pen – there should be some in that dresser up next to the door. Then we eat. *Then* we talk about magic. Your second official lesson, I suppose."

"My second? I suppose yesterday being the first?"

"Yup. Yesterday."

"But yesterday I learnt to listen to Odelia, which literally took five minutes. The rest of the time I just hid in a cubicle while you were killing all the bad guys!"

Eddie nodded. "Yup, lesson number one: magic is dangerous as hell. Don't run with the big dogs if you're still only a pup."

Odelia tilted her head as if to say "exactly".

*

They were on the front verandah, a set of chairs looking out over the driveway. Between them, a coffee table covered in cups and notepads. At Mathilda's feet, which were covered in rainbow-coloured socks, lay Odelia.

"So," Eddie said. "Replay for me how you understand the basic principle."

"Okay," Mathilda moved an errant strand of hair back behind her ear and cinched the corner of her mouth in concentration. "The basic principle begins with the fact that magic is the stuff out of which all things are made."

Eddie nodded, and she continued: "In the beginning, there was a big bang. At that moment, all the stuff that makes matter was created – our reality as we know it was created, and all dimensions as we understand them were created. Basically, one big bang and everything gets made."

"So, you've got the big bang part. Now, what about the rest?"

"Okay. When all of everything, basically, was made, all of time was made with it. Because our universe is in constant motion, time is a record of that motion. Effectively, time and matter as we know them are intrinsically linked. Like they were made together, like...like... conjoined twins."

Eddie laughed. "Not the example I would have used, but sure."

She pulled a tongue at him. "Anyway, because time and reality are joined and are the same thing – or at least both a part of each other, intertwined – then, when you play with the fabric of things, i.e., magic, then you also play with time."

She paused for approval, and Eddie gave her a thumbs up. "Doing great, kiddo."

"So, if you use up a bit of that reality in an act of magic (I know you can't really use it – you more like recycle it, I'm still not exactly sure how that works...) Anyway, when you change reality, for a moment you split the reality and the time, so that you can bend the reality into whatever your spell needs it to be. But then you have the leftover time, which somehow needs to be absorbed back into reality. If you don't do that and direct it back, then pieces of history – or present, or future – change. So, in order to keep time stable, we need to sink that time *back* into the timeline in a safe way?"

"That's right, and that's why all magicians need

to use their powers with a 'sink', as we call it – a time sink. So, you've got the essence of it. Can you tell me the basic principle in less words?"

"Mhmm..." She nodded, flipping through her notepad. "Okay, so here it is: the basic principle of magic is that magic manipulates reality, but costs time."

"And the applied principle?"

"Aahhhh..." Biting her bottom lip, she flicked through pages, squinting at her own bad handwriting. "Ah, here. The applied principle is the basic principle in application, and it is: in order to do magic, you always need a form – like a spell or a ritual or something like that – that can deal with the bending of reality, and then you need a sink to capture the time?"

"Yes. And the actual wording?"

"'The form shapes the manipulation, and the sink holds the cost.'"

"Great. We'll go through the other stuff again later, but I want to give you some things to practice. All the theory in the world won't help you if you can't do the actual work. So, quickly, just tell me again about the first times you knew you could do magic. What did you do?"

"Well, I found a dog that was hit by a car on the side of the road, and I could see he was hurt bad, and I just held him, and I wanted him to be better. I wanted it so much. I picked him up, and he let me. He was small, like a fox terrier, and he whimpered a bit, and I was scared, but when I touched him, I knew that I could heal him and that he could be better."

"And?"

"Well, I felt weird, like somebody had suddenly put me in front of a giant fan, except my hair wasn't blowing and my clothes weren't moving, but I could feel the wind on my face, and the chill in my bones. But there wasn't any, yet it felt like I'd just walked into a cold room with the fan on. And then, all of a sudden, the dog was fine. He licked me on the face, and then ran off. He kept on coming to visit me after school each day at that same space in the road, until one day he didn't. I never knew if his owners moved away, or maybe they just fixed the hole in their fence. I don't know."

"Did you do it again after that?"

"Sure. I mean, at first, I wasn't convinced that it was me. I mean, magic isn't real, right? But I tried again with a bird that was injured at school a few days later and it worked again. After that, I knew that it was me and I thought that I had this God-given gift to heal animals…"

"Which you do."

"Yes, but I never realised I could do *more* than just heal animals. I never realised there was a whole world of magic out there. I mean, you *melted* three guys!"

Eddie's phone buzzed and he looked down at it – it was a message from Sko. He could talk. "Okay, I need to chat to Sko – you know, the guy who found you and put you onto me, and spelled your folks into thinking you're on a scholarship at Colorado U? Anyhow, whilst I figure some stuff out with him, I want you to go to that bush over there." He pointed at a white *camellia japonica* just beside the steps. "I want you to break a small piece of branch, then I want you to heal it again. But as you do it, I want you to feel for the form of your spell – and I want you to feel how the power you are using is peeling away from somewhere – something. You might experience it like a thin, plastic wrapper coming off a sticky piece of candy. That's the feeling I get. Anyhow, the something that you are peeling the power away from – that is the time, and you want to direct that time (the leftover from your spell) into the necklace I gave you. That is your first time sink. Remember the applied principle: the form holds the manipulation, and the sink holds the cost. I want to see a healed bush and a necklace overflowing with time sink when I'm done." He gave her an encouraging pat. "Good luck."

Then he walked into the house to chat with Sko.

*

It should have been silent this far out into the San Luis Valley. Out here there was just desert and sand dunes slipping into rocks and tough, brackish trees – a panoply of browns and yellows and harsh oranges. Beautiful, in the way that rugged natural settings were. Gorgeous and vivid, and a reminder by nature that beautiful can also be dangerous.

As the sun set in the distance, scattered white clouds in the blue sky above, it was aiming to be a cold night. A pack of motorbikes, loud and black, streaked along the R160 eastbound, turning off a dirt road that headed north towards the Great Sand Dunes Park, and skewered off the known road some way in, branching off on an unmarked gravel road, through grasses and rock-strewn paths, towards a hidden and remote destination.

Deep – some miles into the San Luis wilderness outside of Alamosa – sat the cause of all the small town's worries. The Alamosa Brujos. Travelling toward them, headlights the yellow of hellfire, engines revving hot and tailpipes steaming, a large contingent of *los Diablos Cuchillos* rode towards a meeting with the Alamosa Brujos.

The dirt track ended at a large opening in front of a dark hollow in the mountain. There were at least a dozen cars and trucks parked outside the cave entrance, and over 30 members of the Brujos idling around. Mounted on the walls on either side of the entrance was a set of hurricane lamps, burning yellow. Stretching off in either direction from the cave mouth, hanging off spikes knocked into the mountainside, were more hurricane lamps, gilded oil lit, flames flickering as the night breeze shifted some of the lamps, as well as some sand and debris across the cave mouth.

As the motorbikes approached the clearing, all conversation stopped, and all eyes focused on the approaching bike gang. Long jackets were shifted aside to reveal rifles, and shirts were lifted from waistbands to show the grips of pistols and knives.

The massacre at Witch's Teat was a sore point. Three Diablos dead, and two Brujos. That was something that should never have happened, but it did.

The bodies had been found by a group of hikers the next morning, ripped to pieces, hearts pulled out and missing. Drugs and cash left sprawling across the ground.

The bikes pulled into the edge of the clearing, heavy machine growls of the engines winking out one by one, until the area was silent, except for a car radio playing in one of the Brujos' vehicles.

The bikers – a number almost matching that of the Brujos – got off their bikes and stood in front of their machines, arms folded, knives and firearms showing clearly at their sides. All except one. When a solid line of *los Diablos Cuchillos* stood across the clearing entrance, he dismounted. A large, dark figure, clothed in black leather, his face hidden in shadows, long black hair hanging behind his back in braided tails, like a warrior of old. The air near him turned cold, and even his own gang members stepped away as he neared.

The leader of the Cuchillos was no ordinary man. He walked ahead of his gang into the clearing, and the defiant stares of the Brujos – determined for revenge and some kind of justice – withered. The Brujos shrank up against the rock and away from the thing that walked towards them in the body of a man, on the legs of man, in the guise of man, but was no man.

Bethshiel, Demon Lord of the Plains of Torment, felt their fear, and it hungered him. He also felt the aura of power that seeped out of the cave. This was going to be an interesting meeting.

A short, broad figure emerged from the cave. It was a woman, a powerful figure, muscle overrunning to fat. She wore a blue, plaid shirt and had her black hair tied back in a long plait. Black Betty, the second-in-command of the Brujos, came out to greet Bethshiel, and bring him into the cave.

He followed her in, pausing at the entrance to look back at the two groups of men waiting outside. He raised his finger towards them, "If you spill blood, you will answer to me." His voice was soft and dangerous, like the sound of a snake moving across a gravestone. Like the scratch of nails across steel, or a casket creaking open.

Yet they all heard him. There would be no blood spilled that evening.

Bethshiel followed Black Betty into the cave and down the winding tunnel to his destination, the home of Shifting Sands, leader of the Brujos. An ancient shaman who, to date, had successfully avoided death's grip for over 300 years. The demon lord could taste the power on his tongue as they neared, tasting like heartache and desperation and sacrifice. It was a good taste for him. Not the best – not like fear, or hopelessness – that was pure ambrosia. But it was a good taste.

Betty walked Bethshiel into a darkened chamber with a high ceiling, formed over millennia into a craggy room of crevice and shadow. Thin, flickering sconces on the walls held burning candles, and somewhere in there was a cinnamon candle, and also... Bethshiel sniffed appreciatively... human fat.

The private quarters of the ancient shaman were messy, to say the least. He had furs across the floors and runes in blood scrawled down the walls. There were tables with books, manuscripts, and even two laptops flickering blue light into the depths of the cavern, running off an extension cord that trailed off into darkness where it was somehow connected to power.

The gnarled and bent old man, wizened and dark, like ancient paper crunched into a ball and soaked in coffee, shuffled forward. Physically, he was a pathetic human specimen, but the power rolling off him shocked the demon lord. Power like that, he had not felt on the human plane before.

This shaman had power. More than at their last meeting some years before. Many times more power.

As if sensing the demon's surprise, the medicine man's lip lifted ever so slightly, in the beginning of a grin, which could also have been a smirk.

"Welcome to my home, Bethshiel." He waved a hand expansively around the cave, and then flicked his fingers at Betty, who ran over and placed a stool behind him. He sat.

He motioned for Betty to do the same for the demon lord, and she placed a stool behind him. Bethshiel sat as well – no need to cause unnecessary problems.

"So, three of yours died." Shifting Sands was man of few words. He always had been.

Bethshiel sat impassively. "And two of yours."

Shifting Sands nodded. "It was a mistake." He raised his hand above his head and turned it, as if it was a revolving door, and Bethshiel felt something open towards the back of the cave.

A figure drifted in towards them from the darkness. She was beautiful, but dangerous, long, dark hair and wide cheekbones stretched under pale skin, and she had a coat of white owl feathers. Sharpened talons on the ends of her hands were stained red. A white fog rolled around her feet, and she floated forward, as if flying.

She, too, had some power, but between the both of them, Bethshiel knew he could defeat them if needed – he was a lord of Hell, and even in this human form, he had never encountered his match. In his true form, even on this plane, he would crush them easily... but the transformation would cost him power – power he couldn't afford to lose now. He had too much riding on his next move to risk it by fighting a pumped-up human medicine man and his summoned ghost.

He would have to bide his time for a short while longer.

"I was looking for another." The shaman motioned with his hand. "She came and I pulled her through. I let her have the mountains that are her home." That was his explanation, simple and concise – Shifting Sands was a man who said much with few choice words. Bethshiel could appreciate that.

The demon lord sat silently.

"She will not do it again," Shifting Sands declared. "She will hunt elsewhere. I owe her that much."

Bethshiel raised an eyebrow, and somehow, the temperature in the room seemed to drop.

The wizened medicine man knew who he was dealing with, and he steeled himself to continue. "We have another problem. A *brujo*. White man, a Yankee..." His lip curled in a show of contempt. "A wizard." Shifting Sands reached into the furs that draped around him and pulled out a small, leather pouch. Carefully, with liver-spotted hands and brown, bird-leg-thin fingers, he reached into the pouch and pulled out an eye, blood like jelly still clinging to some of the membranes trailing out the back of it.

He crushed the eye in his hand and it released its visions into the air.

A man – a *brujo* – was running into a bar or a club through a flaming doorway – it was empty, except for a handful of people. The man threw something out onto the floor, and suddenly, the room sank into darkness. A magical darkness. Somehow, the eye still saw vague outlines, powered by mage sight. It looked as if the figures were outlined with heat-imaging equipment, in shades of red through green to blue.

The others who had come into the room with the carrier of the eye all glowed a soft blue – slightly magical. But in the room, a man, infused somehow with some sort of bear, was tearing them apart, and he glowed red like the setting sun. He had with him a giant dog that shimmered orange and green. Between them, they obliterated the Alamosa Brujo hit team.

The vision played all the way through until Eddie discovered the pouch and, as he pocketed it, the vision winked out.

Bethshiel sighed inwardly. Potentially, this human wizard was a problem. In his experience, where there was one wizard, there were always more. Always. The good ones, especially. They travelled in packs. But he wouldn't give it to Shifting Sands that easily.

"So?" He shrugged.

Shifting Sands stared at the demon lord in human skin and raised an eyebrow.

The stare of a 300-year-old shaman who had necromantic powers over life and death was something that would intimidate most men. But Bethshiel was a demon lord. He had looked on the face of Lucifer himself. He had walked the halls of Gel Ath Shazor and had literally bathed in the fires of hell. Well. A piqued old man – who was comparatively as old as a newborn – was as inconvenient as a man standing in front of a convoy of tanks.

"So," said the nut-brown medicine man. "He has power. He will have friends who have power. He will now look for the Brujos. And he will find us. He will look for the Diablos – and he will find you, too. Then he and his wizard friends will know about both of us. The sooner he is removed, the better."

"But if he dies, they will come anyway."

"No. That is not how they work. First, they will investigate. They will look, but they will find nothing. All they will know is that their wizard has disappeared. Then we can lead them elsewhere, and go on with our business."

Bethshiel nodded. It wasn't a bad plan. Given that if they left the wizard to his own devices, things could go poorly for them.

"So, we have her," Bethshiel pointed at the owl spirit. "We have the Cuchillos and we have the Brujos. This should be enough to put this wizard into the ground for good."

"Yes." Finally, Shifting Sands smiled. He rubbed his hands together, like a Saturday-morning cartoon caricature villain. "Indeed."

*

Nighttime at the caves was a creepy time. Most of the Brujos had left shortly after the bikers had departed, and the few still hanging about had their own hidey-holes to creep back into. Black Betty, stone-faced second-in-command of the Brujos, sat in the old coven chamber. It was a roughly circular cavity in a larger cavern near the front of the warren of tunnels and caves that was home to Sowapophe Uvehe and the criminal organisation he had built. His Navajo name literally meant "The Lands of Earth that Move" (or, to those who even knew of his existence, Shifting Sands).

He had started the first coven 50 years ago. They all had some power, but not very much – nothing that could challenge his power. Over the years, the bodies in the seats had changed, but the seats, square stone carved from the chamber in which they sat, had not. The table was not a table per se, but a massive, oblong, mostly flat boulder in the middle of the room. The coven had never lived in the tunnels, like Shifting Sands did. For them, it was a place of learning, and worship, and sacrifice. The tunnels were a magical, spiritual place.

To the world, even to the members of the Brujos, they were led by the coven. It had worked well for many years, but last year, the police had somehow been able to bring the coven down, and now she knew how.

The members of the coven had documents in their homes that were covered in ancient charms that were undetectable, unless by magic. Their phone lines were impossible to tap, wrapped in code-talking charms, similar to what the Navajo had used against the Germans in World War 2. And yet, somehow, the police had gotten wiretaps.

The entire coven of five had gone down in a hail of bullets. Somehow, the early detection spells at their houses had not gone off.

It was as if the police had a powerful magician working for them, pulling back the curtain. At the time, nobody had known what had happened, and it had all gone down so quickly: go to sleep on Sunday night; wake up in the morning and everything is broken. La Jolla in custody, four other Coven members dead, and another 13 foot soldiers locked up.

It would have destroyed the Brujos. Would have destroyed most. But they had not even come close to the power behind the throne. Betty had been a captain next to La Jolla, and now she was the number 2. Instead of using the coven to smooth things over at the cops and with the press, now Shifting Sands used the Diablos – apparently, they had someone who was a specialist at this sort of thing. Until such time as they could rebuild the coven, which she would lead. She would make sure of that.

Sitting with her firm, muscled rump on a hard, stone stool, and leaning back against the table with feet outstretched before her, Betty knew that the FBI hadn't brought in a mage to crack the spells of the coven. There was someone local, and powerful, who had done it for them. Either in league with them, or secretly, he had laid open the coven to the scrutiny of the police. Damn! She smiled ruefully to herself. How the fuck had nobody seen it? He'd cracked them open like a *cangrejo* crab and left them with their insides exposed. The vultures had come in and feasted on them, her kind. No one had known.

But she saw it now, and she knew. She walked to Shifting Sands's cave to see if he needed another reason to kill this Yankee wizard.

Chapter 7: The plot thickens

Eddie was in his office at the Vet. It was a slow day, and Mathilda was out front with Maggie, learning how to run the front counter. As far as Maggie knew, Mathilda was the daughter of an old college buddy who had sent her to him because she thought that she wanted to do something with animals, but wasn't sure. It had been a good week, and Eddie had to admit, he liked the girl.

She was a good person, smart, tough, and loved animals. She had ample power and a wonderful level of sensitivity – really good for delicate spells. She had all the raw materials to be a great animal magus and would be a superb addition to the family if she stayed the course.

That was a problem for another day. Now, Maggie was the one he would have to deal with – sooner, rather than later. Someday, Eddie would have to tell Maggie the truth: that he was a wizard and did horrific things in the name of magic to protect how reality worked, and that sometimes the people he loved most died – and would she please stick around? Like, what were the chances of that going well? Eddie sighed.

The phone rang. It was Sko. Eddie answered on the third ring; he had been waiting for the call. "Hey, buddy. What can you tell me?"

"Quite a bit actually, Ed. How's it hanging your

end?"

"To be honest, Sko, I'm not so sure. I think this Brujos thing is more serious than we first figured. This mage that powered those spells I came across has some juice!"

"Yeah, about that... I think that we may be into something even deeper than you think here, Ed. But we'll talk about that in a bit. First off, how's your new apprentice shaping up?"

"Well, she's certainly got talent – I give you that, Sko. If she can keep her head in the game long enough, she's going to be a force to reckoned with some day."

"That's high praise, Eddie."

Eddie nodded to himself. "I think the kid's got something, Sko. Anyway, she's doing okay. Out front with Maggie now, learning how to run the counter. Now, what else can you tell me?"

"So there's a lot going on with the Brujos over the last few months – there's definitely something going on. My nose tells me it's big. Fucking big."

"What, you mean bigger than seven magically armed hitmen trying to take out a nightclub owner and the local mage because of a vendetta with a local drug gang run by witches?"

"Eddie, no offence, but that hit attempt was not even the moisture that evaporates off the drop that falls in this crazy ocean. If I'm right – and you know I normally am – this shit gets big. Ya sitting down?"

"Yup."

"Good. Hold on to your seat. It's quite a ride so far, and I think it's only going to get bigger the deeper we go. I started digging into the Alamosa Brujos – police files, FBI databases, that sort of thing. Then I ran a search charm that looks in news sources for mention of events that could be obvious spell workings. It's like an algorithm, but it's magical and senses magical events, so in its own way it's a bit more effective. Just for shits and giggles, I ran it back 150 years, because that was when we started getting written accounts in the area.

"So, here's some things that you probably didn't know. One: people have been going missing in Alamosa for the past 150 years–"

"People go missing every year, all over the place."

"Yes, they do, but not groups of people passing through the same area at ten-year intervals for the past 150 years."

"Oh. Well, this is an old area... there's plenty of stuff that went down with the Ute and the Navajo before we got here. Besides, the Brujos haven't been around that long. I mean, as a group they were only a few years old when we tussled with them last year and I exposed their coven and we got La Jolla locked up."

"Weeeeeell..." Sko drew out the word until it lasted several seconds, then suddenly cut it short. "No. I think we need to re-evaluate everything we think we know about the Brujos. But I'm getting away from myself. So, just give me a few minutes to line it all up for you.

"First, let's talk about the recent murders. There

were some murders outside of Fort Garland last week, close by The Beer Keg, at a place called the Witch's Teat – a remote outcrop of rock overlooking the Acres Canyon. Five people killed. So that's pretty bad, and you'd think it would have been in the local papers, or on a social media post or something. Anything, right? But nothing. And it gets worse: two of the murdered were members of the Brujos, and three were bikers in the bike gang Diablos Cuchillos, the guys we suspected supplied the Brujos, but we couldn't ever prove it."

"But now we have proof, so this is a good thing, right? Five scumbags kill each other in a drug deal gone wrong, and less bad chemicals on the streets to infect the good people of South Colorado."

"Well, no. We don't have proof, you see. Here's where it gets funky: the police report – the original report on the system – just disappeared. It didn't get deleted, or removed, or even edited. It simply vanished, and a new one was inserted in its place. That could only have been done by a tech mage – someone with powers like me, and there aren't that many of us around. But I'll get to that later, because there's more. So, this tech mage – let's call him Lowlife – disappeared the original file that detailed the murder and the crime scene, and left a replacement file that talked about an accident in which five innocent tourists died.

"What he removed – that was in the original report – was how the hearts were ripped out of all five and that the drug money and the drugs were all left behind. What's more, the puncture wounds looked like they were made by giant talons, and the place was littered with – get this – owl feathers. White owl feathers. I even have the original photos. I'll send them to you now – have a look, tell me what you see."

Eddie's phone pinged and he pulled up the message with the photos. Bikes were knocked over at messy angles on the floor. A dirty, white van was decorated sprays of blood. The ground was churned up and muddy and covered in blood – dark and dried in parts, darker and viscous in others. Strewn around the dead bodies and toppled-over bikes and gunshot shells were dollar bills and clumps of white powder. Littering this classic scene of a violent drug deal, amidst the blood and money and drugs and gun shells, were small, soft, white feathers. Owl feathers, apparently, although Eddie couldn't tell from the photos. It was a scene of absolute carnage. The way the bodies had fallen – given the number of bullet shells and also by looking at the amount of blood sprayed around the scene like a breakdancer with Tourette's had gone crazy with a bucket of red paint – there should have been some sort of wound on the attacker. All they had to go on was the clearly talon-caused puncture wounds and the owl feathers.

Eddie sat silent for a while, lost in thought. "So, what do we know about the hacker who vanished the report?"

"He – or she – was no hacker. This was done by magic, and really well too. If I wasn't the best at what I do, I would have missed it. Almost did. Their signature is faint, almost too faint to pick up, but there were some signs. I couldn't track them back, which has only ever happened to me once before, so this Lowlife is really good. But I'm working on something, so give me a bit of time and I should be able to point you in the right direction. Before we do that, though, I figured that if Lowlife was changing police records, could they not do the same with release dates? There had to be some reason that La Jolla got out of prison early. So, I did a search, ran some algorithms, even more spells, and guess what?" Eddie could hear the smile in Sko's voice. He knew Sko lived for this. "La Jolla's record was changed, in a similar way. Now I've got a search spell looking for characteristic changes on all police and government records over the last ten years. It'll take some time, but I think it may point us in a direction."

"Well, this is big," Eddie responded. "So, what do we know? We know for sure that the Diablos and the Brujos are part of a network that deal drugs, and definitely, we need to look into the Diablos further.

"Also, there is something out there – clearly supernatural – unless a giant white owl has been flying around targeting gangsters and ripping their hearts out.

"And, finally, someone is out there covering their tracks. And all that tells me is that there is more to be discovered."

"I'm on your page, Eddie," Sko rejoined. "There is definitely more to this... way more to this."

"Agreed, my friend. I think it's time you sent more of the team out this way. I get the feeling that things are only going to get tougher from here on in. I mean, I can handle most things, but if their opening bid was a seven-man hit team, what the hell comes next? What if next time it's the Brujos and the Diablos? What if it's them and this new mage that is powering the Brujos and a giant fucking owl? And what if they get Lowlife to hack my life and they start plaguing me with tech magic? My life will get very hard very quickly. And, of course, there's still this damn owl heart-ripper..."

"Yup, Ed, I think you're right. I'll get a call out to the team to see who can join you, and pronto. In the meantime, you watch your back, and see if you can find out more about this new Brujo medicine man that's packing all the juice. You must have some contacts down there on the old reserves? Some old Navajo wisewoman who can give you some insight?"

"Maybe," said Ed. "I have someone, but he's got some issues – I'll try. It's somewhere to start. I think I'll take Tilda and Delia out for a drive to the Sangre de Cristo range tomorrow. Visit my guy. Maybe he can help me out and maybe have a look at that pouch as well. Maybe there's a Navajo story out there about an owl that eats drug dealers?"

"Great, Ed. Good idea – even if that's a whole lot of maybes, at least it's a place to start. Just keep your eyes open. This whole thing is blowing up – from a local coven with a small-time beef to a deadly bike gang as well as a new magic power in South Colorado. Watch your back 'til help arrives, my friend."

"I will, Sko."

Chapter 8: How some things are made

Odelia stood on Mathilda's lap, paws draped out the window, tongue and muzzle flapping in the wind as the Ford made its way to the San Luis Reserve, south of the Sangre de Cristo Mountains.

It was a good two-hour drive and they expected to make it by lunch – and there was still at least a two-hour hike they had to make once they got there.

Odelia was already complaining about the hike.

Mathilda was schlurping down a milkshake – lime flavoured, for the love of God, but each to their own. Eddie was many things, but he had learned not to be too judgy.

"Eddie," she asked between long and concentrated sucks on her straw. "Why don't you tell me the story of how Odelia became a weredog? I mean, I know the summary – but I'd love to hear the whole story."

Odelia yapped – she was in agreement.

"Alrighty, then. Seeing as how I'm outvoted," Eddie consented good-naturedly.

"It was about two years ago, and Odelia had just been found along the R64, and she wasn't in the best of shape. She had been wandering around for some time, and was dehydrated and malnourished and had a wound on her back leg – a deep gash. Jed Foundry – runs the laundromat in town – he picked her up and dropped her off at the Vet. We fed her and nursed her back to health, and after about a week, she seemed just about ready to go back home, but in her case, it seemed like home had left her on the side of the road on purpose, and there was nowhere else for her.

"Maggie had taken a liking to her and so had I, so we decided to let her stay at my place – but only until she had found some place better.

"Meanwhile, I had been hiking in the National Wildlife Refuge north of Alamosa, not too far from the Golden Bear Ranch. I'd had a tough time dealing with a runaway mage from the elven lands..."

"Wait! There's elves? First there's magic, then werebulldogs, and now you're telling me there's elves? Holy shit! With pointy ears and everything? Do they use bows? Do they look like Legolas? I mean... are they all hot and smooth with flowing hair?"

Eddie laughed. "Hell, no. They're not like in the movies. They aren't really elves; they're basically people like us. Well, sort of. We're almost due to check in on them sometime soon anyway, so maybe we'll do a visit – you can come with."

"Aw, yeah! Elven Kingdom, here I come, baby!"

Eddie watched the road, and grinned to himself – it was so good to be young and full of wonder. Maybe he needed this.

"Anyway, I'd had a tough time tracking this guy down and an even tougher time bringing him in, so I was looking forward to spending some quality time at the Vet, and then taking some good weekend hikes. Regular life stuff, you know? So, I was hiking in the wilderness and I saw some wolf spoor – now that is really rare, because basically there's been virtually no wolves in the area since the 40s.

"I cast a simple Apache animal-tracking spell and I found that there were wolves nearby. I found them after a morning of tracking, and obviously I couldn't just walk into a pack of wolves that were clearly way out of their territory. I spelled in Wolf spirit and went to talk to them.

"I was met by Soft Walking, an old male alpha. I was surprised to see an alpha as old as him, but I could sense his power and vitality.

"'Man-walker,' he said. 'I have heard of your breed but have never seen you. Now I do.'

"I kept my distance, respectfully. 'Wolf-kind. I know of your kind well, but do not see you in these parts. Now I do.'

"'I am Soft Walking.'

"'I am Eddie.'

"Soft Walking turned his head quizzically toward me. It was not a wolf name – it spoke nothing of what I was or did. I explained: 'That is my name in the world of man. I am a medicine man – you can call me Golden Bear.'

"Soft Walking looked at me for a while and nodded. 'It is your name, Golden Bear.'

"I nodded back. 'It is.'

"'We are passing through to other parts.'

"Knowing how there had been wolves missing from these parts for some years, I wanted them to stay, but sensed there was more.

"'Why not stay here?' I asked. 'The hunting is good and the water is clean. There are many here who would welcome wolfkind back into these parts. You could raise many pups here.'

"Soft Walking was gentle, but firm. 'We cannot stay here,' he said. 'We are being chased.'

"'Chased by what?'

"'A skinwalker.'

"I felt a chill run across my skin. Skinwalkers were ancient and powerful spirits and were not easily defeated. They were deadly and very hard to kill or dispel. Most shamans simply caused them enough headaches so they moved onto areas of easier prey. Only the most powerful took them on toe-to-toe.

"I asked in soft, gentle tones, 'Old alpha, I don't seek your pack's story – but why is this *naagloshii* chasing your pack?'

"Soft Walking looked aside at his mate, who stood behind him under a low-hanging bough. A gorgeous, slender wolf with one white ear – both turned forward, attentive to the conversation. She raised her muzzle ever so slightly. Soft Walking turned back to me. 'My grandfather fought alongside the medicine man of the light grey people – the Lipan – against this *naagloshii*, and defeated him. Now, he is back in the world – we know not how – and he seeks revenge against our line for his defeat. We are a strong pack, but we cannot face him alone. We do not have the magic.'

"It was an obvious choice, and an easy one. I had fought a *naagloshii* alone before, and defeated it. If this time I had the pack helping me, I was confident I could beat it. 'I will help you defeat this skinwalker,' I said.

"Soft Walking held his frame still, ageing grey muzzle making him look silver in the late morning sun. If ever you needed a portrait of a wolf to adorn the wall above your fireplace, that was it.

"The old pack leader turned to me. 'Golden Bear, the pack accepts your help in ending this evil.' He sat down on his haunches. 'Do you have a plan?'

"As it turned out, I did. We agreed that the pack would track towards the ranch, and would prepare to stand and fight the skinwalker there. I would be in my space of strength, and when the skinwalker appeared, I would bind it and, with their assistance, kill it.

"On the night in question, there was a partly cloudy sky beneath a gibbous moon, which meant that the full moon was on its way. I didn't want to delay any longer, because the moon was friend to all magic users – good and evil alike – and I could not afford to have the *naagloshii* more powerful than it already was.

"The pack had settled in a hollow near the edge of the ranch, within sight of the back of the house. It was a gutsy move from Soft Walking, using the pack as bait – but there was no other way. It was near a space that I had packed with sinks. It was a place of power for me, and I knew that if I could get the skinwalker amongst the sinks, I could tether them together like an electric fence to corral him.

"I dropped my wards on the ranch, and stilled all activity on the sinks. I hoped that the magic that the *naagloshii* would register wouldn't chase it away.

"I lay in a small copse of bush and rocks just over 100 yards along the fence from the pack's camp, and settled down to wait. It wasn't a cold night, nor windy. It was still and calm, but this was no reflection of what was going on inside of me. I was nervous as hell, my heart racing and pulse pounding. A *naagloshii* was no easy fight, not even for me. I knew I could take it, but on any given day, one misstep could end it the wrong way.

"Thankfully, we didn't have long to wait.

"A cloud drifted across the moon as an unnaturally tall and thin man crept across the ranch boundary. He slunk more than walked, loped more than ran, as if a giant, feral spider crept out in the world, in the shape of a man.

"His hair hung behind his back in a long ponytail, his gaunt features obscured by the dark and the distance. But the aura he gave off was distinct. He was a *naagloshii*, and a powerful one. An ancient skinwalker, a spirit of evil that feasted off death – and that aura followed him wherever he went.

"The skinwalker ran swiftly towards the hollow where the pack was camped. It would be there in seconds. I stood up from my cover and activated the sinks. They hummed to life, threading bars of power from one sink to the next, in effect forming a stockade of magical power that the *naagloshii* couldn't easily break through. I ran towards the pack, transforming as I ran, and arrived as a glowing bear amidst chaos. A giant, long-limbed, red-eyed *naagloshii* in wolf form had already killed one of the pack, and was bearing down on Soft Walking and his mate, who were growling and crouched in opposition to the skinwalker.

"All eyes turned to me as I entered the hollow – which was exactly what I wanted – and I leapt at the *naagloshii*. It braced as I hit it, its long, wiry limbs belying the strength it had.

"We got in a tussle, the pack snapping at its legs while I wrestled it to the floor. I was stronger, but it was faster, and it slipped out from under my grip, and was about to bite a serious chunk off my face, when something small hit the skinwalker in the side. It wasn't a fight-ending hit, but it gave me the desperate second that I needed to re-adjust. As I shifted, I got to see what had caused the distraction. Odelia, all 50 pounds of her, had seen the *naagloshii* about to bite my face off and had rushed down from the house and thrown her full weight into its side – every last short-legged, squashed-faced, and wrinkled ounce of her – with the determination that only an English bulldog can bring!

"The creature snapped out at her in irritation, picking her up in its mouth and throwing her across the clearing. Odelia yelped as she landed hard. I was furious, but Odelia's charge had given me the gap I needed, and I got my fangs onto the *naagloshii's* neck, and I snapped it in one savage rip of my jaws. The beast hadn't even finished its death throes and I was up to check on Odelia. As it turned out, she was still alive, but had been bitten by the *naagloshii* and would turn into one at the next full moon – or would die in the transformation. Most died. As curses went, it was bad news. It was a curse of the spirit, a disease, and was a unique and very old form of lycanthropy.

"I couldn't leave Odelia to die after she had saved me. Besides, I'm a vet – saving animals is what I do. So I kept her alive and on a drip while Sko figured out a way to contain the curse. We couldn't end the curse without killing her, but we could route it, and contain it, so that she had control over her transformations. Hence her pink collar. It's magical and crafted by the best in the business. There's a bit more, but basically you have all the important bits.

"And now, you know the story of how Odelia became a werebulldog, and friend of the wolf, and my best friend."

Odelia let out a small yip at that, as if to say, "exactly!" And then she looked back lazily at Mathilda, with a very smug look on her face.

*

Once in the reserve, they parked the car in an empty lot. It wasn't a great time of year for hiking, and, in truth, it wasn't Eddie's preference. But if you needed to see Billy January, this was the way.

"So, who are we here to see again?" Mathilda

asked.

"Billy Jan – short for William January. He's a Navajo storyteller – a medicine man who carries big water in these parts. He's one-eighth Navajo descent, and goes by the name Limping Bear on account of his bad temper and being a really lousy runner." Eddie laughed. "Don't let the look of him suck you in. He looks like a guy you could feel sorry for, but he's mean as a rattlesnake when he needs to be and he plies a tough trade in song magic – I've only met one or two mages who could match him, so if he starts singing, you stop your ears up real fast."

"Why? I mean, he doesn't even know me. Why would he hurt me?"

"It's not about you. It's about him. Listen, let's just get on the hiking trail to his place and I'll tell you all about him."

It was a cold day, and soon enough they were puffing steamy clouds into the air as the three of them hiked up from the parking lot towards Bill's place.

"So the deal is," Eddie began, "Bill was born with a club foot and a foul temper, and even though the foot got fixed, his temper never did. He's pretty young for a medicine man, so he's had a tough time getting a lot of the older guys in the local communities to take him seriously, and of course he's only one-eighth Navajo, which isn't too bad, really, but some say he's not Indian enough.

"So you can imagine how he's not Indian enough, or not white enough, so he never fits in anywhere, and then he finds his power and it turns out he's got juice for days, and so he becomes the youngest medicine man in years – imagine how those kids who mocked him at school would feel now that he's the medicine man of the whole area? But he's had a rough ride, and actually he didn't deserve it. It made him… a bit thorny. He took to drinking to help him cope, and that's just one shit idea. Truth is, I reckon they were jealous of him. He really is one of the finest song mages I've seen. In time, he could be one of the best. Like I said, I've only had some small dealings with him, but I'm mostly sure he's one of the good guys."

"Mostly sure?"

Eddie shrugged. "It's magic – things aren't always what they seem… and besides, I don't know how far I can trust him yet."

"So why are we visiting him, then?"

"Well, those five guys that got taken out at Witch's Teat weren't taken out by any creature I know of – so it must be something supernatural. And if it's in these parts, then it's normally the people who have lived here longest who know. Their roots go back. So, it's off to the only half-decent Navajo medicine man I know, and that's Billy Limping Bear."

Mathilda was brimming with questions. What was the difference between a medicine man and a mage, like her and Eddie? What was song magic; what could it do? Could she do it? She would love that. She loved music.

To be honest, she thought, magic was turning

out to be mostly frustrating, being left in the dark and then sometimes a whole lot of excitement all at once. Eddie was cool, and he clearly cared – he had a heart the size of a city – but he also had a lot on, and he didn't explain things sometimes that he expected her to know. At least, though, he accepted her and he supported her magic. That was a hundred times better than being magic and everyone believing you're crazy (including yourself).

As they walked through the brush that was denser than it looked at first, up hills that were steeper than they seemed at first, Eddie handed a set of earplugs to Mathilda.

She looked at him curiously .

"Billy Limping Bear uses music to cast spells. A great man with a banjo if you need to get a party started – I've seen him literally sing the doves out of the air. But you never know what he's up to, so I'd prefer if you put these in."

"Oh. Well, thanks, but I've got these." Tilda turned her backpack around to show Eddie she had her earpieces and Walkman with her. "But you said he's not a bad guy?"

Eddie stopped walking and tilted his head, thinking about it, and not for long.

"No. I said I 'think' he's not a bad guy. I've never seen him as hurtful. But he may sing you a song and the next time he needs you to come, you may feel strangely compelled to go to a gas station you haven't been to before, and he's standing there, needing a lift. Or if he needs money for booze. He's not bad, but Billy looks after Billy. Let's just say that."

"And we're seeing him because he knows stories about giant Navajo owls that kill drug dealers?"

"Well, he's part Navajo and a medicine man. Like I said, he knows the old stories. Right now, we need some information that only the old stories can give us. So, in these parts, that means Billy."

She grunted, interest taken by something she had seen in the distance.

Eddie bent down to give Odelia a stroke – she was panting along gamely – and they carried on towards Billy's place.

*

The small compound that the State of Colorado had magnanimously given Billy and his family for perpetuity came up in Eddie's view as they emerged from an overgrown path, set upon by closely packed trees. If someone didn't know it was there, it would have been hard to find. Which is exactly the way Billy had sung it.

If you asked Eddie, the young shaman had somehow convinced the locals that his small lot in the San Luis Reserve was his family's, going back some time, and they let him stay there. He was out of the tourist paths, and helped out in the reserve, so it worked out alright, Eddie guessed – but he wasn't convinced that Bill hadn't used some of his power to get the decision swung in his direction.

Coming out of a dense pathway of small trees leaning over each other to form a green, shaded arch, they turned out onto a cleared dirt path that ran down towards a waist-high, chicken-wire fence that had clearly seen better days. Behind it sat a small compound of three buildings: a large, dilapidated barn at the back; a small house of wood and stone near the front; and, off to the side, a tiny shed too small to be a single garage that looked like the sort of place to store garden equipment.

Eddie stopped before they got close to the house.

"Odelia," he said, pointing to the side of the path. She looked up at him inquiringly . "I want you to lay low here. Keep an eye out. Billy sings some strange songs sometimes and these are old and wild parts. Cover our backs, girl."

She snorted, and waddled slowly off towards a large bush she could hide under.

"I'll get us a bucket on the way home."

Another snort.

"Bucket?" asked Tilda.

"Fat girl over there loves KFC," Eddie laughed.

Mathilda's hand shot out and poked Eddie in the stomach. "Not doing too badly yourself there, Eddie!" Tilda teased him. "You got a Snickers there for me?"

Eddie shook his head. Damn teens.

By the time they got to the rusty, pipe-frame gate, hanging on one hinge and barely keeping closed, the front door of the house opened.

Eddie halted and motioned for Tilda to stop behind him.

Out walked Billy Limping Bear, with a harmonica in hand.

He wore sneakers, and old jeans that looked like they hadn't been washed in some time. His face was lean, and he had a slight forward stoop. He looked younger than Eddie had described, probably close to mid-20s, which made him really young for a medicine man. He wore a grey, long-sleeved shirt covered by an old, orange poncho, and on his head sat a battered, brown Stetson with a grey feather in the band. Stubble tracked his cheeks – mostly dark with surprising flecks of grey – and he had a kind look to his face that seemed as if it could truly surface if he ever stopped scowling. But it looked like the sort of face that scowled a lot.

He lifted his right hand, harmonica clutched loosely in it.

"Steady Eddie, the magic vet! Out here looking for a favour, I bet?" His voice drifted clearly across the space between them. He had a voice for song.

Eddie raised a hand in greeting. "Hey, Billy." He thumbed to his side. "That's Mathilda, my new apprentice."

"Look at Mathilda – with beautiful blue hair – out here to visit her good ol' Limping Bear."

"Billy, quit it." Eddie's voice dropped an octave. "There's some things going down and I need to know what some of the old stories say. I'm serious, this is not the time, please. There are lives at stake."

Billy paused, hearing Eddie's change in tone. He nodded. "Alright Eddie, come in. Did you bring a drink?"

Eddie reached into his jacket pocket and pulled out a half-jack of bourbon. "Of course!"

He walked onto the property and up to a set of dilapidated chairs on Billy's porch, and sat down. Tilda sat on the porch edge, near the steps.

Billy took the bourbon and went inside the house. He came out a short while later with three dusty mugs and poured some for each of them.

"Coyote is always out there, waiting…" he began.

"…and Coyote is always hungry," Eddie finished. They both took a big swig from their mugs and both spat some into the bedraggled garden.

Mathilda did the same, her spitting not as practiced, and some bourbon and saliva dribbled down her chin. Both of the men grinned.

Eddie turned to her. "Put on your music, Tilda. We're going to get talking." She nodded and put her headphones on and there was silence across the compound while the men waited and stared off the porch. The click of her Walkman was closely followed by Mathilda getting up and wandering into the garden.

"Smart, Eddie," said Billy. "She won't be hearing any of my songs."

"She doesn't need to, Billy. She's too young."

The young Navajo shaman shrugged. "So, what story do I need to pay you for the bourbon? Good bourbon, by the way. Thank you."

"I'm looking for a story about a killer that rips people's hearts out and may turn into an owl. Or be an owl."

Billy said nothing. Eddie looked up and Billy's face had dropped.

"Are you sure you want this story, Eddie?" He was deadly serious. "This is a sad story, my friend. It's bad medicine, as sure as a white man makes the best whiskey but the worst blankets. Why do you want it?"

Eddie took some time and explained the murders at Witch's Teat, the Brujos and the Diablos. Billy interrupted once or twice to ask questions, and afterwards, Billy sat for a while. Before he said anything, he poured another big cup of bourbon and drank most of it, finally sucking some air in through his teeth before starting up again.

"Eddie, you have a problem." Billy exhaled heavily. "You know, most people think the old stories are just stories. Tales made up by grandmothers to frighten kids to sleep. Morality tales to make sure we behaved, or myths to help us remember the things that came before us. But Eddie, I *know* these stories. These are the stories of my people. I don't just remember them like a memorised set of numbers; I know them, like they're songs carved into my heart. Like they're the song I play when I breathe in and out. Like they're a part of me, woven into me like a thread that ties me to my past and future. I know these stories like I know my own face. I know their tragedies and their joys. I know when they were sung at the trail of tears and I know when the braves told them behind fires in freezing, dusty caves.

"What I am going to tell you isn't a children's story. It is *the* tale of this creature. This is its story, the truth of its life. You understand? I share with you my people's power because I know you are a good man, not because you brought me two cups of bourbon."

Eddie nodded solemnly. "Thank you, Billy."

The wind picked up slightly, and, as if nature was directing the stage play, the clouds overhead grew darker.

"She was once a beautiful woman," Billy began. "Tall and slender; straight and long. Legs that could run all day and arms that could draw a bow and fingers that could deftly weave. Her name was Sacajawea – Little Bird – and her friends called her No-lasso, because many men swung, but none ever caught her. From a young age – too young, maybe – men of many tribes could see that she was going to be special. The wife of a chief, or even a great chief herself.

"Until one day she met Tyee, a Kayenta Navajo down from the north. He was a powerful warrior, big and strong, with hair dark and long, arms tanned, and fingers that rested gently with great power. His smile showed a spirit of goodness, and he was called Smiling Sun. It was a fitting match, and they soon fell deeply in love.

"Little Bird left her tribe, and soon they were married and began to plan for a family, so their hearts could be complete. But, as you know, Coyote is always hungry, and sometimes, he eats joy.

"It was a raid by a rival chief from across the Silver Trout River, eager for the Kayenta lands and horses and crops and women. The Kayenta village of Smiling Sun was the third village that got hit, but it was the one that fought the hardest, and the one that paid the highest price. Smiling Sun fought with ferocity and bravery, and walked to greet his ancestors with pride. Sacajawea fought too, and it ended with her dying slowly in her own blood, left for dead – because all too soon, she would be.

"Around her lay the wreck that was their village. Friends and loved ones gutted like fish, everything taken, children burnt. The stink of burning flesh invaded her lungs – the only smell she could make out over the iron scent of her own blood spilling out through her nose and mouth and down her face. Little Bird was dying, in terrible pain, arrows through her lungs and cuts across her face and arms that had marred her beauty in a terrible way.

"As she lay dying, she prayed with a pure heart. Despite the pain and the longing. Despite the heartache at a life lost, at children she would never have, of years they would never age, of cold winters she would never share with her love beneath blankets, and of sunshine days they would never again laugh in beneath the gold of the setting sun. Despite this loss of the promise that the Great Spirit had woven into her life at birth, she prayed.

"And Owl, who announces death, heard her. Soft, silent wings carrying her on the winds of passing mortals, the spirit of Owl glided over the devastated Navajo village. She heard the moans of Sacajawea, she heard the breath whisper out her lips, and she smelt the blood seeping from pierced lungs feeding the earth. But, most importantly, she heard the call for vengeance.

"Owl landed next to the dying Little Bird, and with the peace and serenity that only a messenger of death could convey, Owl spread her wings over the dying Navajo woman, and allowed her spirit to enter.

"She devoured her heartache and misery and pain, and knew that she could use her for other things. For Owl does that – with her there is always a plan, within a plan, within a story. She sees further through time almost more than any other spirit, with her giant, round eyes.

"And the spirit of Owl that lived in Little Bird lent her speed and silence and the hunt and the night. And her claws. So, the stikini was born. A woman with an owl's cloak of white feathers and talons, who rips out the hearts of those she slays, and eats them whole. The way Little Bird's heart was ripped out in grief. Some say the favourite feast of stikini is the heart of a child, but that is not true of this stikini. It is not true of Little Bird, the stikini who is the white feather-coat that lived in these mountains."

Billy Ti iki Oah bowed his head, spent after what was clearly an effort. The emotional impact of living that story had taken its toll. Eddie, who sat close, felt tired. Even Mathilda, who had patently heard more than she had let on, and whose Walkman had definitely not been playing, stood slumped, leaning loosely against an old tree stump in the garden.

Eddie refilled Billy's cup and took a long pull from the bottle, finishing it.

"Jesus, Billy. That was one helluva story."

Billy nodded and slumped back into his chair.

"Are the stories always this powerful?"

Billy shook his head. "No. If the spirit is near, or alive in this world, then the story carries more power. This means she is here, in this world again. And near. That means we have work to do."

Eddie was shocked. "We?" Billy was normally a loner and never volunteered for anything, unless it involved free beer and cigarettes.

"Yes, you heard me, white man. We. There's still more to the story. I think you and the little lady better come inside. I'll go put on the kettle." Billy stood, stretching his back, and walked over to his front door, pausing before he went in. "Oh, and tell your dog she can come and lie by the fire while we settle this thing out."

Eddie tried not to show his surprise, and Mathilda grinned. The rustle in the grass outside showed that Odelia had heard, and she was on her way. Lying by the fire happened to be one of her top three favourite things.

With the kettle hung over the flames in the fireplace, Odelia sprawled out on an old rug that was so dirty its original colour was impossible to determine, and the three humans sat in chairs around the hearth in a dusty, brown cabin – Eddie on a stool and Mathilda in the one rocking chair. Billy settled down to continue his story.

"So, you see, the Navajo stikini was made by the spirit of Owl, who could fly between the world of man and the spirit world, in the same way that some shamans can see or talk between the two worlds. All people move between both worlds – when they die, they pass from our world into the spirit world, and from there, into the Land of Eternal Summer. All souls must get the chance to go to Eternal Summer."

Mathilda was confused, "Wait – all souls? Even bad people?"

"Yes, even bad people. They will go to the Land of Eternal Summer and, over time, may come back as someone else – or maybe even some other animal. But we will never know."

"But how can bad people come back the same as good people? That isn't fair."

"That's because Great Nature is not about what is fair according to you. Great Nature is about what will bring you closer to Great Nature. So you can live a life of joy. Also, how do you know that a person is bad – by whose standard are they bad? How do you judge?"

"Well, it's obvious – what about Adolf Hitler? I think we can agree he was a prize asshole!"

Billy laughed. "Well, he probably may have been the biggest asshole since Custer, but what if what you call his 'badness' served a greater good?"

"Nah, Billy. I call Bullshit. I mean, he orchestrated a world war that resulted in, like, 100 million people dying. I mean, he is responsible for the murder of six million Jewish people."

"Of course, I agree – Hitler did some evil stuff. But what if that evil stuff was meant to happen, so that better stuff could happen afterwards? Like winter killing the trees so that they can bloom in spring again, even better than before? Like the war throwing our scientific advances forward by 50 years in the space of five. Or the fact that Israel was formed and the Jews got a homeland after the war, something they hadn't got right in the 2000 years before that. Or what about the fact that the global population has exploded and now we live in a time where we have the highest quality of living we've have ever had AND the highest level of population – that means that we now have more happy people on the planet than we ever have had before. All brought on because of World War 2.

"What about the women's rights movement? In the war, women showed that they could work in factories and contribute to homes and incomes just as well as any man could. The equality of women – another outcome. What about minorities who fought in the war and showed that the racist ideas about them were bullshit? Without the war, where would they be now?

"Governments changed, ancient monopolies toppled, human rights soared and technology advanced. So, Hitler may certainly have been an evil ass-hat, but if you lived forever, and wanted to see as many souls as possible elevate themselves over time... then was the war a bad, or a good, thing? And, if Hitler started the war, and the war ends up as net positive for mankind, then is he truly evil? If he is doing his heart's bidding and it was twisted by Coyote, because even Coyote listens to the Great Spirit... then was he really evil?"

"But..." Mathilda hated this line of argument. "But if that's how you think, then basically no one is ever evil, no matter how bad a person they actually are."

Billy winked. "Smart girl."

"But..."

Eddie raised his hand. "Please, guys. Let Billy just finish his story – we can argue ethics another time."

Mathilda gave Eddie a dirty look, and Odelia let out a gentle sigh.

"Thanks, Eddie," Billy said with a wry smile, looking at Mathilda. "I think you saved me there!"

Mathilda shot him a look as well, then leaned back in the rocking chair and folded her arms.

After they had all had a cup of coffee, steam still wafting out of the steel kettle mingled with the woodfire smoke, Billy began again.

"Sacajawea is the stikini of the Sangre de Cristo Mountains, moving with our people as we spread south over hundreds of years. Occasionally, someone would go missing, and, generally, they weren't the best of us. Sometimes though, it was a child, or a mother.

"Over time, she became a part of our legend, and a part of the stories of our people. Then the white settlers came, and we fought, and we died. Over the years, our land shrank and our numbers diminished. Until almost 80 years ago, just after the end of the Second World War, our elders decided that there had been enough death. As a people, we were tired. We wanted to live and to find a way to embrace this new world, but still hold onto the best of our heritage.

"That meant the killer ghost of a woman tormented in the times when the deep spirits still walked the land had to go. Her time was done, and, in truth, it was a mercy. We would send her to peace, to the Land of Eternal Summer, where she would no longer be the stikini, but rather she could be Little Bird again, and she could reunite with Smiling Sun and their love could be made whole by Great Nature.

"But the ritual is difficult, and something went wrong. I do not know what, but my grandfather was one of those involved in the ritual, and what happened that day haunted him until he died.

"As the medicine man of my people, it is my duty to return the stikini to her rightful place in the circle of life, for she has suffered enough. And you two are going to help me."

"I'm in!" Mathilda volunteered instantly, beaming ear to ear.

Eddie held his enamel coffee mug in both hands, sitting forward, elbows resting on his knees. "If we catch her, would you be able to find out her connection to the Brujos and Diablos?"

Billy nodded. "Her story will then become my story – the story of my people, don't forget. I will know what she knew."

"Okay. Will it be difficult?"

"Very."

"Will it be dangerous?"

"I think so."

"And how soon do you want to do this?"

"Well, there's no time like the present, my grandfather always used to say. But I'll need to gather some supplies. What do you say to tomorrow night?"

Eddie handed his empty mug back to Billy. "Top me up, Billy, and then tell me about this ritual you have in mind. Mathilda, take notes on supplies."

"Yesss!" Mathilda shrieked. "We're doing this! I love being a mage!"

Billy eyed Eddie.

"You sure, Vet Man?

"I'm sure."

*

The time disappeared in a blur.

Eddie had helped erect the totem pole behind Bill's barn, and they had spent the day consecrating the area around it and digging holes to put wards in. Mathilda and Odelia had done food runs, coffee runs, hardware store trips, and journeys to parts of the reserve that produced exceptionally specific plants.

It seemed that being a shaman was very different to being a mage. On the way back home that night, Eddie explained it.

"So, shamans have power, right? But how do they sink the time? They use plants. This was why the Druids were such a big thing and why the Romans took them out. They could sink power into oak trees, and the best ones, entire forests of them. They were really tough."

"Well, if they were so tough, how did the Romans beat them?"

"Lots of reasons to do with the fact that the Romans had a more efficient way of sinking power – human sacrifice. And they had a lot of humans they could sacrifice."

"Geez, that's really sick. But then who beat the Romans? I mean, they're not around anymore, so someone must have beaten them?"

"Are you sure?"

"Duh. I've read history books. The Romans got their asses handed to them by a whole bunch of barbarians."

"Sure, the empire did. But the mages?"

"Uh..."

"Yah, not so snappy now. Well, they're still

around and still as twisted as ever... You ever heard of the Roman Catholic Church?"

"Oh my God! You mean the Vatican are ancient Roman mages who practice human sacrifice so they can keep using magic?"

"Clever girl!"

"Holy shit! Tell me more, Eddie – I need to know."

Eddie grinned. "Being a mage is cool, huh? But let's get some takeout, then chill for tonight. My brain hurts already with the amount of magic I'm going to have to cast tomorrow, and I'm going to need you to do some casting, too. You know the animal-summoning spell you've been working on? You're going to have to use that, big time. So let's take it easy for now, and once this is done, we'll take a week or two and I'll tell you the *real* history of the world."

"Thanks, Ed. That'd be nice." She mock-punched Eddie on the arm.

"Sure, Tilly." He reached out and ruffled her hair.

They drove the rest of the way home not speaking, a bit embarrassed about their displays of affection and growing closeness. They were mages, but still human.

*

Paris, France, 19 March 1314

The crowd was packed closely on the bridge nearer the city side, which is why Miriam had decided to view the execution from the landward side.

The *Île aux Juifs* – the Isle of the Jews – had been used for executions going back hundreds of years, and today's rushed affair was simply another state-sanctioned killing of the wrong people, in a long history of the state killing the wrong people.

Even though this day had been building for six years, the final decision had come hurriedly. Philip the Fair – that stone-faced, money-grabbing, back-stabbing, scheming gambler – was just the sort of man that she had needed to bring about the fruition of her plan.

This day had finally arrived, and she knew that something would be sealed today. It was a day marked by fate, dripping in destiny and heavy with meaning at an epochal level. Those who stood around the pile of sticks and wood in their drab clothing with their dirty hands and faces and their short lives – they would never know what the events of the day would truly herald.

The fate of many would rest on what Jacques de Molay did as he died. It was execution by immolation – death by burning – and the pyres had been hastily built, the pair of tall stakes firmly and quickly planted on a wooden platform.

This was it. There was no going back now. This was the end of what she had begun all those many years ago, the end of it achieved. After this, the Tufaahatan would finally be brought to mainland France, hidden, as it was, amidst the treasures of the Knights Templar. She felt like a proud parent and, at the same time, she was sad. De Molay did not deserve to die. Neither did De Charney. They were pawns in a game much bigger than them, that had been in motion for longer than they could even conceive.

Her hood up against a slightly overcast day, a chill wind nipped at her with the prickly wet teeth of the river, and gusted at her cloak. It was new, and red – more flamboyant than she had allowed herself in some time, but her stint in Paris was over now. Philip, the king, had delivered as she knew he would, and Clement, that arse-licking stooge of a pope, had gone along as they'd known he would.

Soon, the riches of the Templars would be in the hands of the king, and that would set off another set of events that would allow them to finally find and receive what was rightfully theirs. The Tufaahatan. A treasure so ancient it was beyond the counting of men. It had other names, of course, but Tufaahatan was what it was first known as. From a time before time was counted, when they walked the earth like gods.

A murmur in the crowds from the far end of the bridge brought her out of her reverie. The cart with the accused was winding its way near. Guards of the king wearing the gold and blue fleur de lis of the house of Capet marched in front and behind the wagon, as well as guards in the blue and red of the office of the provost of Paris.

The two captives were very heavily guarded, but then again, they weren't any two normal men.

Jacques de Molay was the last grand master of the Knights Templar, sentenced for execution by the king, for crimes against God and men. But every single one of them was total fiction. In truth, the king needed the immense treasures that sat in the knights' vaults, and he needed to be free from his debt to them – a debt so deep it could cripple the nation.

And Geoffroi de Charney was a lord from Normandy, a master among the Templars, and particularly important to her. She knew his line intimately. She had shepherded it and watched it well.

For the past 150 years, she had watched the line of Mathieu Gardanne de Rein closely, like a ghost in the shadows. With her as a wife, Mathieu would have no children, but she had loved him well, until he finally died underneath her, his heart going the way that all hearts did when their men were between the legs of a succubus.

She had loved Mathieu truly. He was a unique and genuine man and the power of magic ran strongly through him, even more strongly than he knew. His brothers and sisters had been sheltered beneath the umbrella of his success, as was her plan, and they had flourished well, the family association with the Knights Templar running true until this very day. The last day of the Knights Templar: 19 March 1314.

She found a rickety, wooden box, braced it against some raised cobblestones, and stepped atop the box, seeing clearly above the heads of the crowds. She saw the cart arriving with the prisoners, and even though it was almost 50 yards away, she had to hold in a gasp when she saw Geoffroi. The family genes had run true – she felt like she could have been looking at picture of Mathieu in old age – an old age he had never reached. Only 46, but stooped and thinned after six years in prison, Geoffroi de Charney looked almost 60, and carried the hawkish looks of his great-great-uncle Mathieu. He had once been a handsome man, and remnants of that still remained. But it did little for him now, because he was minutes away from an awful and lingering death for something he had not done. A recipient of the king's justice.

Behind him on the platform came De Molay, grand master of the Knights Templar. He radiated power, a power that spilled out of him like a dam about to burst. Which was exactly what was about to happen.

This is why the king should have used the pope's men. They were fewer, but their magic was puissant, even if Clement was a bumbling arse-lick. There were still some in Rome that knew the old ways, and they had power. Real power. Power to change the world. Entire worlds.

But, like all these things, they were finely balanced. This moment, in front of her now, was a tipping point. She felt it. What De Molay would do now, she wasn't sure – but she was sure it would be bad for the king and the pope.

The king's men watched on, a steel-encased cordon of soldiers draped in blue and yellow around the pyre. The provost himself, clearly rattled and pulled out of bed early for the sudden execution, stepped up on to the wooden platform alongside the pyre, and faced the two men.

His loud voice carried over the reducing hubbub of the crowd.

"You, Jacques de Molay, grand master of the once-holy Knights Templar, now disgraced in the eyes of God, king and man, are faced with crimes against God, against king, and against country – all abominable and insufferable and each on their own punishable by death. Of the specific charges, there are five, and they are listed, in no particular order, as follows…"

He was drawing it out, making a spectacle of it, the crowd oohing and aahing as he listed the crimes so vile he could barely bring himself to utter them. It was all bullshit, of course. The devotion of the Templars to God was unshakeable, almost as unshakeable as their love of coin. The leadership of the Templars took their vows very seriously, and as he read out the charges around sodomy, Miriam grinned ruefully to herself, because the provost was a known sodomiser. No man, woman, or child had a safe anus in his place of work, and he abused his position frequently and abundantly. Everybody knew it, and yet it was De Molay and De Charney who stood before the pyre, about to pay in flames for their successes in matters of collection and their failures in matters military.

The crowd was growing restless, and the provost – a longstanding reader of crowds – cut his proclamation short, and signalled to the pyre. Two men led the ageing Templars to the stakes, and tied them to them.

On the side looking away from the city, towards

Miriam, was De Charney. Again, his similarities to Mathieu struck her, and she was surprised that she still felt what she did, after so long. She had genuinely loved Mathieu – his wide, high cheekbones and broad chest so similar to those of De Charney, now tied to the stake... and she had loved Mathieu to death, as was her way. She was, after all, what she was. She could be nothing else.

De Molay was tied facing the city he was born to protect. He had fought and bled for the king, Paris, and Christendom. He was a puissant mage that called down on power few had access to. With the destruction of his order, all of the spell sinks available to them had been removed, and she knew why he carried such a powerful curse in him, and what it cost him to bear it.

Death curses were extraordinarily powerful because, usually, knowing they would die, the caster didn't give a damn about curtailing the power of the spell in order that they could control the sink. De Molay had been imprisoned for six and a half years, and he had been working on this spell for that entire time. Layer after layer – intricate, delicate cobweb upon gossamer-thin layer, until he had built around himself, through himself, and within himself a curse so powerful that it was about to destroy the balance of power in Europe.

It was more than she could have hoped for, and she was eager to see what the death of the grand master would release.

Some said the grand master was a magical genius, but, given what his order did, he had few opportunities to display his aptitude. When every problem was a nail, one tended to use only hammers.

When his was an order that encased themselves in armour and fought infidels, it didn't leave much latitude for genius.

The crowd murmured as a guard carried a lit torch away from a sconce near the side of the bridge and walked towards the pyre of the condemned men. Some of the mob cheered. Little did they care for innocence or guilt – all they wanted was condemnation and spectacle, and the great news that it wasn't them on the pyre, it was somebody else. Today, it was De Molay and De Charney.

She knew the guard had lit the pyre, because of the gasp from the people near the front. A wisp of smoke crept into the air, like a snake climbing up a rockface. Miriam smiled wryly to herself at the thought. Or like a snake in a garden, she thought, curling its way up a tree to whisper in a woman's ear.

The crowd seemed agitated, and with the amount of magic rolling off De Molay, she didn't wonder why. De Charney was muttering under his breath, using his meagre magical power to support whatever it was that De Molay was doing. There was a chance he could have used his power to escape, or to dull the agony and die painlessly. The grand master tied with him definitely could have stopped the entire affair in an instant, especially with the Church mages not present. But he didn't. He allowed the farce of an execution to continue... all the while muttering his final curse – his death curse – under his breath.

The thing about being burnt at the stake is that most people died before the flames actually hit them.

Usually, the rope around their necks that tied them to the stake would tighten as their weight came off their legs, trying to escape the heat, and they would be strangled to death – unpleasant, certainly, but far more preferable to death by burning. If they weren't equipped with a noose (De Molay and De Charney were not), then asphyxiation from the smoke would do it. Again, a really bad way to die, but still preferable to being roasted alive.

Miriam had seen many deaths over her years, and some burnings at the stake. At least at this one, the wood was not wet. It would smoke, and they would most likely die within minutes, as the smoke filled their lungs. They would expire before the flames took to their skin and they burnt like human candles as their own fat became fuel for the fire.

It seemed, though, that the smoke was staying clear of De Molay, so he could utter the words he needed to, in order to cast his curse. The fire grew, and De Charney's head began moving as he wriggled and squirmed on the stake, the heat becoming increasingly uncomfortable. His movements became more frenzied, and his head bobbed, his chest heaving up and down, and then his head fell down onto his chest. A few seconds later, his legs sagged, and he fell forward, only the strap on his chest affixing him to the stake keeping him from falling forward into the flames.

And sadly, and yet mercifully swiftly, Geoffroi de Charney, the descendant of Mathieu, the man from the line that she loved, passed away.

De Molay seemed unharmed, and his voice grew

louder. Now the fire was crackling – a blaze big enough to burn two whole men, flames licking up as high as his waist. The smoke should have been choking him, and the flames should have been searing him, causing unbearable pain, but Jacques de Molay kept on working his curse, until in an instant, a soft sheen of light passed from him, and suddenly, he visibly paled. The shield – he had had one after all – had dropped, and now he was in the full heat of the furnace. He continued his spell, through a mounting and infinite world of pain, and finally, the capstone piece.

In an upraised voice he cried: "And so it is with the line of Capet, and so it is with Philip the Fourth, and so it is with Clementine, as it is now with I, Jacques de Molay. I bequeath this to be real in power and in time. Let it be done, in the name of God!"

He hung his head, inhaled one last time and, slowly and dramatically, breathed his last.

The curse released.

Miriam felt the power spread out from the dead grand master – a circle of light, like sunlight as it breaks through the veil of clouds in the morning. A circle of power that echoed throughout the world. Its power rushed through the crowds. Some stumbled, some swayed, but all felt it. Miriam braced herself, for she knew what was coming. The power of the curse hit her, and lifted her off her feet, throwing her back into the family that stood behind her.

All present knew that something momentous had just happened, except none of them knew exactly what.

Scrambling to her feet, and muttering quick apologies to the family, pausing to help the old mother up, she turned and headed back to shore off the bridge. The history of Europe – and the world as they knew it – had just been changed, and in line with their agenda. She would have to get back to London – she and Samael would need to talk about this. Plans would have to be made. The future was no longer what it was meant to be.

*

The night was still and dark; cloudless and cold.

Behind the barn, a circle of ground had been cleared and pounded hard. The heavy, flat-bottomed iron pole that Eddie had pressed it with, leant against the barn.

The circle had been outlined with white-painted stones, each with a different symbol smeared in blood or paint or saliva.

Bill had drawn more symbols in the sand outside the circle, and even more inside it. Within the circle, Eddie, Billy, and Mathilda stood, peering towards the totem pole that they had erected earlier. It stood over 9 foot above the ground, each one-foot segment representing a different god or spirit.

In case she was needed, Odelia hid in the barn close by.

Bill Limping Bear, shaman to the Navajo of

Southern Colorado, was dressed in jeans, boots, and a fading blue Adidas zip-up top smudged in brown dirt. He also had a red headband tying his braids back, with three pure white feathers stuck in the band.

He held an ancient tomahawk in his left hand, and a bowl of liquid in his right, and he was going over his chants in his head, committing some complex rituals to memory.

"Why don't you just read it?" Mathilda asked.

Billy stopped, obviously peeved. "Because that is not the way of my people."

"No," Mathilda acted as though she was explaining to a child. "That was the way of your people because they had no written tradition. That was why they had to remember everything. But now you have tech-no-log-y." She drew each syllable out to emphasise how slow he was being, and then pulled her cellphone out of her pocket and waived it in front of Billy's face. "Look – fancy thing – lights up in dark and has words on it for reading. Big whampum magic."

"Aaah, fuck off, white privilege. I've got some serious magic to do here."

Mathilda smiled sweetly at him. "Yessir. I'll jus' head back on to your tepee and start your cooking and cleaning for when the big men are done their mighty magic. Too complicated for us little women."

"Aah, f–" Eddie stepped in between the two of them, separating them with his hefty hands. He had been loading up on energy all day – every charm he had was stocked and charged, he was channelling a powerful bear energy and he was radiating aggression and menace and power. "Shut it, kids. We've all got our own shit on tonight. We can't get this wrong, so stop behaving like high school dropouts and get your heads in the game.

"You," he turned and pointed at Mathilda. "Your part of the plan is critical – if you fail, the whole damn thing doesn't take off and we have to kill the stikini, you get it? That means an innocent woman who has suffered under possession by an owl spirit for 500 years gets to die in the spirit world, and NEVER gets eternal rest. That's fucking eternity. So don't you fuck it up."

Mathilda stilled immediately.

"And you," now Eddie turned on the Navajo shaman. "If you need to read under a glow-in-the-dark teddy fucking nightlight, I don't care – you do WHATEVER IT TAKES to get her here and cast the spell, understand? You of all people know the cost of this, and you're too proud to take some advice? Do you want to be right, or do you want to win?"

Chastened, Billy replied with his head down: "We need to win."

"Good." Eddie stepped out from between them. "Now you two sort your shit out. We've got 15 minutes to go and I'm not letting teenage angst, first-time stage fright, or fucking tribal ego get in the way of us fixing this. Tonight, we right some wrongs. Now, I'm going for a piss."

Hulking, like a bristling bear, Eddie strode out of the circle.

When he was out of earshot, Mathilda commented out the side of her mouth, "Geez, sorry, Dad."

"Is he always this way?"

"Nah. It's the bear in him."

"Maybe. That and the fact that he's got more juice running through him than I've ever seen running through a human being."

"Wow." Mathilda was genuinely surprised.

"Yeah. If we make it through the night, I'll tell you some of the stories about him. I never believed even half of them until now. He's pulling down the kind of power that I've never seen in one man before..." He paused for a second. "Sorry for being shitty about the reading – it was a good idea. Thanks for being here."

"Yah, I'm sorry too. It was a dick move to tease you about the tech."

"And the tepee thing."

"Yeah, that too. Sorry." She held up a fist for a bump. "We good?" This time, a genuine smile.

He bumped back, and, for once, the smirk on his face became an actual smile. A small one, but a smile nonetheless. "Yeah, we good."

Eddie headed back into the circle, and they carried on their preparation for the ritual to come.

The next few minutes showed the immutability of time. They were both the quickest, and the longest, minutes of their lives. Each moment dragged out as they went over their parts in this strange pantomime of ceremony and spell. Each moment shot by as they rushed towards a tragic and intense moment in history.

Finally, as they stood in silence in the circle, around the totem of the Navajo, Billy stepped forward. He looked at each of them, standing either side of him, and nodded.

"It's time."

He lifted his small, wooden bowl from the ground and drank every last drop in it, grimacing at the taste. Then he started to chant and sway, tapping a rhythm with his hand against the side of the tomahawk. Mathilda found the rhythm alluring and started to move her body side to side as the shaman chanted, his magic filling the circle. She shot a glance at Eddie. He stood as still as a stone, unmoving in the circle, entirely unaffected by the pull of the shaman's song.

For almost an hour, Billy sang and danced his ritual, weaving in movements and phrases and rhythms into a summoning spell of great power. One did not easily summon a stikini.

With a final stomp on the ground, Billy finished his spell, and walked back towards them for a rest before the next phase of the plan.

Now Mathilda closed her eyes and reached out with the only actual spell she knew – an animal call. She pictured in her mind the image of an owl. She felt it fly past her. She heard the flap of its wings and its hoot at the night. She called on owls, and dumped the sink into the totem pole in front of her. In the circle, she had more power than she had had before, and she had never worked with a sink as large as this one. She threw her power into the task, calling out every owl for miles around, pouring her entire being into the spell, straining to pull them in, call them in by the dozen, until she felt a meaty hand rest gently on her shoulder.

"Well done, Mathilda. You have called more than we need."

She opened her eyes to see Billy giving her the thumbs up. Eddie nodded at her, and then gave her a shoulder a tender squeeze. His hand felt like it was twice the size it should be, and the power that coursed through it felt like he could easily crush her shoulder like a discarded candy wrapper.

She was glad he was on their side.

Around them, the sounds of owls landing on the barn, on the trees, and some even on the dirt, reached their ears. There seemed to be hundreds of them. If that didn't call to the spirit of Owl, then nothing would.

The night was not soundless, but it was eerie. The owls that roosted around the ritual circle and their totem stayed quiet, in an unnatural way. They shifted and moved wingtips and adjusted weight on branches or creaking gutters along rusted, corrugated rooftops. But still, for as many as were there, their silence was overwhelming. It was the silence of waiting predators, and it had a weight all of its own.

In the circle, the three humans breathed quietly. Billy and Mathilda, more laboured. Eddie, slow and easy. He took the time to scan around the circle, his night vision enhanced by a small, bronze circlet he had around his neck – a vision ward from Bex, the glamour mage. She would be here soon, and Eddie had a horrible feeling that they would need her. She was travelling in with Tod, who was as dangerous and surly as Bex was friendly and unassuming. But underestimate Bex at your peril. They were part of the small group of mages founded by Sko ten years ago, and had become a power for good in the region. There were only seven of them, but each a powerful mage in their own field, each one a world-beater in their own right.

He knew that tonight was just the beginning of this operation, and having Tod and Bex by his side would be essential if they were going to take out the Alamo's coven and their drug-peddling partners, the Diablos.

Eddie dropped his weight and leant slightly forward; something was coming. Despite his night vision and his enhanced sight as a bear totem, he couldn't see it. Nor could he hear it. But he felt it. The hair on the back of his neck stood up and, unconsciously, he released a low, scary growl. Guttural and promising death. As he realised he was doing it, Eddie saw Billy and Mathilda back away from him.

He raised a hand in apology. "Something's coming," he whispered.

Mathilda pulled some rope out of her pack and placed the pack on the ground.

Billy held his tomahawk tightly in both hands.

Eddie crouched low and prepared to pounce. If he were a dog, his canines would be bared and he would be growling. If he were a cat, his hair would be lifted and he would be hissing. But he was a mage, and he prepared to unleash his bear totem power.

The bronze choker around his neck shone lightly, charged as it was for a night of use. His deflection charm had been burnt out and he couldn't get a new one until he saw Tod again. Hopefully soon. But Eddie had other tricks in his proverbial bag of them. He had a plastic ball that morphed on impact with its target into a thick plastic web – courtesy of Colm, the plastic mage in their group. Around his waist (beneath his long, brown coat) he wore a thin piece of lion skin that he'd been given by Cassiopeia – she was an actual Greek muse and she claimed that the piece of skin was from the original Nemean lion slain by Heracles, and it would give Eddie incredible strength. He had never tested it, and Cassie was sometimes a mite unreliable – as muses were wont to be – but when she was bang on the money, then she over-delivered. Either way, Eddie figured it wouldn't hurt, as long as the piece of old lion skin didn't abuse him in some way, and it wasn't giving him those kinds of vibes.

A feeling began to drift across Billy's compound. Odelia crouched low and growled. All animals know that when there is something dangerous in the dark, you crouch low and growl. Humans know it too, but we've forgotten that feeling for other things – like how to Android and iPhone. Eddie, unlike most of us, hadn't forgotten it, and the bear in his totem began clambering to come out and bare its teeth and claws and rage against whatever was coming and warn it that a bear lived here and that the bear would kill it.

Mathilda shivered in fear. She found herself wanting to run – an unreasonable fear, because nothing was there yet and this was something she could never outrun – but at a deep, primal level, her genetic memory of when people went missing to predators like these, of times when the dark held innumerable and unspeakable terrors, told her that she needed to run, because even if she lived for five seconds longer, she would live for five more seconds. Mathilda had never experienced anything like this, and gritted her teeth and dropped to her knees and clutched the dirt beneath her, to prevent herself from running away.

Billy walked over to her slowly, as if wading upstream over slippery rocks, and, softly, he touched her with the tomahawk. The fear melted from her, from her head down to her toes, like a wave of warmth sliding through her body, and she stood up and looked ahead in the direction that she felt the fear was emanating from. She clenched her teeth and set her jaw against it. Now, she was filled with defiance. She would defy this fear, this thing, even if she died doing it.

She lifted her hand to wipe a tear that had slipped out only a few seconds ago, when the fear had threatened to overwhelm her, and she marvelled at what the tomahawk had dispelled from her. Billy nodded at her, and then turned to face the direction that they felt the stikini would come from.

Fog – the type that was unnaturally dense – grew in ever-expanding, thick, ropey strands, reached across the clearing and up from the ground. In a very short space of time, anything below waist height was obscured in a white mist. The feeling of fear grew more intense, and the mist grew taller. The owls started to hoot – every single one of them – and then they began to beat their wings, and the space amidst them – the circle with the totem pole and the three humans waiting for an ancient, undead spirit of vengeance – very soon became noisy and chaotic. For some reason, this just made the fear worse. It was as if the owls were panicking and were trying to fly away, but the fear held them firm and fast, paralysed on their perches.

Billy squatted, Geronimo's tomahawk in his hands. Sweat ran down the sides of his face. The stikini had to come, unable to ignore the summons to the circle. But nothing said she had to come slowly or gently or peacefully. Because she had been summoned to this plane by another, he couldn't control her – that was what Eddie was for – but he could break her curse and dispel her, setting her free from an age-worth of torment.

Except, of course, she would fight him tooth and claw to not let that happen.

There was an instant before she attacked when they all knew that she was about to attack.

A sudden rushing sound, the intake of air, and the stikini exploded out of the mist, straight up into the air, rising like a phoenix from the flames of its rebirthing fire, white fog rolling off her outspread arms beneath her white, feathered cloak, and cutting on her talons. For a split-second, in that way that fast and violent encounters sometimes happen, everything stood still and she seemed to float in mid-air, a transfixed Navajo wraith cloaked in great beauty and sadness and vengeance.

She landed and in an instant back-handed Mathilda across the face with a claw and blocked a tomahawk strike from Billy – he had hit at her with the flat of its blade. As she touched the axe, a shock ran through her body as the powerful magic of Little Hat – Geronimo's medicine man and one of the most powerful shamans of modern times – attacked the fear-based curse that lived inside her. As this happened, a giant, brown bear with fangs the size of a large man's fingers barrelled through the fog and tackled her to the floor.

Crawling back to her feet, Mathilda looked at the bear and saw Eddie, but at the same time she saw the bear, as if both of them filled the same space. It was mind-bending, but she shook her head and scrambled for her rope and ran towards the fray.

Eddie had one of the stikini's arms in his giant paw and was snapping at her head with his maw, but her free hand was moving at lightning speed, slicing at his thick bear hide, talons arcing through the air, leaving icy, white streaks behind them. She landed deep, gouging strike after strike and Eddie couldn't match her for speed.

Billy rushed in and the stikini lashed out a foot and caught him on the side of his face, sending him flying across the circle to lie still, blood seeping from a cut above his cheekbone.

From behind the barn, there was a deep, unholy howl, as deep as an ocean trench with the base of a lion and the high notes of a wolf. Suddenly, Odelia, now transformed into her 500-pound wereform, bounded out from her cover and leapt high in the air, over the circle boundary, and collided bodily with the stikini, the spirit of vengeance now caught grappling the giant dog and the giant Eddie-bear.

The stikini was as strong as two men, but she didn't have the strength to fight a weredog that hit like a truck and a giant bear with the strength of the Nemean lion. Eddie was crazy powerful and, despite bleeding in a dozen places through a tough fur and hide, his grip was unbreakable, like soldered iron around her wrist. If he could just get his other arm on her...

Odelia went for the stikini's hand and got a viscous slash across her muzzle that would've cut open the face of normal dog, but the werebulldog barely flinched. The momentary distraction allowed Eddie another crack at grabbing the stikini's hand, and his time he got it. Pinning her arms down, he wrapped her in a bear hug, hands behind her back, and then he fell to the floor, holding her in place like a bad mimicry of a modern-day MMA match.

This was Billy's time to shine, but he was still out cold from the kick to the head. Odelia looked around her, left and right, her giant head trying to figure out what to do next. She bounded over to Billy and licked him on the face with a tongue wider than his head, and then barked at him to get up. Mathilda ran over and gripped Billy by his collar, and shouted his name in his face.

Screaming, panicked, she felt a surge of power jolt through her hands, and Billy's eyes shot open. Wide-eyed, he looked around and saw what was going on. He scrabbled in the dirt for the tomahawk.

"The Owl spirit!" he shouted to Mathilda.

He ran over to where Eddie wasn't getting it all his own way as the stikini spirit was kicking and biting at him, pulling chunks out of his upper arms and shoulders. Despite this punishment, his grip remained steady.

As the stikini writhed in Eddie's arms, Billy laid the flat of Geronimo's tomahawk against her face, and he began chanting. At first, she just screamed and writhed more, her beautiful, statuesque face a rictus of pain, but then a form began to rise up from within her. It was the curse of vengeance – it was the essence of the spirit of Owl.

It would not come out easy, striving to keep in its form, not seeing another open home. These things needed a space to go and could not exist without a host, but Sacajawea was no longer the host for it.

Meanwhile, Mathilda focused on the owls and poured what was left of any power she had into them, joining them as one amorphous mass, as if they were all powered by one spirit, one being, because that was how they had first come into this world.

United as one, the owls contained the spirit of Owl, and so summoned by its own, the spirit of Owl, called from its place in the world of spirit, arrived in the world of man.

Sensing its owner, the curse flew back to Owl, and Owl welcomed it in gratefully. The owl spirit, one of the mightiest of the spirit animals, saw the circle, and, with it, the body of Sacajawea.

It nodded its beaked head, its giant eyes like two moons in a floating spirit form of the prime owl.

"Ahehee adeezhi." Thank you, sister, it uttered, and spread its wings from where it floated, and in one sweep of its mighty wings it took off into the heavens of the night sky, to float into the stars, taking the curse of Sacajawea with it. The owls all left to follow, and in an instant, every single owl had fled from the scene, after their primeval creator.

The mist was still there, but slowly sinking back into the ground, and Eddie lay, holding the still body of Sacajawea, who now looked like a beautiful woman, proud and strong, and not a cursed spirit of Owl's vengeance.

Billy was slumped over, tired from his efforts, but he was not done yet. He held out his hands – Mathilda ran up and took his right arm, and Odelia slid her massive head under his left. Buoyed by them, he sang an ancient Navajo song – older than time, older than even the oldest of his people could remember. It was a song from before the time of men and it was the pathway to Heaven. It was a song, somehow, we all know.

Billy was opening up a pathway to the Land of Eternal Summer. If Sacajawea had no way to go to her rightful afterlife, she would become a ghost, and in some respects that could open her up for worse use than what she had been through already. There was no way Billy would allow that, and so he sang the song that lived in the heart of every Navajo, that most sang only once, when they died. The way to Heaven.

The stars above seemed to form a circle around a moon that had not been whole earlier on – but was sure whole now. Then the moon became a hole in the sky, and the stars became pinpricks of light illuminating a path. The hole turned a soft yellow, and it looked like a wan, yellow sunlight was streaming through the hole in the sky. All standing there, in awe, could feel the gentle heat of the sun shining down on them, like it does on the best of summer mornings.

A figure, indistinct and small at first, appeared in the hole in the sky. As it walked towards them, it grew larger and more defined, into the shape of man, tall of limb, dark-skinned and tanned with a muscular physique, lean and strong. As he neared the edge of the hole, he peered through, and smiled a smile of indescribable joy. It was Smiling Sun.

Sacajawea – or, at least, her spirit – rose from the body that Eddie was holding, and as she stood from the ground, passing through Eddie's grip, her body crumpled away, like the dust it had already been for hundreds of years. She burst out laughing, tears streaming down her cheeks as she raised her arms out wide, and she was pulled up towards Heaven along the trail of starlight, towards the yellow, sunlight-filled entrance in the sky.

She ascended, slowly at first, and the higher she got, the faster she flew, until the spirit of Sacajawea soared into the sky, into Heaven, and into the waiting arms of Smiling Sun. And, after over 500 years, their heaven was complete, and Sacajawea was redeemed.

And down beneath the united couple, there wasn't a dry eye in the totem circle.

*

Shifting Sands awoke with a start. His power had been broken – somebody had broken his hold on the stikini, and he knew who. He didn't know how, or why, but he knew that, somehow, Eddie Burma was responsible for this. It seemed like it was the kind of thing he would do – besides, who else could pull that off around here, anyway? He was the only one with enough power, and the will to do it.

Eddie would have to go, and he would have to go soon. The evil old shaman ran his tongue across his teeth, as if tasting the idea of killing Eddie. He knew he'd have to do it – he'd always known that, from the moment he saw him through his vision pouch. He just never thought it would be so soon.

Before he went back to sleep, he formed a plan in his mind. And as he lay in his cave, wrapped in furs and blankets against the cold, his ancient, magically powered body tossed and turned as the thoughts of vengeance filled his mind.

He had literally been made for vengeance. As he dozed back off to sleep, he thought of a time when he had not known vengeance. It was a time when he had not known much of violence, or of the wars between men. As he grew older, though, that had changed...

Some smells never leave a person. They stay enmeshed in their mind forever, trapped there as long as their faculties will hold it. Those who die young forget the smell sooner. In the case of Shifting Sands – Sowapophe Uvehe – the smell stayed with him for hundreds of years.

The smell of burning bodies, sizzling human fats and acids, sharp-tanged, burning hair. After all these years, he could still smell it, taste it on his tongue, amidst the grey-blue smoke from the green pines that had got caught in the blaze.

Alone, tired, covered in cuts and bruises, with blood streaming from a deep gash on his head, the young warrior had run back to his tribal campsite after their party had been ambushed by the Spaniards. They had known the Spaniards were coming, and had rushed out to meet them. But the steel-clad conquistadors had lain in wait. It had been a trap, and this time, his people had fallen for it.

A musket butt to the head had laid him low amidst some savage hand-to-hand fighting. He awoke amongst a pile of dead men – some Spaniards in there, also some other tribesmen, but mainly his Navajo brethren.

He had sprinted back to his family camp, hoping for the best, expecting the worst, but as his heart pounded in his chest, sweat pouring down his body bruised from combat, he knew the truth.

The smoke rising grey and white through the trees was the first sign.

The smell was the second.

By the time he got there, everyone he knew was dead. His father, his mother, his friends, his entire family, his entire tribe. Either dead or taken captive, something the Spaniards often did, killing the men and taking the women to work in their homes and in their beds.

He moved from behind the tree that hid him, and walked out into the clearing of his people, now decimated and burnt. As he did so, he felt himself go dizzy, head spinning. It could have been blood loss, or shock, or too much smoke, or a combination of all three, but whatever the cause, it all meant the same thing. He fell to the floor in a sweat, and began to dream crazy things.

He had a vision of himself moving amongst the sands to the south, older than ancient. In this vision, he tapped his staff to the floor, and the swirling desert winds parted to reveal a cave in which he could safely live.

He saw shamans from other tribes, teaching him their ways, a long and lonely journey from tribe to tribe, campsite to campsite. The path of a lone warrior, a powerful magic man.

He saw marches of Spanish, Mexican, and American men, waging war after war against his people and others like them. He fought them bravely and powerfully, using magic, deceit, and treachery to defeat them. But, despite his growing power and many victories, the attackers came in a never-ending tide.

He could never win.

The vision in his dream shifted again, and this time he saw himself as he lay on the ground in the clearing. Dead. Still and at peace, his soul at rest in the skies, with his people.

He was too angry to rest. He would seek out his people, when his time came, but now... now was the time for revenge.

The young man woke up suddenly, and with clarity, as though he had not been asleep at all, merely thinking something else.

In a dream that he would never forget, Shifting Sands gained clarity of his choice – he chose to live, even though it meant a life of vengeance.

Some smells, people could never forget.

Despite the memory, Sowapophe Uvehe slept the deep, energising sleep of innocents and crazy men. Or, at least, men who had accepted what they had become.

*

The sun seemed to shine a little brighter the next morning, when they woke up in Billy's lounge. Tired and aching, the three of them sat in grinning silence over some bacon and beans that Billy had fried up. Even Odelia seemed slightly less surly.

They had done a good thing. In fact, that didn't really cover it. They had done a great thing. A soul restored to Heaven – last night, they had done the work of angels.

In between spoonfuls of beans, Billy spoke to Eddie. "So, I now know the stikini's story – she was banished from this realm by my grandfather, to the realm of spirit – they had tried to do what we did, but something went wrong. She was brought back by a name from legend. I still can't believe it. If it's true, then we have a bigger problem than the stikini."

Eddie looked up from the last few beans in his bowl. "What do you mean, 'bigger problem'?"

"If she was brought back by this medicine man – Sowapophe Uvehe – The Land that Moves Back and Forth – then he hasn't died in 300 years... and some worse news for you: he's the head of your old friends, the Alamosa Brujos."

"Wait. The Land that Moves Back and Forth? What kind name is that?" asked Mathilda.

"It comes from the desert sand dunes," said Billy. "His name – Sowapophe Uvehe – means Shifting Sands. His has been a cursed name amongst our people for generations."

Eddie shook his head, as if clearing fog from it. Heavy scratches ran down his face and arms, and he was bandaged in parts. He healed quickly – way more quickly than he should – given the powers he had, but he wouldn't look fine for another week. "Thanks, Billy. I think that name was the information we needed. But today, I just want to sit in the sun, feel it shine down on me. I want to take this win. Tomorrow, I'll give you a call – maybe I'll get Sko, a friend of mine, to join in. He thought there was more to this than what appeared at first, and I've learnt to listen to his hunches. But not today, okay? Today I'm tired, and I'm happy, and for once, I know we did some good. Let's take it up tomorrow, okay?"

"Sure thing, Big Bear. More beans?"

Eddie grinned. "Obviously."

Later, as Eddie, Mathilda, and Odelia drove home, the Ford raising a trail of dust on the dirt road behind them, Eddie put on some music.

As they turned onto the tarred road out of the park, the radio belted out the unmistakable sound of Norman Greenbaum's "Spirit in the sky". With two people and a howling bulldog singing along.

Chapter 9: The oddly dressed gentlemen
Southern France, November 1314

Miriam ran. Faster than any human had a right to, but despite her more-than-human heritage, she couldn't outrun horses, and couldn't avoid mobs converging from seemingly every direction. And she couldn't fight them all, either.

Miriam still ran, and even though she had immense energy reserves, they weren't limitless. She couldn't run forever.

Her breath came out of her mouth and nose in steaming gusts of white, the setting sun painting the woods red.

She paused after she crossed a small stream, and looked around her. There was no one to be seen, and she stood still, catching her breath, chest rising and falling heavily, amidst the thundering of her heart in her ears and her own lungs trying to fight for more air. She heard the howling of the dogs and the distant shouts of the mob.

A horn trumpeted through the air, followed by more shouting. They knew that if they didn't get her before nightfall, their task would be even more difficult. But this bunch were more determined than most. More organised, more driven.

She couldn't explain it, but she felt an intensity

in their hunt for her that she hadn't felt on other chases. It wasn't the first time she had been called a witch, and she hoped very much that it would not be the last. But she wouldn't die at the hands of peasant rabble, not she who had been a wife to kings and a consort to sultans. She aimed to live, to be accused by the ignorant again.

The horn went once more, this time closer, and she turned and began running again, deeper into the forest. As it got darker, that would suit her – she could see better in the dark than those chasing her, but she couldn't outrun the noses of their dogs, and to run at speed in the dark, in the woods – well, that brought a risk of its own.

The sun was setting faster now, the gorgeous orange and amber receding before the darkness, turning it from an autumn-coloured fairy tale into a potential nightmare in pitch black. As the horn went again, now for the third time, sounding louder still, she wondered who this nightmare would favour: her, or her pursuers?

As she ran onwards, the woods seemed to become even more dense, the space in between giant, grey boughs diminishing. This would slow their horses – but not their dogs. She caught her foot and fell, not heavily, cushioned as her fall was by a mattress of autumn leaves, but the extra effort it took to get up again told her that her strength was close to spent. She didn't have much run left in her.

She noticed a slight uphill slant in the land as she continued weaving through the trees. More rocks coming up, some almost invisible in the deepening darkness – soon, it would be full dark, and overcast. If she could just find somewhere to hole up, keep them away from her through the night, they would give up by morning, and she could make fresh her escape.

Gradually, the incline grew steeper and the trees began to thin as more rock and shale lay underfoot. She looked up, and through a rare gap in the trees, she saw a rocky outcropping that seemed to tower up above the woods. If she could get there before the sun finally set, she might be able to get some bearings, get a sense of the direction she should be headed – see a river, or a road, or a distant mountain, even – a landmark of some sort, anything really, that she could use to orientate herself.

It was risky – getting higher up, she could be exposed – but in the failing light, she felt it was worth the risk. If she could get her bearings, then she could even move that way steadily in the dark. She just needed to know which way to go.

Furtively, like a hunted animal, she made her way through the rocks and up the ever-steepening slope, until she was scrabbling on all fours up a rockface – sheer at brief moments – scraping hand and knee as it got darker. She clambered up as quickly as she could, and by the time she got near the top, the last rays of the sun disappeared, casting the world in a mystical array of black through purple through pink and orange, with a small hub of red at its core. The setting sun was truly gorgeous, but its fading light spoke of a deadly danger for her.

She reached the top, and spun around on the rocks, looking in every direction for something she could head towards, searching desperately and hurriedly, hoping for something.

And she saw it. Just before a hill, not more than a two-mile distance: a river. A full-blown river, difficult to cross in these parts, it could only be the Garonne, running south from Langon. They would guess to track along the river, but if she could stay ahead of them, then at least she had a way out. If she had a small boat, then she would leave them behind her. That would be asking for too much – even the impossible – but if she could just get to the river and work her way upstream, she had an idea where she would come out. If she could just get to that river, she would be free come morning.

Hope, a kindling flame, sprung warm and alive in her breast.

As the sun finally and truly set, she made her way down the outcropping, into the close dark of the forest, her new direction firmly fixed in her mind.

When she was two-thirds of the way down the outcropping, two horses sped into the clearing at the base, lathered in sweat, steam rolling off them, their hooves thundering underfoot, as the men on their backs reined them in and they ground to a halt in the soft turf. The horses panted heavily. One of the men was tall, thin, and draped in dark, waterproofed leathers, their exact shape indistinct in the darkness. Except for one thing that she could make out: he seemed to be wearing a bright orange shirt, covered in woven suns, bright yellow and gold. The second man uttered a word, a whisper of power, and the lamp in his hand came alight. She could see that beneath his heavy riding leathers this shorter and wider man also rode with one incongruous piece of clothing: beneath a dark and heavy hood for rain, his tricorne hat was as green as the grass of a desert oasis.

So, they were mages. Green Hat, the shorter of the two, raised the lamp. Orange Shirt, who seemed to be in command, scanned the area where she was hiding.

For a little while, the only sound in the space was the puffing of the horses as they recovered their breath. They had been pushed hard.

"I know you are here, Qarinah!" the tall rider – Orange Shirt – shouted into the night. "I can feel you. In the same way that you can feel, we are also blessed, as users of the infinite gift. I know you are here. We will find you. I promise you, we will find you. If we catch you now, or we catch you in ten years, or a hundred, or a thousand. We will catch you. We will never rest. You will be ours."

Miriam held still, her air coming in small, short breaths through her nose, striving to be silent, striving to be small and unheard.

The horses of the two men fidgeted as Orange Shirt turned and conferred in hushed tones with Green Hat. She couldn't hear what they said, but shortly afterwards, she felt the pull of magic in the air. She had no idea what they were about to do, but she knew it couldn't be good – at least, not for her.

She detected no sink on them, and this was clearly not their death curse, or their dying wish. That normally only meant one thing: they were evil. They either had no care for the damage that magic performed without a sink could do, or they achieved their magic sink through human sacrifice. It was abominable, but hugely effective – the Vatican mages were specialists at it, she knew. Either option spelled bad news for her.

A rustle in the trees behind the two men made them pause to turn and look – a group of villagers, bedraggled and tired from the chase, walked into the clearing. Ten or 12 of them, at least.

She felt the growing pressure from the buildup of magic slip away.

Saved, by the very men who were hunting her!

Orange Shirt looked down at the lead villager with disgust clearly etched on his face. "La Montagne!"

The villager gave a short, quick bow. "Sorry m'lord. We ran as fast as we could, but we could not keep apace with your horses. I have this group with me now – where should we search?"

Orange Shirt let out a sigh, and pointed towards the hillock on which Miriam hid.

"There. Look there, and down behind it. Tell me what landmarks you see from the top. Go now, do not tarry."

La Montagne bowed again, and motioned to his men, who – although weary – moved quickly, lest they provoke the two horse-riding lords.

Miriam had limited time, and so – quickly, hunched low to the rocks – she made her way to the back of the small hill, and down as quickly as possible. The men would be on her position soon, and she couldn't allow them to spot her. Or the direction in which she ran.

As quickly and as carefully as she could – because her life truly did depend on it – Miriam ran into the woods, towards the river and her salvation, away from the oddly dressed men and their pack of witch-hunting villagers. There was a new player in the game. She would need to escape first, then lie low. Later, she would make contact with Samael; he would need to know about this.

*

At first, it was bewilderment.

Then came shock. And finally, as realisation dawned as to what was going on, then came terror.

This, Shifting Sands acknowledged as a fact by now, was the way of things.

He enjoyed the hunt, after all these years. Still the hunt, still the chase. Followed, of course, by the satisfaction of wet, salt-and-iron life flooding into him. It was funny, but he had hated the hunt as a child. As a young boy with his tribe, he had been shy and retiring. He had not relished the hunt. But now, it was the thing in life that gave him the most joy.

He flew with the wind, the air cool beneath his wings. Another dry night, cold, no snow. It had been an unusually dry beginning to winter, and he knew that meant something significant, but he had enough on his plate to not worry about what that was.

For now, he needed sacrifice. Bodies whose lives could power his own. People whose lives of scurrying and possession and rat race and new sneakers would finally become something worthwhile. They would become sinks for his spells and would allow him to carry out workings of great power.

The report had come in of a family of five on the road. Mom, dad, an aunt, and two kids. A giant, gas-guzzling western steel family wagon had loaded up on fuel and his Brujos had noted them, and passed their details on. The vehicle had tracked to the R107, travelling east, and it looked like they would be pulling into one of the motels along the roadside for the night.

On spread, giant vulture wings, he glided on the thermals rising up off the road.

The headlights of a lone vehicle – packed full of pointless lives about to find meaning – travelled down the road at speed, but now began to slow as they approached a row of motels, three alongside each other, locally known as "the Three Sisters". Three one-story, peach-walled, and ugly sisters, alongside a sparsely-parked gravel and tar parking lot.

As the car slowed and approached the motels, Shifting Sands, in vulture form, floated in towards them from on high, his target getting bigger in his sight as he neared.

By the time it was off the short driveway and onto the gravel section of the parking lot, he was almost overhead, and he banked to the left, dropping down to the ground as they nosed the vehicle underneath a stuttering yellow light.

In an opulent display of power, a large and perfect specimen of a red-headed turkey vulture landed in a dark patch between two light poles, and turned into a man. A short, bent man, tanned and wrinkled, long, grey hair hanging in lank clumps on either side of his head. Lips downcast in a permanent scowl.

Shifting Sands, wearing jeans and moccasins and a crumpled, tan leather jacket, stepped out of the darkness, and walked slowly towards the parking car.

It was dark coming in off the road, and the traffic was sparse this time of year. The motels were far from full, however there was some movement happening around the motel entrances – but that was not too close, and the ancient shaman had no concern for whoever was in the motels. They would never know he was even there.

The engine of the car died and the headlights shut off as the shaman approached. A large man got out of the driver's side, talking back into the car, then stretched up towards the night sky, pulling out the stiffness of a long haul behind the wheel. As the man finished his stretch, he pulled his shirt down back over his belly, and turned at the sound of feet scuffing the gravel behind him.

He saw Shifting Sands, and, though small, the shaman was not a sight he expected, or welcomed. Bent and dishevelled as he was, wrinkled and surly, he was not a friendly sight. The man raised his hand to warn the old man off, but in an instant – faster than should have been possible – Shifting Sands crossed the gap between them, and he slapped the man across the face, knocking him back to the car, almost back into his seat.

A large Bowie knife appeared in the shaman's left hand, and he plunged it into the neck of the man. The father clawed at his neck, his eyes wide in disbelief, not understanding what was happening to him. He opened his mouth to speak, and tried to force his way out the car, but the shaman was blocking him. The last thought he had before he died was that he should have hit the horn to call for help for his family. He died with his hand reaching for the steering wheel alongside him, his semi-severed neck falling to the side, sightless, dead eyes facing the rearview mirror. A small plastic tag hung off the mirror: "World's Best Dad".

Shifting Sands grinned at the terror that was pouring out of the car, at the shock of the family inside. He could taste it already. It was glorious and life-giving. The youngest, taken last, were the best.

Screams emanated from inside the car. Shrill, desperate, despairing screams, and the sound of scrabbling for door handles. He nonchalantly raised a hand, and the doors all immediately locked.

With one violent tug, he pulled the man's body out of the car, and it fell to the ground. He climbed into the blood-covered front seat and closed the door behind him. From the front passenger seat, the mother flailed ineffectively at him, and the sound of her arm snapping in his grip gave him perverse pleasure. The panicked screeches from the back seats filled him in a sick way –

in the worst kind of way a human could be fulfilled. But after 300 years, was he even still human?

Chapter 10: Get by with a little help from my friends

The sounds of laughter echoed across Golden Bear Ranch.

Outside the back of Eddie's cabin was a trestle table, covered in a pale blue sheet as a tablecloth, weighed heavily with platters of food. Barbecued meats, pastas, salads and breads, beers, and a big tub of ice-cream, along with a pile of miscellaneous chocolate bars Eddie had grabbed on the way out of the store.

Around the table sat Eddie, Mathilda (for once without her earphones in), Billy, and two others: Tod and Bex. Odelia lay alert beneath the table, waiting on scraps that Mathilda always seemed to be providing.

Eddie, still covered in small cuts that had healed much in the days since the fight to release Sacajawea from the Owl spirit, had a chicken drumstick in his hand, and he was using it like a conductor's baton, telling the tale of only three nights before.

Tod – a small, dour-looking man, like an irate accounts auditor in a crumpled trench coat – wore a paisley blue and white scarf and a light pink, long-sleeved shirt, along with sneakers and jeans. He sat forward, taking in every detail of the story, asking pointed questions about the spells cast, and nodding his head.

Becca sat listening, silent, doodling absentmindedly on a napkin.

Mathilda watched Becca. This was a strange thing to do, not because it was inherently a weird thing to sit and stare at someone you hardly knew, but more because of how Becca's appearance changed in some small way every time she looked at her. When they had first arrived, Mathilda was sure that Becca's hair was longer and lighter... and that maybe she was a little taller.

Now she looked a bit larger, and darker-haired. Becca looked towards her, smiled kindly, then got up and walked over.

"Hey, Mathilda." She sat down next to Mathilda.

"Er, hey, Becca – sorry for staring, it's just..."

Becca, still smiling, nodded. "Yes, I get it. I change all the time. It's my magic. It works the opposite to yours."

"The opposite? What do you mean?"

"Hang on," Becca told her. "Eddie, us girls are going for a walk. You and Tod don't do anything crazy without me, understand?"

"Yes, mom!" Eddie joked.

"Sure," Tod popped back, as tight-lipped with his words as he looked.

Becca and Mathilda walked away from the house, down towards the rear fence of the ranch. It was largely grassland and the occasional tree, sets of rocks and some light bush, interspersed with totems and stone circles Eddie had set up as giant power sinks. Becca avoided those and was more interested in clumps of wildflowers, and she walked for a while before speaking up.

"So, Mathilda – how did you know you had magical power?"

"Well, I think it was about a year ago when I first felt it, more or less, and then I healed an injured dog. Then I knew, but wasn't sure – you know, it could've been some sort of weird coincidence. But then afterwards I tried again, this time with a bird – and then I really knew. I'm good at healing animals, just like Eddie," she said, with some pride in her voice.

"Well..." said Becca. "Not exactly like Eddie. His first magical experience was him turning into a giant bear to rip some guys apart – thankfully, he never got that right. The healing side only came later."

"Oh! I thought because he was the vet guy... I suppose I just assumed... oh, fuck. You know, Eddie never really tells me anything."

"But he has been teaching you, right?"

"Yeah, but... I feel like there should be more, you know? I feel like Eddie's holding back somehow. I have a suspicion that I'm getting only the barest minimum. I hardly know anything, except how to call animals and heal them, and if I'm not working in the Vet with Maggie, then I'm practicing magic sinks – and then every now and again I get in a crazy fight where Eddie turns into some kind of creature and basically becomes the Incredible Hulk, or he melts some guys into shit.

I don't know... It's been crazy... I just feel all at sea. I mean, Eddie's cool, but he's not big on details. And I know he cares – he seems to care about everybody – but... I don't know. I just wish he'd teach me more, you know?"

Becca nodded. "I get it. Eddie is a great guy, and he's got the biggest heart in the world, but he's still basically a guy who is convinced that biting somebody's face off is a good way to win an argument. Don't forget, there's a lot of bear in him! Also, he's doing the best that he can. We don't get many apprentices, so he's probably out of practice. But Tod and I are here for a bit of time, so I can help to teach you some more stuff, if you'd like?"

"Really?" Tilda's face lit up. "That would be awesome and amazing! Awe-zing!"

Becca laughed. "Ama-some!"

They fist-bumped.

Becca bent down and picked up a small, yellow prairie flower and put it in her hair, which was turning blonder again. "Okay, so here's your first lesson from me: you know how at first you never knew you had magic, and then suddenly one day you did?"

"Yes?"

"And you can use magic sometimes – like when you heal an animal, or when you called the owls at Billy's place – but then other times you don't use magic, like when you go shopping, or work at the Vet – you know, normal stuff."

"Yeah. So?"

"So, I don't have that. You see, magic is a continuum. Think of a slide along a ruler. On the one end, it's very magical, and the other side is totally non-magical. Most people spend their lives at the one end of the slide, barely ever experiencing any magic – but probably experiencing more than they know. They just never figured it as magic."

"For example?"

"Well, childbirth, for one. That's a pretty magical experience."

"I heard it was all pain and screaming?"

"Well, yeah, the sink has to go somewhere, right? We can talk more about that sort of thing later. There's a lady out west who is a specialist in magical events masquerading as normal ones. It's an amazing study. Anyway... look – so you lead a life where you have no magic, and you occasionally draw magic into your life, but I was built the opposite. Apparently, my affliction is pretty rare – but my magic runs all the time, and only when I call the normalness into my life, then I get to look how I look when there is no glamour."

"So..." Tilda was trying to figure out what that meant.

"So, unless I actively jump in and take charge, my glamour will run rampant and change how I look constantly, and will keep running and never stop switching and changing."

"Erm, so how do you sink for that? Surely, you should – I mean wouldn't you damage time – you know, the space-time continuum and all that?" She waved her hands in the air when she said "continuum".

"No. Glamour magic, especially with my affliction, happens on me, and so my body automatically pays the cost. A few months after I first started exhibiting, I started to have health problems. After about a year, I almost died of a heart attack – my organs had begun to fail. That was when Sko found me, and he built me a magical pacemaker to help keep me alive. He's pretty much the best tech mage out there ever, and if it wasn't for him, I'd be dead.

"Cassie, a friend of ours, knew someone who suffered from the same thing as me, and she taught me how to control it. So now I keep it under control most of the time, especially in public – but here, I let it off a bit, and she also taught me how to sink the cost into my jewellery. I can lead a mostly normal life, but it can be tough when I get too excited, because then my magic gets out of control, and I can't afford to not have a big enough sink around, because it's like a crazy horse at a rodeo that nobody can ride."

"So, what happens if you let out more magic than you can sink?"

"Well, it takes its toll on me – so it could affect my health. And I suppose if I take on too much, it could hurt me really bad, maybe even kill me. But I've got some pretty big sinks, and I've never had to do anything that even comes close to filling them."

"Oh, wow! That's pretty hectic! I mean, aren't you scared that one day you'll pull on more power than you can sink?"

Becca shrugged. "Sure, I mean, that's a risk. Luckily I have my affliction under control now, and sometimes I let loose and I can have fun with my powers, but magic is a dangerous and risky business. You should have figured that out by now. If you survive to Eddie and Sko's age, and you've been using your powers, the likelihood is that you've been through some crazy stuff. I'm way younger than them, but I grew up an orphan – a junkie mom – and when I started exhibiting at 13, Sko took me in and he's been my family for almost six years now – him, Ed, Tod, Cassie, Colm, and Elle. That's our group – we're like a family."

"And maybe me too?"

"Sure, you too. If you want to."

"Well, of course I do. I mean, what other choices do I have?"

"For a regular user like you, you have options. I've heard that there are ways you can shut it down permanently, if you wanted to. There are techniques. But once you've done that... well, then it's gone for good, and some people don't respond to the absence so well. You know, like a missing limb you're always looking for. Anyway, why don't you show me what you can do, and I'll show you a bit of glamour magic? Maybe I can give you some tips – my magic can be far more subtle than Eddie's, so maybe I could give you some tips he would never look at. That is, if you want to?"

Mathilda nodded her head. "Sure. I'd like that, thank you."

*

Tod had a half-empty beer bottle in his hand and, for once, on a very rare occasion, seemed to relax a bit.

Eddie sat across the table from him with a Snickers in one hand and a full beer in the other. "So the deal with Chance was that he was creating ripples, changing events – some big ones – by doing random, unsupervised magic shit. Some of it calling on power too big to shrug off. Some events too big to ignore. Sko told him to rein it in. We even offered to bring him into our group – we could teach him and he could learn the right ways."

"Obviously, judging by the way things went, he wasn't interested," Tod remarked with a sardonic smirk.

"Well, no. Also, what's interesting is that he ran to Ghent – interesting because it's an ancient European intersection. A lot of old lines intersect across that city. What's more, Chance got taken out by a pair of mages who gave me the impression they were part of something bigger – Chance was terrified of them, and they killed him to keep his silence. The whole thing was pretty unsettling, and Sko is looking into it, but it really got me thinking."

"What are you thinking?"

"I'm thinking like when Sko and I started out 20 years ago, there was a coven led by a guy called Kishinski. He was an absolute genius. A magical savant.

He'd figured out a way to plot out which events in history he could influence through the manipulation of time sinks. His plan was to change past events to access missing sources of power – mythical grimoires, legendary artefacts, that sort of thing."

"Sounds like a bright guy. What happened?"

"Sko, me, and a mage friend of his out of Canada happened, that's what. We cornered them in a cult-style sacrifice session after one of their goons kidnapped a mom and her baby in a stroller out of a park. We followed their panel van to an abandoned construction site that Kishinski's calculations put right at the centre of a nexus of intersecting lines from old times. We caught them halfway through a ritual, two bodies on the floor and another three to go. It got pretty ugly. A lot of people didn't make it."

Tod nodded understandingly. "We get the fun jobs, don't we? Be a mage, they said… see the world, they said… bathe in wine, women, and song… glory and power…" He snorted. "Get to wipe the world's ass and clean its shit, more likely."

Eddie laughed. "Eddie Burma, world's best toilet paper – extra thick, double-ply."

"Sorry, Ed, if I'm a bit more tetchy than normal. There's a new director at the CIA and he's pushing for me hard. He's one signature away from declaring me a person of interest on the national high security list."

"That bad?"

"Well, what government wouldn't want an assassin that couldn't miss?"

"I've seen you miss."

"When?" Tod challenged.

"Fine, you don't miss, Tod. I think we're going to need that. Sko reckons we're in it deep and I reckon we don't know the half of it. It's mostly conjecture for now. But to finish this thing with Chance... I have some old manuals in a box somewhere that we liberated from Kishinski's cult. I want to have a look at some of the calculations in there and I want to put in the time and place of Chance's 'random' uses of magic without time sinks. See what comes up."

"You couldn't have asked him before, you know, he shuffled off his mortal coil?"

Eddie shook his head and took another bite out of his Snickers. "Nah, he wasn't the kind of guy to open up."

Tod finished his beer, stood up, and walked over to the cooler and brought back two more open bottles. He put one down in front of Eddie. "So, old friend, you've released the stikini. That sounds like a great job done. I've shaken the CIA hounds off my ass for the time being. We've got a new apprentice. Becca and me are here for you... so what's next?"

"Well, to be honest, I'm not 100% sure. I can tell you what we know: we know that the Diablos and the Brujos are probably working together. Not only was there the murder scene with the stikini, but also Billy got her memories and he saw her with the leader of the Brujos and the leader of the Diablos. Both gave off vibes bad enough to scare a stikini, which means they are pretty bad *hombres.*

"We also know that what we thought we knew about the Brujos is bullshit. We thought they were a coven of small-time mages, whom we helped bust up. Turns out, the power behind the throne has always been a 300-year-old shaman who's a Navajo cautionary tale about when medicine men go bad! I've felt some of the power this guy has, and he's no joke. As far as we can tell, he's been killing people every ten years for the past 150 years… but if he's 300 years old, then he's probably the most prolific serial killer in the history of the US. We need to draw him out, and we need to shut him down.

"Lastly, someone has been throwing some pretty heavy-hitting tech mage spells around, and you know how Sko is about someone being as good as he is. Whoever that mage is, they just entered a world of pain they never knew existed."

Tod laughed. "Do not fuck with Sko! That should be, like, the first commandment!"

Eddie laughed. "Amen to that! So, I guess we should probably check where Sko is on the tech mage, and in the meanwhile, we try and get a sense of what the Brujos and Diablos are up to next – and then we've got to look at shutting them down."

"Well, I say we go for the head. Kill this evil medicine man. Then we rid the world of evil – fucking aye! And the Brujos lose their mojo – fucking aye number two! And that probably breaks the deal between them and the Diablos. He's the lynchpin."

"Yup. I think you're on the money, Tod. Let's chat

with Billy tomorrow and see if he can access the stikini's memories to try and point us towards Shifting Sands."

*

And finally, it snowed.

That night, the temperature plummeted as winter finally seemed to remember that it was running late, and it caught up with Colorado with a vengeance. Snow fell thick as temperatures crashed, and the next morning, all were grateful for the fireplace, and the cosy confines of Eddie's small cabin.

Mathilda made coffee and Eddie fried eggs, while Tod worked on a charm that he had started the night before. Becca wrestled playfully with Odelia.

It was, in Eddie's life, as close as he could get to a scene of domestic bliss. A little while later, they were consuming eggs fried in butter, toaster waffles with maple syrup, and coffee by the pint.

Tod wrapped a bracelet around Mathilda's wrist. "That's for you. Next time anybody shoots at you, they're sure to miss."

"Oh, wow, my first charm!"

Tod casually waved away her excitement with a dripping waffle, spilling syrup on the table that nobody seemed to really worry about.

"So," Eddie muttered between giant schlurps of coffee and crunches of waffle. "Now I don't have enough food to feed one, let alone four–"

Odelia barked.

"Five! Sorry, girl."

As if suddenly reminded, Mathilda pulled a piece of waffle down off the counter and held it at lazy bulldog height.

"So, I guess we need to do some shopping, and then take a trip out to Billy to see if we can get some more info on Shifting Sands."

"Does Billy know we're coming – with friends?" asked Mathilda.

"No. I sent him a message, but it's unread. You know Billy and tech!"

Mathilda reached for her phone. "I'll let him know we're coming."

Eddie wasn't quite sure what had just happened there, but was pretty sure he should be knowing more about it, seeing as he was Mathilda's actual guardian. "Aah, okay then... Tod and Becca – what do you guys want to do?"

"Well," Becca piped up, a hint of her farmgirl drawl slipping through her glamour. This morning, she looked platinum blonde with striking grey eyes. "We're going to Alamosa, right? So I was thinking I could take a walk around town while you're shopping, and sense for subtle magics – I'm more sensitive to that than you. Maybe I could pick up something? It could point us in a direction."

Tod patted Bex on the arm. "Yeah, I'm not into shopping. I'm happy to walk around with Bex in case, you know, something pops up."

"Sure, travel in pairs. Not a bad idea. You guys can take an hour or so walking around town – the girls and I will get some shopping and grab a coffee or something until you get back. Then we'll go catch Billy, and you guys can meet a kickass Navajo medicine man!"

*

The phone rang for some time before Maggie picked up.

It should be a quiet day at the Vet, and Eddie felt guilty for not even looking in, but between getting Wayne Munston and Candy out to Red River, exorcising ancient Navajo owl spirits, getting shot at, teaching a new apprentice, and trying to figure out this crazy situation with the Alamosa Brujos, he had his hands full.

"Hi, Eddie." He could hear the tension in her voice.

"Hey, Maggie. Sorry for not being in the last few days – I know you've got it covered, but something's come up and I need to handle it."

Silence.

"I know, Eddie. I know how it works with you. With us. Something comes up and you can't be in. I've already called Vince from Underfield to ask if he could work locum for a while and he's coming in a bit later."

"Oh." That caught Eddie by surprise. He was that easily replaced, and in his own practice too. And by Maggie.

"You know, Ed, you're the best vet I've ever seen by a country mile. No one comes even close. You're the most caring guy I've ever met, you've got a heart the size of Texas, and you know I've got your back through thick and thin. It doesn't hurt me that you vanish, or that you sometimes fly off on a fanciful trip to God-knows-where. It hurts me that you won't tell me what the hell is going on."

"Maggie, I..." Eddie didn't know what to say. What could he say? The truth wasn't an option, and she deserved more than a lie. If he did lie to her, then at least it had to be a good one, a much better lie than some lame-ass piece of shit-fakery that he would come up with. He was an appalling liar. It turned out to be a tough, emotional decision, and Eddie knew exactly what to do with those. Ignore them, and deal with them another time.

"What, Eddie? Spit it out."

"I'm sorry, Maggie, I can't talk now. I probably need another week, maybe two, and I should be done, and I'll be back in the Vet. We'll talk then."

"Eddie..."

"Got to go, Maggie. I'll call you later. Look after yourself."

"Eddie?"

"What, Maggie?" Eddie, frustrated at himself, was beginning to get irritated.

"Promise me that in two weeks, once this is done, we'll talk, and what you tell me will make sense, and I'll feel better?"

"Sure," Eddie breathed out a giant sigh. "We'll talk, Maggie. I promise. I don't know if it'll make you feel better, but at least you'll know the truth."

"Thank you, Eddie. That's all I ever wanted from you. Look after yourself, you hear?"

"Will do, Mags."

He ended the call.

The Fort Garland General Store was up ahead, and he slowed down and signalled to turn into the parking lot alongside the store. Eddie focused on the parking lot so he didn't have to address the raised eyebrow of Mathilda, or the panting grin of Odelia, who was clearly enjoying the sight of Eddie squirming. Now, on top of everything else he was juggling, he had to figure out what the hell he was going to say to Maggie in two weeks' time. Like he didn't have enough on his plate already!

*

Sometimes it's not important HOW you know, but it is important THAT you know. Like how you know that shit is about to go down isn't as important as actually knowing that it is about to go down.

Possibly, it was the roar of the multiple motorbikes running down an otherwise quiet street that alerted Eddie.

It could have been Odelia, who began sniffing the air uneasily, as a pack of Brujos in long jackets and Diablos in black leathers all walked into the front of the store.

Or maybe it was the way the front of the store suddenly fell silent.

A split-second later, it was the look of shock and surprise on Mathilda's face as she saw who was coming through the entrance.

Sound. Smell. Sight. Eddie would rather look like a fool with his tool in his hand, than die like a fool, too cool to pull his tool. He could always explain away a nervous reaction. He couldn't explain away being dead.

He hit wolf totem hard and fast, and as he did so, Odelia triggered into her weredog form. Mathilda dropped to the floor instantly – good girl! – then Eddie focused on their assailants, as a hail of bullets churned their way across the store.

People around him, who had been oblivious to anything other than an easy Thursday morning shop at the local store, were suddenly confronted by a dozen gunmen pouring gun shells towards the back of the building. Flashing muzzles were directed at Eddie, and after three immense rounds at the giant bulldog charging through aisles and knocking aside people and shopping carts to get to the gunmen, they immediately registered panic.

Wolf form lent Eddie strength – not as much as bear, but it also gave him agility and alarming speed. And sharper claws. And longer fangs. Witnesses were later not able to describe exactly what they saw. Some said it was a wolf, others a man, and some said it was both. Along with the tales of the giant bulldog, it was enough crazy to be diagnosed as mass hysteria amidst a gang turf war. Sometimes people need a story in order to feel safe.

As it turned out, Eddie was not feeling all that safe at the time, as he ran and bounded over an aisle, onto a wall, then off the side wall and back down onto the shopping area... just as a set of gunmen were drawing a bead on him. He pulled a massive Bowie knife out of his jacket, heavy and thick, blade tip rounded like the shape of a blue whale, chunky and with enormous slashing power. Just the thing for a melee when you have the speed and power of a giant, magically powered wolf man.

Between claw and knife, Eddie dismembered or dispatched three gunmen in the first few seconds, as they scattered for cover. Two others ran from Eddie, only to be grabbed in a mouth big enough to swallow their heads whole. Five gunmen were on the floor dying, or dead, and the others were scattering for cover, shooting over their shoulders in an entirely unheroic way.

The smell of blood pumped rich through the air, along with the smell of orange juice, from a small display of bottles that had been blown apart in the bullet storm.

In the millisecond lull when gunshots spat out singly, other sensations assailed Eddie. The wailing of the mother at the end of the aisle who was lying over her child, using her own body as a shield against the death threatened by the gangland gunmen. The scent of gun powder. The deep, arterial red of blood creeping across the white tiles and pooling around a pile of damaged cans fallen from the shelves.

Then there was the low, deep-to-your-toes, heavy base growl of Odelia in her most violent and powerful mood. They had attacked in her favourite store, and the ladies at the counter ALWAYS gave her treats. Now the cashiers were cowering behind their counters, except one, who was on the floor, quite still. With a small but persistent trickle of blood pouring out from behind her register.

Outside, a heavy V8 motor revved and tyres screeched loudly as a pickup ground to a halt and more gang members bailed out of the back, all armed with guns or blades.

As if woken by the arrival of reinforcements, the violence escalated again.

The front of the store was dominated by six cash registers and a small office on the far-right side. Behind that, eight aisles stretched down the length of the store until they reached the back, where a string of refrigerator doors lined the entire back wall, except for one patch, that held a door to the storeroom and restrooms.

A Diablo gunman popped his gun up from behind register one – Eddie sensed it as it happened, spun on his heel, and tossed his Bowie knife end-over-end, into the Diablo's head. The knife curved through the air to hit its target, and embedded itself firmly in his skull. After almost 200 years, Undefeatable, the Bowie knife of Davy Crockett, still would not miss a mark.

Eddie leapt over register 3 and tore out the throat of a gunman, while three others opened fire at him. Two others opened fire on their worst nightmare – the giant weredog that ripped bandits apart and tossed them through the air like rag dolls.

Black Betty and La Jolla were the last to get out of the V8, engine still turning over, gurgling out its low, petrol-guzzling growl.

The surly number 2 of the Brujos and the captain watched as another four hitmen ran in towards the grocery store after jumping out of their pickup. Betty reached into the car and pulled out a hickory staff, 5 foot tall, carved, and festooned with feathers, skins, sticks, and stones. It was a powerful sink that had been in the Brujos for some time and, with it, she could cast the most powerful spell she knew. She was going to take this *pendejo* down. Him and his fucking giant dog.

She placed her feet firmly on the tarmac, staff held in both hands, planted in front of her. She began to sing, her loud voice – louder than it should be – carrying far further than one would think it could. Her voice was strangely elegant, from such a hard-looking woman, with such a savage visage. There was a touch of real beauty in her voice, so ironically missing from how she appeared to the outside world. There was a tenderness there, which her face gave no hint of, and some femininity in the working too. She was singing an ancient spell, born from a woman wronged, who called on the power of death to avenge her.

The sink was massive, and the casting complex. It needed some serious ability and power, but Betty knew she was up to the task. It was also a spell that one couldn't cast too many times in a life, lest death begin to look for you. Or so they said.

La Jolla bent into the car on the side away from the store and pulled the seat forward – he was rummaging around for something big.

Meanwhile, just inside the front of the store had become a scene of bloody mayhem. Odelia was seeping blood from a number of places on her fur where bullets had penetrated. Her muzzle was dark red from ripping gang members apart, and she had a slight limp as she slunk, belly low, forward towards the cash registers as the four new gang members ran into the store.

Eddie was in full werewolf rage now, with Undefeatable – the blood-covered, 200-year-old Bowie knife – back in his hand. He had a Diablo biker bent backwards over a counter, one hand pulling down on the biker's head, the other mashing the butt of his knife into the biker's body, each blow breaking ribs and mangling organs. After a minute of repeated smashing, Eddie left the body to pulp and leak vital liquids and small shards of bone onto the floor.

He turned towards the incoming gunmen, a growl releasing from his throat, like a chained madman.

Then, a howl. Odelia joined, and the customers who hid behind aisles, office doors, and the still-standing displays were terrified. Some of them loosed their bowels. It was instinctual, and from before the time that humankind walked upright. Sometimes, we aren't so complex.

Of these newcomers, only two had guns. Submachine guns, and ammo bandoliers stacked tight with extra magazines. The other two carried twinned sets of machetes. They were Diablos Cuchillos, full members, armed with the Devil's own knives.

They neared, and Eddie could see the enchantment misting off their machetes like dark smoke.

As they moved in closer still, he could see the wrongness in their eyes. In the set of their shoulders. In the way that they loped liked hunted, haunted men. To become actual Knives of the Devil, you had to give up something. In return, you got speed, and strength, and lost all fear. Your soul? Yes, you would give up your soul – but that was what many had given up already, for much less. To become a Cuchillo, you had to give up your hope. Your life, your loves, anything that sparked joy in you, the hope that it would be yours again – you had to give that up. It was surprisingly hard to give that up. But Deribo and Pablo had both done that, and had truly become evil, evil men.

Chucho and Niki, the other two Brujos, ran in, submachine guns blazing, forcing Eddie and Odelia to duck for cover. Niki was a gorgeous brunette with covergirl looks who had always been able to cast small cantrips. Her specialty was fire, and with an SMG in one hand and a ball of flame in the other, she emptied her mag into the store, then threw her ball of flame towards the cash register that Odelia crouched behind. It lit up instantly and the magical flame spread across the counter and along the ground, reaching out for Odelia. Niki changed mags. As the flames reached for her, Odelia leapt – and Niki opened fire, sinking slug after slug into the giant werebulldog.

Eddie roared in a blind rage and swept over the counter only a few yards away. Chucho poured rounds at Eddie, but they kept on missing as his deflection charm, recently renewed by Tod, was working at full strength.

Chucho threw his empty SMG at Eddie in fury, and pointed all fingers at the charging mage. Suddenly, webs shot out of his fingers – his one spell. Green and purple strands of fluid jetted out of his fingertips and stuck to Eddie, solidifying instantly. Liquid tendrils turned to goo and then toughened into fibrous strands, and as Eddie ripped one set away, another stuck to him, slowing him down, until, after a few steps, yet another set was clinging to him, drying as he slowed.

Within seconds, Eddie was held firmly in place, struggling against the webs.

And then Deribo and Pablo – the two Devil's Knives – attacked. Deribo charged in towards Odelia as she limped away from the flames that reached for her.

Eddie was struggling against ever-increasing webs that seemed to grow out of everywhere. The rational part of his mind was struggling to surface through the tide of werewolf rage, but at the speed that the webs hardened, he wouldn't be able to rip them apart, and he would need to come down from the berserker wolf rage to dispel the webs.

Maybe the wolf had been a bad choice, but it had seemed right at the time. Now, he needed to come down fast – unbelievably fast, or he would eat pain and shit bullets. If he survived.

Pablo jumped next to Eddie and started to hack at him with his devil-cursed machete.

Meanwhile, Niki had emptied her mag again, and had dropped her gun to focus on the spell, now using both hands to pour power into the flames that were rushing towards Odelia, the limping dog backing away as fast as the flames licked at her face, body, and paws. Blood dried on the dog as she retreated, her weredog healing kicking in, but as flames singed her, parts of her fur started to blacken. Blood dripped out of holes in her chest. Given time, she would heal, but time was at a premium. Deribo stepped in towards the weredog, black smoke trails drifting in the wake of his machetes. Niki's fire moved around him, to allow him through untouched.

Deribo lunged his first blade at the dog, who scrambled out of the way, but stumbled into a burst of fire that knocked her to the side, and the next machete sliced across a heavily-jowled muzzle. Odelia backed up further, lowering her stance on injured legs, and growled even more fiercely.

Then Odelia sprang, her massive power hurtling her forward, but Deribo was faster than a normal man –

stronger too. He leapt aside, only partially being caught by the giant dog's charge, forcing him a step backwards, and breaking his balance – but not so much that he couldn't lash out with an ensorcelled machete and cut heavily into the side of the bulldog. As his machete bit deeply into her left shoulder, smoke poured in, and she howled in pain. Some of the light in her eyes dimmed, and she seemed to shrink a little. As the smoke poured into her, hope drained out. Deribo piled into the giant dog, his arms a blur of motion, each movement slicing black, smoking blades through the air, threatening to carve into the dog even further. Niki stepped behind him, her power now growing to maximum, calling on all she had, opening up her sinks to full effect – amulets, necklaces, and rings glowing with the cost of her power spent.

Flames grew in height and suddenly surged forward to surround and jump at the battling bulldog, parts of her fur catching alight.

Pablo's first strikes bit into the webs surrounding Eddie, who screamed in pain as machete blades sliced through the webbing and into his arms and chest. Pablo was grinning evilly, while Chucho focused on using the webs to keep Eddie in place.

Eddie sunk into himself, retreating from the rage of the wolf, through his own rage and pain – there were some old wounds there, still festering, leaking into his life.

Knives hacked at him, partially absorbed by his wolf totem power and the webs, but still some got through. Black smoke seeped in. Hope seeped out.

Eddie's resolve to fight the rage weakened. More cuts tore through and made it harder to focus, harder to hold onto what was good – it felt easier to sink back into the rage, but Eddie held fast. He needed something else besides the rage. He needed something better.

He heard Odelia's howl of anger and pain. He cared about her so hard, he shouted out to her. Eddie loved that dog, and she would die for him – by the sounds of it, that was what she was doing.

In that instant, Eddie felt something other than the tug of anger. Love, concern... care. For Eddie cared greatly. He was known as the angry man. The bear. The wolf. The jaguar. An angry predator. The anger drove him to violence... but it was the care that drove him to action in the first place. He turned to anger so he could deal with the violence. But it was the care that came first. It held some pain, like all love does. He could see why he avoided it, often. But in this moment, Eddie embraced how much he cared, and the rage subsided.

Power rose up inside him, and in that moment, he cast his spell. A spell old as time, cast across every tradition. He preferred the tradition of old Albion, of Merlin, the father of modern mages. The power welled up inside Eddie as the spirit of the wolf subsided, as the machetes descended towards him in a rain of deadly blows. Eddie muttered the words, and gave the power form: *"Draoidheachd Falbh!"* Magic be Gone.

With a deep "whoomp", the power spread out from him in a circle. The webs evaporated, blown away like dust before a storm wind. The circle expanded, hitting Niki's flames, and in an instant, they winked out of existence. Odelia stopped peddling backwards, and bunched her legs for another charge at the Diablos Cuchillos in front of her. She leapt forward with renewed power, and they engaged in a deadly tussle of blade versus fang, beast versus man.

Deribo struggled with the massive weredog, one hand poking towards her face with a machete blade, the other with black smoking blade raised high, waiting for a gap to strike. She stumbled, and he brought it down fast, and powerfully. The blade sunk heavily into her thick-browed, heavily wrinkled head. With a bright spray of red blood, her head bowed, and she sunk forward under the impact of the heavy blow. Deribo pulled his machete back for another strike, and for a split-second, it stuck.

A split-second was all Odelia needed. She pounced, each paw striking down an arm, and as Deribo shifted backwards, she closed her massive jaws around his head, and crunched it in two. Deribo's body fell to the floor, and Odelia looked up, the top half of the Diablo's head still in her mouth.

Niki had scrambled for her SMG after her flames had been dispelled, and she was reloading it frantically. Odelia hit the Bruja like a freight train, breaking her neck on impact, and then, with the vengeful nature that only a bulldog endowed with the size of a lion and the strength of three could exude, Odelia snapped her in her jaws and shook her like a wet towel, before finally dashing her almost lifeless body onto the floor, and ripping chunks off her.

It was not pretty or nice. Niki's life choices had

not worked out for her.

And that left Eddie, backpedalling before a rampant Pablo, who was whirling black blades through the air at an inhuman speed, whilst keeping the Diablos Cuchillos between him and Chucho, who was reloading his gun, and planning to mow Eddie down.

Outside, Black Betty had readied her power and called on her spell.

She raised her staff, and slammed it with all her might back down on the ground. And, theatrically, and as loudly as she could, she sang out the final words, the closing... the name of the spell:

"Beso de Muerte." The Kiss of Death.

Power left her body and filled the air in front of her, in mere seconds forming small eddies of air and buffeting wind, throwing up dust and debris, and changing colour into a dark grey cloud... almost. A patch of darkened air – what one might expect a good CGI ghost to look like – flew directly towards Eddie. Fast, precise, and deadly. Aimed.

Slightly tired from her casting, yet satisfied, Betty leant on her staff, and reached to the back of her belt for her chrome- and gold-plated Desert Eagle. Who's to say a girl can't have her bling?

Pablo was a skilled knifeman, and Eddie had been in scraps with some pretty tough guys before, but normally he was in some sort of animal form that gave him the edge. This time, Pablo had the edge with his demonic gifted speed and strength. Eddie needed a gap, just so he could get another spell off, or he could pull another form out of his totem necklace.

And that was when the Kiss of Death hit him. The cloud of darkness enveloped him. Instantly, he went cold, and felt the fear of the grave, the cold embrace of death reaching for him. He had never cast it, but he had heard of the spell – it was quite infamous – and he knew that he was literally feeling the kiss of death itself. Very few survived.

As the mist sunk onto him, and into him, his chest started to tighten and his breath became laboured. Out the corner of his eye, Eddie saw Odelia charge across the store and catch Chuchu, the Brujos' spell-casting gunman, in the side. He didn't see her coming, and it looked like one of those accident clips where the pedestrian is facing the camera, and the bus hits them from the side, totally unexpectedly and without even slowing.

A white blur, and he was gone. A scream, a crunch, and Chucho – bless his dirty, unwashed little cotton socks – was no more.

Eddie turned and lumbered towards the back of the store. He needed some time away from Pablo. He needed to figure a counterspell to the Kiss of Death. It was not a normal spell, and his dispelling would not work. It was more of a curse. An invitation to close with one of the primordial forces. Pablo chuckled – an evil sound, for it was mirthless... the sound of a being delighting in the fear and hopeless actions of another. But Eddie wasn't fearful, or hopeless – he was buying time.

Outside, La Jolla had finished pulling a large,

dark, steel case out from behind the pickup's seat. It was a black oblong, almost as long as the seat was deep, and about a foot wide. He opened it up. It was a rocket launcher! The Brujos' captain grinned malevolently. He might not be able to sling magic around, but he figured that a rocket launcher was good enough. That would put this mage down once and for all.

Ahead of La Jolla, Black Betty – golden Desert Eagle in one hand, and staff ringing with power in the other – walked towards the store, where she could see that unstoppable monster dog take out Chucho. It was a shame. She had never liked Chucho – the man was an insufferable brag – but he was one more gun to shoot and one more body to take hits. Wherever that mage and his dog went, people seemed to take hits. Especially hers. She saw Eddie get enveloped in the dark kiss of her spell, and felt happy – although you couldn't tell by looking at her, surly as she was – because Eddie would soon die. All she needed to do was to keep her spell powered up, and it would kill him. Very rare was the mage who could counter that particular spell, and she doubted it would be Eddie. He was too blunt an instrument for the subtleties needed to overcome it. He had power in spades, but subtlety? He had that in thimbles.

She checked her revolver again – it was fully loaded – and she readied to drop her silver-tipped slugs into that dog and finally put it down.

Mathilda, at the back of the store, had been peeking out every now and then for a view of what was happening, but she had seen very little of what was going on. She had kept her head down and out of the way – there wasn't much she could do in this fight. She was hoping to remedy that in the future, but she was panicked, and scared, and needed to survive. But she also needed to see what was going on, and she needed for Eddie and Odelia to be safe. The sounds from the front of the store were horrendous. Snarling and ripping, screaming and gunshots, along with the sounds of mortal struggle. Also, the smell of blood, thick and iron, in the air. So potent she could feel it on her tongue.

She dared to sneak a quick look and saw a scene from her worst nightmare.

Bodies were strewn over counters, ripped open, guts and limbs spread across a shopfront spattered in carnage and bullet holes. Cash registers were shot in half. Cans, bottles, and packages were ripped open. Staggering down the aisle, rushing towards her as fast as he could, Eddie was trying to get away from a devilish man attacking him with two machetes trailing black smoke in their wakes.

More disturbing, was the mist that surrounded Eddie. She could feel the cold streaming off it, a deadly-feeling thing that struck terror into her. It seemed, somehow, to be choking him. He was trying to cast a spell, but was under chase by the cursed Diablos. She had to do something, but what? All she could do was call animals... That was what she could do... she had an idea.

She closed her eyes, clutched her small wooden sink tight in her hand, and reached out to the animals she was calling. She felt them hear her call, and respond.

More and more of them. She poured out, calling them in, though she had far less power than she had had at the healing of the stikini – still, desperation forced her to pour out everything she could.

Within seconds, she felt the response. After a few more menacing moments, a dark shape on grey wings hurtled in through the front of the store. Then another, and another. They started flitting through in ones and twos, then in groups, then in flights. Very soon, there were hundreds, diving in through the shop entrance, suicidally charging towards their target.

Pablo, the Diablo Cuchillo, truly one of Satan's knives, was hacking at Eddie, who was slowly having the life sucked out of him by an enveloping, freezing, deathly black mist. Eddie was putting Undefeatable to great use, using the aged Bowie to catch machete blow after blow, but too many were starting to get through, and by now he had cuts running down his arms and on his head.

Suddenly, a pigeon flew its small, grey body into the Diablo knifeman, hitting him in the head. The pigeon died instantly, and fell to the floor. Pablo stepped back from Eddie and looked over his shoulder, only to duck another brace of pigeons that swooped down towards him. Suddenly, Pablo was set upon by hundreds of kamikaze pigeons, cracking into him bodily. He waved his arms, fighting them off, claws and pecks, small bodies smashing into him. He stumbled a few steps further away from Eddie. And as his breath squeezed out of him, Eddie fought to keep concentration. His vision was blurring now as Pablo was covered almost entirely in flapping grey figures.

But Eddie could not miss. Undefeatable, once thrown, would not miss. Eddie, taking the brief gap he was given, raised his arm high above his head, and brought it down, hurtling Undefeatable through the air. Pablo cleared a clawing pigeon off his face to get a clear view of Eddie, and a clear view of the massive Bowie knife flying through the air like a gleaming silver torpedo. His eyes went wide, and Undefeatable sank into his chest. Pablo raised his head to breathe in, a breath which never came, as his heart split in two, destroyed by a 200-year-old magical Bowie knife.

Pablo sunk to the floor as his lifeblood trickled out of his mouth. His eyes closed and one could hope that his soul would go to a better place. Unfortunately, it would not.

Eddie sunk to his knees as the Kiss of Death stole the breath from him. Mathilda screamed and ran over, as her pigeons idly pecked at the body of the dead Diablo Cuchillo.

"Eddie!" she screamed, and grabbed him.

Eddie looked at her, his eyes increasingly lifeless.

"No, it can't be... No!" Mathilda screamed, as Eddie struggled to stay conscious, his brain struggling for lack of air, muddled, scattering thoughts and emotions. All the while, his mind was racing to come up with a solution.

Outside the store, Black Betty walked towards Odelia, staff in one hand, and Desert Eagle in the other.

The giant dog was growling and crouching just outside the doorway, ready to pounce, but in truth she was largely spent. Blood ran freely down her front, left paw, and her chest was peppered with bullet holes. Her right eye was swollen shut from a massive gash on the top of her head that pushed it closed. But if ever there was one creature that had more heart than any body she was ever in, it was Odelia. She would not – not ever – die easy.

Black Betty fucking hated dogs. Especially the one crouched in front of her. She raised her gun, to end this once and for all. She heard a sound behind her, turned to look, saw nothing, and flicked her head forward again.

"Goodbye, mutt," she muttered with venom.

As she heard the small shick of a bolt whistling through the air, she felt its sting in her neck. She opened her mouth to utter a spell, but nothing came out. She was paralysed. Black Betty couldn't swear, and as her legs fell out from beneath her, she used whatever control she had to turn to face whomever or whatever had shot her.

The air shimmered in front of her, and an elaborate camouflage spell fell. Becca dropped her glamour, and walked forward, small crossbow in hand.

"Can't cast if you can't speak, can you, bitch? You can't live if you can't breathe. And the poison on my bolts paralyses instantly. At least you said goodbye to the dog!"

Black Betty closed her eyes as the curare-based poison took hold of her heart and lungs, and her system shut down. As she breathed her last, the light dimmed out at the top of her staff, and her spell on Eddie died.

Eddie breathed in – a huge breath, like a man who has struggled through ice and water, and finally burst through to the surface. The black mist dissipated, and warmth rushed back into his body.

Mathilda held him tight as he lay against her and she rested her head on his. As relief flooded through her, she sobbed and held him close. Eddie reached up with a hand, and awkwardly placed it on her shoulder.

Outside in the road, La Jolla looked around, panicked. He was a Brujo, he was a bad man, but he'd never seen anything like the shit he'd seen today. Betty had fallen to the ground, and a woman had appeared out of nowhere. Sixteen hitmen in the team, and he was the only one left alive. But one pull of the trigger would change all of that.

He registered a movement to his right; a solitary man walked out into the road, almost 30 yards away.

Tod eyed the Brujo about to launch a rocket into his friends. He pulled his coat back to behind his gun handle and he launched his signature accuracy spell. He never missed. Any shot. Ever.

The Brujo pulled the trigger, and the rocket launched. Tod's hand flew for the holster and, coming up instantly with a six-gun in his hand, snapped off a shot.

La Jolla heard the crack of a gunshot and saw the pistol pointed at him. He expected to feel the thud of a bullet against his body, but it was too late, because he had already pulled the trigger on the rocket launcher.

Tod was not aiming for La Jolla. Even if he shot the Brujos' captain dead between the eyes, the rocket would still travel into the store, killing his friends and all the innocent shoppers with them.

Tod wasn't a gunman, a hitman, or even a sniper. He was an accuracy mage, and he never missed. Even if he was shooting a rocket being launched out of a launcher tube.

Everything paused. The world stopped spinning and time took a deep, slow breath in nervous anticipation of what would happen next.

The world exploded in front of La Jolla, as the TBG-7V Tanin, 105mm thermobaric warhead was blasted out of the air by an unbelievable shot by a ludicrously precise accuracy mage.

La Jolla was sprayed all over their massive pickup that was then thrown back, spinning out of the explosion, into the shopfronts across the road. Becca flew ten yards through the air, landing with a lucky pounce on the tar. What windows were left in the grocery store were blown out, and Odelia was bodily lifted and thrown over the threshold, and back into the store. Fire rained down on the street as if Lucifer himself was tossing out balls off flame, and chunks of asphalt spattered around in a shower of hard, black rain.

Tod grinned. That was one helluva explosion. He reholstered his gun, and walked in to check on his friends, before the sirens started and the police arrived.

Staying with Eddie, he always had the best of

times.

Chapter 11: Consequence

Shifting Sands was not a man who was summoned. He had no respect for white man's law or their lawkeepers. There was no man whom he had met that caused him fear. It was something he did not feel anymore, had not for hundreds of years. This magician in Fort Garland was proving hard to kill, but he caused no fear in the undying shaman – in fact, his strength was a beacon to him. He sought to hunt him, pursue him, and overcome him.

He had sent his followers to do what he should have done, and now he had been summonsed. Bethshiel, the demon lord, had called him, and there was only one choice.

Bethshiel had called him, by tapping into the intrinsic nature of things, and reaching across space and time, dispensing the power and sinking the cost, and speaking directly into his mind. Through the veils and wards he had in place, through the enchantments woven about his 300-year-old person, there should have been a presence, and then request to open and communicate. But Bethshiel's voice had knifed right through his defences and lanced directly into his mind. That took power he had to respect. And, possibly, fear.

Bethshiel had summonsed him to a meeting just over the New Mexico state line, at Tse Bit Ai – Shiprock. The irony was not lost on him. Shiprock, in the Navajo nation. The Rock with Wings, a place of power for the

Navajo. Their first home in the south, where they had been deposited by the great bird. A peak raised by beings of power that the world had not seen in aeons.

Shiprock was a holy place and held much puissance.

Shifting Sands was not welcome there, and had not been for a long time, but the shamans of the Navajo nation could not stop him. They were even weaker than the boy in Alamosa. And if they could not stop him, they would not even consider approaching Bethshiel.

It was a fitting place for a meeting, and only four hours away by car. He did not fly; he decided to save his strength. If Bethshiel truly wanted him dead, he could not prevent it – but he could delay, and run. The indignity of even considering running caused him irritation.

He had crossed the state line a short while back and Shiprock was ahead of him, silhouetted by the clear, white halfmoon. There weren't so many people out here, so the night sky was still clean.

The ancient, megalithic rock formation that reached over 7000 feet tall had towered over his people's origins in the south of the continent. A place of ancient power for the Navajo, and a fitting and ominous place for a meeting with a demon lord.

The gates to the reserve were open as his beams shone on them, with nobody in sight. The lights on either side of the chain-link fence were both out. The old shaman hoped that the guards at the gate hadn't been harmed – he was not accepted by the Navajo anymore, but in his normal life he once had been. His magic tradition had once been of the Navajo, and he knew they were the last vestiges of a way of life he had seen and lived with his own eyes, not just in a book or on a stupid moving picture box on a wall.

Maybe there was still a small part of him that wanted to be a Navajo. A full human, part of something bigger. He sniffed derisively at the thought. But still, there was something there, no matter how small. On a still night like this, in a place as solemn and powerful, it was worthwhile being honest with oneself. He had chosen a difficult journey – a dark one. He did not regret what he had become, but sometimes – well, he had been a sensitive child once. He would leave it at that.

Up ahead, in the dark shadow of The Rock with Wings, three bikes were parked, each with a black-leather-clad rider leaning against it, arms folded.

The middle one was tall and wide, and the darkness practically oozed out of him. Along with the cold. It always felt cold around Bethshiel, and when you were cold, well, it felt even colder. Shifting Sands parked the car some distance away, switched the lights off, and soft-shoed in his moccasins over to where the demon lord stood with two of his captains.

As he neared, the familiar freeze in his brain started to set in. The freeze that came from being near a being that was so powerful, and not of this plane. As if reality as we know it was protesting. Which, in a way, it sort of was. If he had to describe it, he would say that it was like the time some *naabaahii* hotheads had taken over a steam train – they had fed it bad coal and had driven it too fast in the wrong places and ended up with a literal trainwreck.

Being around Bethshiel felt like a trainwreck had happened inside your head. Reality was bent and squeaked out of shape like so much broken metal, and steam poured out of places it was not supposed to.

The human mind was not designed to deal with a demon lord – well, at least as much of him as could fit on this plane. It was anathema to this version of reality and so the brain, in its inborn urge for self-preservation and internal and infinite wisdom, treated demons as predators. Fight, flight, or freeze alarms went off in their presence and at a level that was beyond what we thought was possible.

Amongst men, Shifting Sands was an apex predator. There were none who could stand against him and not many who could simply stand before him. But the awkwardness that others felt in the presence of his undying power was a mere shadow of what people felt in front of the demon lord. As unnatural as Shifting Sands's state was, he was still, at least, a human in origin. Bethshiel was not.

Shifting Sands stopped a short way away from the demon lord, the cold pressing into him like knives against his skin.

The figures on either side of Bethshiel were no mere men – their eyes were dull and stared off into space in a facsimile of conventional life. They stood motionless, their chests rising and falling at the minimal rate required to allow continued human life, to sustain the last vestiges of humanity that remained inside them. Shifting Sands felt some mirth rise inside of himself – he felt like he'd just described the basic modern, corporate white man.

"And?" Bethshiel's mouth opened, but Shifting Sands felt the voice in his head, rather than heard it out loud. It sounded like fingers dragging across chalkboards while an arctic wind blew on his exposed balls. He shivered all the way down his spine.

Shifting Sands sighed. "We failed."

"You had two of my best knives with you. How many of yours did you send?"

"La Jolla, Betty, two gifted, and 12 others."

Bethshiel visibly winced, scrunching around the corners of his eyes. "Eighteen. Including a full mage, two gifted, two Diablos knives and one of your captains?"

Shifting Sands nodded his head. "The other 12 all had guns – shotguns, submachine guns, the works. He can't be that strong! Betty cast the Kiss of Death. The others expended their power to the fullest. La Jolla used a rocket launcher. Your knives, with their cursed machetes, were flicked aside like insects. This is no mere mage."

Bethshiel nodded slowly. "Was he alone?"

"He had a dog with him."

Bethshiel's eyes flared, suddenly angry. "A fucking dog?" his voice roared and echoed through the dark and still night.

Shifting Sands winced internally, although his face remained stone still. He nodded. "A weredog of some sort – it shifts to lion size."

Bethshiel leant forward, his eyes shifting into a glowing red, his voice dropping to a dangerous growl. "So, you're telling me that a human wizard and a magical dog killed 18 of our people?"

Shifting Sands shrugged, in a very Navajo kind of way that he knew irritated just about everyone that wasn't Navajo.

By the look on the demon lord's face, it worked on him too.

Bethshiel lowered his head, closed his eyes, and raised his right hand to his head, thumb and middle finger rubbing his temples. He breathed in and out, deeply and slowly, silence filling the space between them. A heavy, pregnant silence.

"Alright." He moved his hand, raised his head, and looked at Shifting Sands. "I think this will need some personal attention. I will be coming to town next week. I will bring a team with me. In the meanwhile, you get everyone you have and then we're going to squash this fucker. I'll get Sunny to scan the web and find out everything she can about this mage and when we meet next week, it'll be to finalise a plan. Once and for all, come Lucifer ascending, or Jesus falling, I'm going to nail that mage to a tree while an imp eats his guts out."

"I'll be ready."

"If you aren't, shaman," Bethshiel raised a finger

at the ancient Navajo spellcaster, "then it'll be you on that tree."

Bethshiel shooed Shifting Sands away with his hand, motioning that his audience was over. Fuming at the indignity, but powerless to rebel, Shifting Sands turned back to his car, to begin the drive home.

*

It was a late morning in at the Golden Bear Ranch. The light snowfall from the night before meant that the ground outside was part half-frozen, brown slush and part snow, speckled over frosted grasses and shrubs, and trees showing their winter dressing.

Inside the house, there was little movement. Eddie lay in bed, coughing fitfully, his lungs still recovering from their brush with the Kiss of Death. His body was covered in cuts and deep gashes. Usually, he recovered very rapidly – sometimes, within a day of the injury – but his wounds were too many, and also, had been made with cursed blades. That made for a different story.

Lying on the floor next to him, on a thick pile blanket, surrounded by cushions, Odelia wasn't faring much better, her small body working hard to combat the extent of the injuries that she had received in her wereform. For a 500-pound werebeast with accelerated healing and a high level of trauma resistance to drop into the form of a normal dog, 50 pounds, max – that was a serious cut in capacity to heal. Changing back badly damaged could mean the death of her inner, normal form. Unless, of course, there was a healer present. Like Mathilda. She had been at Odelia's side all night, and had passed out next to her, totally and utterly drained.

Mathilda woke in the morning covered in a blanket, and as she stirred, Becca and Tod had come in and brought her some coffee and toast.

Eddie was still asleep, but he had magical reserves to call on. Odelia didn't have magical reserves in her normal form. She, in effect, had a magical disease that was managed through her ensorcelled collar.

Eddie woke late, to a busy scene in his room.

Odelia slept on her bed, next to his. Mathilda, wan and pale, was healing the bulldog and, from what he could tell, she was doing a damn fine job of it. Becca and Tod were coming back in with more food and drink that they had prepared, and it seemed as though they had found his stash of Snickers. As they walked in, he sat up and called to them. "I see you found my stash. Damn, thieving city folk!" He followed this with a weak smile. "Send me a few of those."

Becca grabbed a handful of chocolate bars and carried them over to Eddie. "You're looking pretty banged up, Ed. They cast some helluva nasty curse on you."

"Mmm," Eddie groaned. "One of the worst I've heard of. But I shook it off. I'll be good. How's Odelia?"

"Mathilda has been healing her almost nonstop since we got back yesterday. So, she'll have to sleep it off, but she'll be well soon. The one I'm the most worried about is Mathilda, actually. She's pouring so much into healing Odelia, I think she may harm herself."

"Ah, hello? Actually here! In the room, three feet away," Mathilda piped up weakly. She had one hand resting on Odelia, who was breathing steadily, and in her other, she raised a cup of coffee to her lips. Dark bags lay heavily under her eyes.

Eddie threw her a chocolate. "Here, take this while you're still in the room and eat it, then grab a pillow and rest up. We need to have a family conference. Unpack yesterday's clusterfuck and figure out what we do next."

"Easy," Tod interjected, leaning against the doorframe to the room. "We go find this fucking medicine man and we feed him some of his own bad medicine. And we kill every single one of his leather-wearing, bad-attitude, facial-haired, drug-dealing motherfuckers."

Tod was pissed. He hadn't seen Eddie or Odelia down like this before, and was not the guy to show it, but it hurt. If he and Bex had arrived a minute later, both Eddie and Odelia would be dead. The group was the only family he had. They had been there for him and saved him in countless ways. He wouldn't lose them, no matter how many bullets he had to shoot, no matter how many he had to kill. It seemed that the Brujos were going to learn one hard lesson – there isn't much more dangerous than a pissed-off accuracy mage.

"We can't just go charging in," Becca shook her head. "We need a plan – some intel."

"I'm for charging in," Eddie reckoned. "We find a Brujo, we hit him until he tells us where Shifting Sands is hiding out. And then we get in there and I rip his head off."

"Not unless I shoot him first," growled Tod.

"Hold on," Mathilda spoke up. "What about Billy? He found the stikini. He still holds her stories, don't forget. Maybe he could find the Brujos' hideout?"

"Good point," Eddie commented. "Also, don't forget that the old shaman is a Navajo medicine man, and Billy would want to clean that up – or at least help. He's a good kid and he could definitely lend a hand." Eddie concluded by biting the ears off a chocolate rabbit out of his candy stash.

"Listen," Becca cut in. "I know you're all upset, but if we go into this half-cocked, we're going to get ourselves killed. What if there are more of those psychos with black blades and those other real spellcasters? We have no idea what we could be walking into if we track him down and just charge in. I'm calling Sko – maybe he can rustle up some info."

"Alright," Eddie agreed. "You call Sko. Let me get a shirt on. Tod – you want to get the fireplace going?" He leant over the side of the bed to get a look at Odelia. She was resting deeply, but the worst of her damage was removed. Now she just needed a good sleep – something, it turned out, that bulldogs were champions at. This one in particular.

Five minutes later, they gathered in the lounge. Tod had packed the fireplace high and the fire was roaring with an excitement that it had no place to be roaring with. Magic had some advantages – fire-lighting cantrips being one of them.

Becca walked in. She had gone and grabbed a pink jersey from her room, although it flickered in the light, changing colour every so often, and once even turning into an emerald-green, 80s power-suit blazer. Becca focused a little and the jersey settled down into its natural shape and size.

She was frowning. "I can't seem to get Sko."

"That's odd," said Tod. "He literally has the most secure lines you can get. He doesn't lose signal, and he always takes our calls."

"It's unlike him to not take a call from any of us," remarked Eddie. "Especially with what's been going on lately. He may just have stepped out for a bit. Give him a few minutes and try again. In the meanwhile, Tod, please can you get me that small, green box out of the cupboard next to the fireplace. Sorry you're having to do the chores, but I'm recovering, and normally I'd get my apprentice to do it, but she's recovering too!"

"No problem, Ed," declared surly-lipped Tod. "I know you'd do the same."

Tod had to stand on tiptoes to reach the small, green box – dark bottle-green, and about the size of a shoebox, but half the length. He gave it to Eddie, who put it on the side table, opened it, and pulled out a crystal ball the size of a large tea mug, resting on a small silver platter that had a dragon carved into the edge, swirling around the outside. Popping up from the platter, supporting the ball, were four silver dragon legs.

Mathilda gasped. "Is that...?"

"Yup, a real crystal ball!" Eddie grinned at her amazement. Compared to her wide-eyed enthusiasm at everything he threw her way, Eddie was positively blasé.

It was easy to get excited when you were still discovering the world of magic, and Eddie supposed that after some time, having been through what he had been through, it became easy to get jaded.

Becca slid her phone into her pocket and clapped her hands. "Oh, goody – I love a crystal ball!" She was easily the most skilled amongst those in the room at using them. She had the sensitivity. Eddie brute-forced the damn things, and Tod chased the images too aggressively, and so they were always fractured. Becca had the knack of coaxing the images out of the mists. She called them, and they came easily and clearly.

Becca kneeled alongside the table and waved her hands around the crystal ball in a way that looked as though she was stroking the air. She closed her eyes and focused for a short while. A tiny wisp of white smoke appeared in the ball and it swirled over itself and expanded, in a few seconds covering the entire inside of the crystal ball.

Becca's eyes flicked open, and she called to the crystal ball. "Sko? You there?"

Silence.

"Sko?"

The mist flickered, and a vision of Sko's face appeared, from the bottom up, as though there were a camera resting on his chest. From this view, they could see a squashed view of his face and the top of his bald head over a mountain of white beard.

"That you, Becca?"

"It is, you old goat! Move your ball so we can see you properly."

Sko laughed. "I can't – it's the mini ball on my amulet."

"You mean that cheesy golden disc with the cracked marble you got at a flea market is actually the real deal?"

Sko chuckled again. "Because I'm the real deal, baby! No one's got a nose for a magical artefact like me. But yeah, I'm on the amulet today – there's been some, aaah, complications. I've had some technical difficulties."

"What!?"

"Never!"

Eddie and Tod both shouted at the same time. Sko did not have technical difficulties – he gave them.

"What the hell, Sko!" Becca exclaimed. "We can't get you on your normal phone. What's the deal?"

"Well, you see, it's kind of a long story...

*

In a penthouse apartment, high up in a bustling city, sat a man at a large desk, facing five screens.

Sko, tech mage extraordinaire, bent over the keyboard, his fingers dancing over it. He was a big man, tall and wide with a bald head and a massive white beard. Gandalf-massive. Dwarven-massive. Thick and imperious. Sko was proud of his beard, and kept it well groomed.

The big man hunched forward, his eyes glued to his central screen. At first glance, he resembled any technical maestro, plying his trade and writing code. On second glance, it became clear that this was no ordinary techie: intensely packed, minute streams of ancient script were carved into the desk and they ran up over the screens, like an army of red, encrypted ants. A circle of esoteric text was written in something that looked alarmingly like blood around the chair and desk, and along the power cord that ran to them. The power cord linked to a room that had every square inch covered in arcane runes and symbols, where batteries and inverters received the solar and generator power from outside that powered Sko's entire apartment.

The fibre cable coming in was wrapped in lead casing and covered in Apothshiek's impermeable hide – an intrusion-proof measure developed by the famous Russian tech mage from the Cold War, Anton Apothshiek. Sko had modified it further, and it too was covered in additional runes and scripts.

There were no cameras on any of the screens. There was a webcam, but that sat beneath a case, at the far left of the table.

Sko had three cellphones on the desk next to him, all of their cases inscribed with fine script and binary code, his primary phone having additional code on its casing, specially crafted in a magical forging process that blended a range of conventional metals with arcane elements, and made the device a very powerful magical item. Incidentally, it was the same process used to forge Excalibur.

Sko's server room was probably the safest server room in the world, ever. It wasn't only his server room. On the servers sat his magical library – his original and found grimoires. Logs on all the activities of all the special interest groups that needed watching. Most of them ran way beneath the notice of the average government, but they needed watching nonetheless.

Angel lived on his servers. Part AI, part djinn, she collated and archived, controlled and guarded. If, by some miracle, you got into the server room, Angel would kill you. If she didn't, and the 15 separate security spells and counterspells didn't get you, outside of the emergency-release gas, then the explosives would probably take you out, along with the upper two floors of the building.

Sko was nothing if not thorough. As far as he knew, he was the best at what he did. Kids were learning fast, but they weren't taking to magic for the same reasons he had, when he was coming up. Sure, they were more tech-savvy, quicker to believe in the power of magic, looking more readily to grasp it. Anything that would give them a quick leg up, an advantage.

What they didn't realise was that it all took work. Normal tech took work. Building a business took work. Magic took work. And if you didn't put the work in, it would get you killed. It was that sort of business. In fact, magic was worse than that. If you didn't put the work in, then other people got killed along with you.

A noise came from directly behind him, but he did not look around. The old tech mage knew what it was – the familiar whir of his house robot, R3. By the laws of conventional engineering, R3 could not exist. By the laws of magic, he could – and by the combination of the best of both, R3 was an absolute marvel.

As a homage to Sko's childhood fantasies, R3 looked almost identical to R2-D2, the Star Wars droid – but he was no droid. He was an animus; to be precise, he was an animated, steel golem. Except he had Rajput's levitating carpet spelled into his interior framework, and he could float across the floor smoothly enough to not spill Sko's extra-large cappuccino. He was also armed with a number of anti-personal spells, some exceptionally lethal.

Sko waited for R3 to reach to him, then he took his coffee and leant back in his chair to take a good, long sip. Whoever it was that was doing a number on the Alamosa police records was good. Begrudgingly, Sko admitted, they were fantastic. Maybe he hadn't even encountered anyone that good before.

It excited him. There were surprisingly few tech mages in the world, and amongst them, he was acknowledged as the best. The king of the magical geeks. Hell, yeah!

Sko could easily set up some programmes and spells to make him dazzlingly rich. He could buy an island and retire somewhere on his own piece of paradise.

But what drove him was the chase, the hack and secure, the spell and counterspell. The strategy of it – the patience of cat and mouse. The need to figure out the next conundrum, find the next puzzle. It was the challenge that kept Sko going... and now, in this mystery figure, he had found a new challenge that he didn't know he could beat.

Well, not now, anyway. But later, sure. He would find a way. He always did.

It took a special kind of mage to use magic to hack software – they needed to understand two uniquely distinct worlds and find a way to marry them in the best possible way. Each field required a certain artistry, but the combination was like finding an accounting genius who could oil-paint Van Gogh ambidextrously.

Not that he meant to blow smoke up his own ass, but tech mages were the brightest of a bright lot. And he was the brightest.

An alarm sounded from his furthest-left monitor, and he scooted over in his wheeled chair to get a closer look.

A grin spread across his face.

"Gotcha!"

Someone had sprung his trap.

It was a classic breadcrumb trail. He had snooped around the Alamosa police files, the museum and library archives, the newspaper records, as well as every public office report he could find. Each time he had gone from one search to the next, he had left a sign. Enough that if someone was looking, and they could track a magical signature, then they would.

He hadn't left a trail a mile wide, but he hadn't made it too hard either. He did want them to track his magical scent, and he definitely wanted them to track him back to machine 5. Once their spell entered the machine, there was no way out, and he would have a clear and unmistakable sense of their magical signature, as singular as a fingerprint.

Once he had that, then as long as there was some kind of internet connection, they would be his. That could be swiping a credit card, getting pegged on a CCTV camera, or using the Wi-Fi in a café.

And if they hid, he would find them. His search engines and magical algorithms were unrivalled and any number of government agencies around the world whose names could reduce to acronyms would have committed any number of evils to get his skills. He kept his tech under the highest of security, because of that.

He clapped his hands and rubbed them together, then leant in towards the screen, pulling out a keyboard from alongside it. The keyboard was rune-covered and encrypted – he'd had a mage out of Canada carve it, and it left a heavy magical scent that, to the casual tech mage out there, made it seem like he was someone else. If they tracked him, they would spend their time chasing ghosts.

Sko logged in – as he did so, pouring a surge of power through his hands into the keyboard and then into the screen and chasing into the ether. His trap was a virtual machine set up on a server in Iceland that had been routed through two other fake IPs, but always leaving a small smidge of essence behind. Not enough for it to be conspicuous, but it was on a piece of code, some software, always something.

And when the piece of search software or spell arrived, he would dismantle it and he would have the essence of his opponent. He would be able to track them, comprehend their spellwork, and understand their software.

He had algorithms that would look for programming flaws, and others that sought out holes in their weaving of the fabric of reality. In other words, he poked holes in their witchcraft and undid their magic, like unpicking the seams of a suit and watching the clothes fall off the king, as he strode naked down his own hallway.

Sko was a master of his craft.

A small, red light flashing at the top-left corner of his screen showed him that the trap had been sprung. On the centre of the screen, the search software – interwoven with a spell of some kind that he couldn't make out at first sight – squirmed beneath some thick, black bars on his screen. It was caged in a simple, yet powerful and very elegant spell called Grace's Black Box, that he had modified slightly, to make it a truly mighty piece of work.

Sko's fingers skipped along the keys as he pulled scripts down from a storehouse and dropped binary probes into the cage to start finding out what he had caught. He reached within himself, to that silent place where his power slept like a coiled snake, and slowly allowed some to whip down his arm, into his fingers, and delicately, like God caressing the first white petals of spring, he let it hop into the keyboard and become part of the programme he was running.

Everything was moving according to plan – and then he heard it for the first time. Within the Grace Box, he heard something. It sounded like... humming. Curious, he edged his spell in towards it cautiously, but specifically and with intent. He picked up a clear melody, and as he surveyed it more closely, the strength of the tune grew, and became clearer. It was Johnny Cash: "Ring of Fire".

It was about that time that he had a bad feeling about this operation.

Sko started to draw his spell back, but it was too late. It began sliding across the screen, down towards the cage. He typed his cancel protocol, but it was as if the power for his cancel command got sucked into the growing whirlwind in the centre of the screen. The Grace Box disappeared, pulled into the whirling ring of fire. The ring began to glow, and cheap thumbnails of cartoon fire flickered along its edges. Heat began to radiate from the screen.

Sko poured power into the keyboard and into the screen, countermeasures beefing up into gushes of water and foam, and hundreds of small, caricatured firemen sprayed the ring with hoses and extinguishers. The ring took them in, and grew bigger, and hotter.

Sko threw the keyboard aside, ducked beneath the table and pulled the power from machine 5. Next, he pulled the wired connection. He backed away from under the table in time to see that the screen had not gone off. In fact, it was glowing bright, pulsing even, with flames that had become hot enough to singe him if he approached any closer. The edges of the screen were melting, the glass dripping into the portal of fire that had now become a metaphysical channel between Sko's apartment and God-knows-where. The screen throbbed as the spell sought power from other sources for its final surge, which could only end one way.

Sko scrambled out of his defensive circle, calling down shielding spells as layer upon layer of shadow and light descended from the ceiling, enveloping machine 5 like layers of cake and icing. Sko backed up, scooting along the floor, and stopped as he bumped into something hard. It was R3, standing over him protectively, emanating a forcefield of strength around them both.

Then machine 5 blew, beneath its protective blankets. A soft, deep whumpf sounded out, and some flame and black smoke escaped into his home. Not much got past his runic protective circle, but seeing his machine totally destroyed and every single countermeasure that had held countless hackers and mages at bay simply sucked into a spell, and then melted, was too much to bear. The leftover pieces of machine 5 burnt for a short while longer beneath the protective shroud, and he could hear, as if somebody was playing a song whilst driving into the distance, the fading strains of Johnny Cash's "Ring of Fire", dwindling away.

He had been played, and he had been played hard. Sko was furious. If this fucker wanted to play, then bring it on. They had just crossed a line and there was no turning back. Sko stood up and dusted himself off. He went into his bedroom and got his number one backup laptop, and started running counter-intrusion measures across his work desk. He cast spells at a rate he hadn't cast in years, and called down the most obscure enchantments he could remember – and he could remember a lot in his steel-trap mind.

After an hour, exhausted, Sko sank into the sofa in his lounge. It was a fine, black Nappa leather, and as he sat down, a wispy trace of soot puffed up into the air. He would get R3 to clean it in a bit, but at least his house was safe and, as far as he could tell, there was no trace of that Ring of Fire spell. It had a been a very well worked, energy-sapping spell that used alternate sources to fuel it, above the power of the caster. Very clever. It had also been like a homing missile. Fly into the target and simply blow it up. It would have done that too, if he hadn't been as well defended as he was.

Even though it had been a pretty close call – closer than he'd had in a long time – Sko felt alive and satisfied. He put his head back to think, closed his eyes, and in a surprisingly short time, faded off to sleep.

*

"So now I'm keeping low on my devices while I make sure that nothing else has been compromised. I'm sure that things are safe, and out of what I could recreate from the attack, I think I've got a pretty good profile on this caster.

"But enough about me – why don't you tell me what's happening on your end? Give Uncle Sko a little update?"

"Sure," Eddie offered. "Keep sitting down, brother. This one's going to be even more interesting than your story!"

Over the next few minutes, they all took turns recounting the events of the attempted hit in the general store. At the end of it, Sko let out a long, heavy breath.

"Jesus. They really came at you hard! How you holding up, Ed?"

Eddie laughed it off. "It was a close thing for a bit there, Sko. That fucking black mist choking death spell nearly had me! Those demon machete-wielders were also pretty tough…"

Odelia growled at that.

"That's right, girl!" Eddie translated, "but they weren't as tough as a pissed-off bulldog."

Everyone giggled, and the bulldog shook her head and snorted as if to say, "Damn right!".

Tod spoke up: "We need to get clear on an action

plan here. What happened at the store wasn't a hit, it was the first assault in an all-out war. There were almost 20 bodies in that team – they had automatic weapons, at least three mages, two demon-possessed, and a rocket launcher. A team that big could take out a whole city block, not just a guy and a fucking dog!" Tod was getting heated, and fast. He wanted instant action, revenge for the attack on the people he loved. His family.

Becca, as usual, was the peacemaker. She reached out and placed a gentle hand on Tod's forearm. "We'll get them, Tod. We always have. Let's just get them in a way that gives us the best chance of winning."

Tod turned and flopped into a chair like a petulant teenager. He sat back and threw his hands in the air. "So, what do we do, then? Hide out here until they strike again?"

"No," Becca reassured him. "We plan. We prepare. We heal and we regroup. Then we take them on our terms. We take them so that they can never defeat us, never come back, and never hurt anyone ever again."

Odelia growled in concurrence.

"Alright," Eddie chipped in. "I think we're all agreed that we need to go back, and make sure we get the win. So, what is our plan?"

"We call Billy to come with us," suggested Mathilda. "And you teach me how to kick magical ass!"

All nodded.

"Agreed," said Ed. "Get Billy; teach Mathilda some

offensive magic. That gets us two more guns in the fight. What else?"

"I have a scent on their hacker now," said Sko. "She's good – really good. Probably the best I've ever come across."

"Better than you."

Sko dropped a withering, filthy look through his amulet, at Tod. Nobody was better than Sko. Nobody.

Patently ignoring Tod, Sko continued: "I can drop some interference on their mage to keep her busy. In the meanwhile, you've got a Navajo shaman to find."

*

As they approached Billy's place, they knew something was wrong.

The gate to the property was torn completely off its hinges and lying to the side.

On instinct, Eddie charged his totem, shifting as he charged forward, then shambling with a bear-like gait into Billy's compound. Odelia's transformation was also triggered by the time she pounded through the broken gate, followed by Mathilda, Tod, and Becca – all running.

The place was wrecked. Shattered pieces of wood and concrete chips were strewn across the compound grounds. The moss-covered cherub fountain in the middle of the front yard was shot to pieces, its head lying upside down amongst a bullet-case-strewn garden. Or what was left of it.

The front porch of Billy's small, wooden house was riddled with bullets and the chairs that he and Eddie had sat on with cups of whiskey were shot to shreds. Hurtling like a crazy bear, Eddie ploughed up the steps and shattered the front door without even slowing, his giant frame blowing bits of door aside as if it was made of paper.

As he ran in, he shouted back over his shoulder in a half-growl, half-yell, "I've got the house – check around the back."

"On it, boss!" Tod ran past the house to the barn, six-gun in each hand. Becca, right hand covered in a glowing ball of purple light, left with a loaded hand-crossbow, followed closely after. Odelia, in full wereboar form, charged right behind them – but slow enough to keep close to Mathilda.

Barrelling from room to room, Eddie saw that the house was a total mess: furniture was tossed over, the TV kicked in. Whoever had been there had done a real number on the place, but at least there was no Billy. The bear in Eddie roared, and he turned to make his way out the house, to join the others.

Tod was in the barn, rummaging through piles of wood and dust-covered stacks of hay. Billy's bike was lying on its side, tyres newly slashed. There was an old birdcage smashed on the floor amongst the dirt, strewn hay, and rubble, but at least here, the shooting had stopped.

"Where is he?" Mathilda screamed, panicking.

Odelia charged into the barn and started snuffling, her giant werebeast nose against the floor, sniffing for scent. She scurried around the place, tossing aside haybales with her head like they were cardboard boxes. She flipped the bike out of the way and pounded both front paws on the floor.

"Odelia, can you smell him?" Mathilda cried. "Is Billy there?"

Odelia double-woofed, excitedly.

Mathilda sprinted over, dropping to her knees, scrabbling the dirt and rubble aside. There was a trapdoor beneath it all.

"Billy, you in there?" she hollered. "It's Mathilda. We're here. Eddie's here. There's no one else, you're safe!"

She called again as Eddie barged through the doorway, ready to rip heads off.

"Mathilda?" It was faint, but it was Billy. His voice came from beneath the floor.

"Billy?"

"Mathilda – wait, I'm coming."

There were some scratching and shuffling noises, as well as the sounds of bolts sliding back, and then the floorboards lifted up. Billy emerged from his dark, cramped hidey-hole. Beneath him was a cavity not much more than a yard deep, with symbols etched into the packed dirt and rock.

His hair was tousled and fell across his face as he climbed out to face a giant bear, a bulldog, a stranger with a pair of six-guns, and an unfamiliar mage with crossbow in one hand, the other hand glowing purple.

He clutched Geronimo's tomahawk tightly to his chest. "Mathilda," he nodded at her, then looked up at the bear. "Eddie."

"Hey, Billy," Eddie's voice came out gruffly, with too much bear. "What the hell happened here?"

"Well, help me the hell up off the ground and get me a whiskey. I've got a story for you."

*

Back at the Golden Bear Ranch, Billy held a cup of coffee loaded with whiskey.

"They came at me hard and fast, but I had warning. The coyote warned me. I saved him from a trap a few months ago, and he howled the kind of howl that meant trouble. I didn't have long, else I would have got going on my bike, but he gave me enough time to get to my hidey-hole. I used to hide my stash in there, back in the days when it was illegal, but nowadays it just stores cobwebs. Anyways, as I hit my hole and slid the cover over my head, I heard a squadron of feet stampeding onto the grounds, then voices, and then gunfire. They shot out my house, my barn. They punctured my bike tyres – I heard them. They were Brujos for sure and Shifting Sands had told them how to find me.

"I had grabbed Geronimo's tomahawk before I went in, and it helped hide me from their search. I could feel they had a Bruja with them, someone with power, but she couldn't find me through my mask.

"Then they left, and I was lying around in my hole, hoping it was safe to come out. Thought of maybe, you know, singing out to bring some small creature near the barn to the hole so they could scout for me – but then I heard that commotion and what sounded like a bear charging through my house. I thought it was you guys – I hoped – and this time, I got lucky. Maybe next time, not so much."

"Well, if we get things our way, there won't be a next time," said Eddie.

"What you mean?"

"We're going after Shifting Sands!" Mathilda blurted out excitedly. "We're going to hunt him and his Brujos down and we're going to take him out. The Alamosa Brujos are going down for good!"

Billy looked confused. "Sure, Shifting Sands is a bad guy and he's been a bad guy for 300 years. I know you guys were looking into some stuff around him – but what's got into you all of a sudden? What's changed?"

"His hit squad trying to take us out, that's what."

"What?"

"You heard her right, Billy." Eddie set a hand on Billy's shoulder. "They sent a small army after us. Three Brujos, two Diablos, over a dozen gunmen. One had a rocket launcher. We can't sit back and take that. And now they tried to use their gunmen to silence you. It's time to end this."

"Holy shit!" Billy took another slug of his whiskey coffee. He shot a look at Mathilda. "You guys are all okay?"

Mathilda smiled and nodded.

"We sure are," confirmed Eddie. "And we got pretty worried when you weren't taking calls, but we're glad you're in one piece."

"That's right," Tod chipped in. "Can't say the same for your ranch, though!"

Billy sipped more coffee and shrugged. "I can always rebuild – I've needed to fix the place up for some time anyway. At least they never caught me."

"Good attitude!" Becca piped up from the kitchen, where she was pottering around at the stove.

"Sure, Bill, and we'll all help you rebuild when the time comes," Eddie offered. "But now we need to sort things out. You up for a war council?"

"Damn straight! Let's get this on."

"Alright, then. Becca, you good?" Ed shouted into the kitchen.

"Coming. Lasagna's about ready."

"I'm dialling Sko now. Everyone get comfy."

Tod grinned. "It's about time we sorted this shit out. These hedge-witches are going down."

Eddie set his laptop on the coffee table in front of the TV, facing into the lounge. He, Mathilda, and Odelia sat on the couch, with a space for Becca to squeeze in on the side. Tod sat on a small stool next to Eddie, and Billy on a dining chair on the other side of the couch. All sat facing into the laptop, fire crackling on the far side of the lounge.

Sko's big, bearded face filled the screen.

"Hey, my people. How you all doing?"

They all chimed their hellos.

Becca rushed in from the kitchen to drop a dish of lasagna on the table. "Coming!" she sang, running back into the kitchen and returning with a pile of bowls and handful of spoons. She put them on the table and squeezed into her spot next to Mathilda. "Supper's up! Okay, Sko, I'm all yours."

Sko chuckled. "Damn, Becca, I can almost smell your lasagna from here."

"Right!" Eddie clapped his hands. "Sko and I have had some chats since our last meeting. We think we have a plan." He turned to look at Billy. "And there's a place in there for you too, Bill. Over to you, Sko."

"So, there's some things we do know, and some we don't. We do know that Shifting Sands is near Alamosa and the Great Desert, but we don't know exactly where he is. From my tussle with his tech mage, I've figured out some of how they bind spells to software. Every tech mage has a way that they do this and hers – I'm pretty sure it's a she – is the most unique and inventive I have ever seen. She is really brilliant.

Anyway, now that I have a good sense of her signature,
I'm able to track down her work more reliably.

"For the last year, she's been altering reports
– police files, archives, scans of the first newspaper
pressings in the area going back about a hundred
years. Old diary entries from the first settlers, even.
I've run the best search spells in existence on this. He's
been murdering settlers, vagrants, and holidaymakers
moving through the area. Check this out."

The screen flipped from a closeup of Sko's face
to a map of the area, major roads and towns marked
as sky-blue lines and dots, the terrain showing up as
light yellow to green, depending on the amount of
vegetation .

"Here's a map of the area for 100 miles either
side of the town. And HERE," (he placed a really hard
emphasis on the HERE), "are kills that have similar
body markings, modus operandi, etcetera, for the past
hundred years. Check out the red dots!"

Smaller, red dots appeared on the map like a rash
spreading across the screen.

"Dozens of people murdered and consumed to
sustain the life of an ancient, soul-sucking shaman."

"How many?' Billy was distraught.

"I've easily got a hundred blips here that I would
say are over 90% probability."

"Jesus! A hundred people?"

"Well, that's what we can figure from the reports,
but if you take the deaths caused over the years by his

little covens and over the last few years by the Brujos and all their drug-related issues, I reckon it's hundreds more. This guy is a total psychopath. But that's not why I pulled up these things – I pulled them up to show this…" A thin, red circle appeared around a dense collection of red dots. "Just over 60% of the deaths over the past 40 years have happened in a ten-mile radius, and given how far he could most likely travel and make it back to his lair, this radius here," the red circle expanded ever so slightly, "is the most likely area for his hideout – and here," a black dot popped up, "is a set of motels that are right, slap-bang in the middle of his range. The perfect place in his reach, with three deaths attributed to him over the past 20 years, one as little as two weeks ago!

"What's more, Billy can confirm my accuracy by reading the stikini's memories. If she was controlled by him, maybe she was in his lair."

"But hold on," Mathilda interjected. "If Billy can tell us about Shifting Sands's lair, why not just go there and hunt him down?"

"He'll be too well protected in his lair – he's pretty tough anyway, got dozens of gunmen, an alliance with the Diablos Cuchillos, and a small coven of his own witches. If we walk into his turf, bear in mind that we're walking into a place that he may have had up to a hundred years to prepare for unwanted visitors. We have no idea what kind of hell we'd be walking into. So that's a hard 'no' on getting there while he's alive. The plan I have in mind is to catch him out in the open, so Tod can get a clean shot at him."

"A shot?" Eddie probed. "But a bullet – even shot by an accuracy mage – won't touch a shaman as powerful as him!"

"You're right, of course – but that's because you're talking about a normal bullet. I'm talking about something completely different. I'm talking about a god-killer!"

"What? A god-killer? What in the two courts of Fey is that?"

Suddenly a rasping, high-pitched hoot rang through the room. Tod – surly, dour-faced Tod – was laughing! "By the gods, you did it, old man! You really did it!"

"What?" Every face in the room turned to Tod now.

"Well," Tod explained. "Years ago, when I was tackling a dryad problem in – of all places – Florida, I found a collection of ancient writing this dryad had. It seemed to be the old Greek myths, but told in a slightly different way, each one revealing more about the Greek gods than the regular myths did. I brought them back to Sko and he got Cassie on it – seeing as how she's actually a Greek muse – and she went about translating them. She got a bit freaked out by one part, because it detailed the construction process for a spear of Ares. Bear in mind that Ares wasn't cool or fine-looking like the statues. He was mean and gory and sat on a throne of human skin and delighted in the deaths of men and cries of battle. He wasn't the god of war, so much as the god of rage and war – the god of slaughter. He thrived on violence, the bestial nature of men in mortal conflict, the moving mass of men hacking and dying in bloody combat. According to Cassie, he was a real shit. Not that she moved in his circles much. She came around a bit later, but she knew enough people who had met him, and the consensus was that he was unpredictable and dangerous to be around.

"Anyway, a lot of the Greek stories contain tales of Ares being humiliated by the other gods, but actually, that was some retelling for the sake of politics. The truth is, the other gods all feared him, and he wasn't often taken down easily.

"So, you can imagine, when the old scrolls revealed the spells that Ares infused in his spear whilst Hephaestus was forging it, that was a big deal. At first, it seemed impossible to reconstruct, but now it looks that, somehow, Sko has done it. He has made Ares's spear, in bullet form! I can't wait to shoot that! Imagine."

"I wouldn't be so keen to shoot it," Sko warned. "Wielding it has some side effects. It is imbued with the characteristics that made Ares such a happy-go-lucky guy!"

"Now I'm intrigued," Eddie confessed. "What the hell does an Ares bullet do?"

"Well, unlike some of the more famous spears in myth," Sko explained, "Ares didn't just wield one spear, and he also used other weapons and armour as well. So, with that and some other research, Cassie and I deduced some time back that it was a working on his weapons that made them so dangerous – not just his innate godly strength and savagery. Also, it wasn't that he had simply a unique, imbued item – like Excalibur or Gungnir, for example. He spelled his weapons and armour, and took the sink on himself, for as long as the spells worked – this is what drove him mad in battle, and ultimately led to his downfall. In fact, the whole Olympus pantheon, actually…"

"Sko, the bullet…"

"Sorry, I digress. The demise of the ancient pantheon is really interesting, but okay… the god-killer bullet. So, Ares layered a number of spells over his spear, each designed to penetrate through different types of shields. We thought at first that it was impossible, but then I realised that it only seemed impossible for mortal minds because of our limited and four-dimensional perspective of reality: that's the three physical dimensions, plus time. It is conceivable that a god – especially a crazy one – would have a less conventional view of reality and may see in more dimensions, allowing him to layer the spells onto the object across more dimensions. It was too much for my mind, but not if I created a magically enhanced AI to comprehend it for me. So, Charles was born!"

Sko smiled a massive grin as he said it proudly.

"Really, Sko? You named your AI capable of multidimensional thought 'Charles'?"

"Of course, after the inventor of the first computer! Anyway, Charles figured out how to embed spells using some clever teleportation spells – which are very powerful and very costly, I might add. We realised how we could embed spells into different dimensions of the bullet. So now, we could weave spells across eight dimensions of the bullet, not just its normal physical three. Also, I chose just about the biggest bullet I could find. So it'll hold the mass together, but it's not like it's as big as a sword or spear. Still. The Ares bullet is an absolute god-killer – do not underestimate what it can do. I am 100% sure that it will work. How *well* it will work... well, straight up, I'm not so sure. We haven't really had the chance to test it. But I reckon this could take down a demigod or even a god – fully shielded. This is, in my opinion, the most powerful weapon I have ever seen. And, in Tod's hands, we know that whoever gets in his sights has no chance."

Tod was giggling, and almost shaking, his face split into the widest grin that any of them around the table had ever seen. "What calibre?" he asked. "What rifle?"

Sko smiled widely. "You'll love this, Tod. It's a .50 BMG. That means the Ares bullet gets fired from a Macmillan TAC-50!"

Tod shrieked, whooping loudly as he jumped up and fist-pumped the air.

"It's getting packed as we speak – expect it to arrive in two days."

Tod fist-pumped again and ran around the house, like a child getting their first PlayStation for Christmas.

Eddie laughed and shook his head. "Okay, so we get him out in the open and Tod puts him down. We get him out in the open... how, exactly?"

"Easy – he's out looking for you, Mathilda, and the bulldog. We know where he hunts. We just place you where he hunts."

"You mean, like bait?" Eddie asked, eyebrow raised.

"Wait – you mean *we're* the bait?" Mathilda sounded concerned.

"Listen," Sko reasoned. "This guy is going to come for you anyway. He probably won't do it at the ranch, because every mage knows that going after your enemy on their home turf is just a crazy thing to do. So that means he's going to catch you some other time. Maybe next time you go to the mall, or the store, or when you pop out for gas. Who knows where it'll be and how many other people he'll kill in the process? As it is, it was a miracle that there were no fatalities amongst the bystanders during the last hit attempt.

"This way, we get to control the surroundings and have some sort of say. And, of course, when they do hit, we'll have Tod lined up with a sniper rifle and a god-killing bullet to put Shifting Sands down. Plus some other surprises that we've been cooking up."

"Oh? Like what?" asked Tod.

"Well, Becca has been working on something to take the gunmen out – next time there's a mob, she'll have the means to take them down. Not lethal, but unbelievably effective – plays right into her glamour mage sweet spot, and it's just about ready to roll. I also think we'll need to beef Mathilda up, though – do you guys think you can get her some half-decent shield and offensive spells in the next three days? I know it's tight, but she has power, can cast pretty well, and, well, she needs to be a part of this."

Eddie shook his head. "Great plan, Sko, but I don't want Mathilda to be a part of the bait. When it goes down, I'm going full bear totem – that's supernatural speed, heightened strength, Nemean lion belt, deflection charms, blur glamour from Becca – but with me maintaining all of that so I can wade in and take on everyone I need to, it means that bear gets full rein, and he's a pretty gnarly guy. We know what happens when he gets full control. That's where the 'ber' in berserker comes from! I don't want her around for that – for any of that."

"I'm going," Mathilda said, a bit too loudly and a bit too strongly. "I made a difference in the last fight, and I'll do it again in the next one too. Especially if you actually teach me some spells."

"Listen, Ed," persuaded Sko. "It needs to be real. This guy will pick up something if you show with Odelia and no Mathilda. Besides, I think she's right – she's got some muscle. If you guys can help her use it, she'll come in handy."

Eddie gnashed his teeth, clenched and unclenched his hands. He breathed in deeply, and then slowly out again. He said nothing. The room went silent.

"Ed?" Sko's voice sounded tinny through the laptop speakers.

"Fine," Eddie said, through gritted teeth. "Let's work out the details later." He pushed himself up from the couch and walked outside.

Odelia jumped lightly off the couch and followed Eddie.

Chapter 12: Shit's going down

Of the three motels that clutched to the side of the R107, the Flamingo was the largest. It had 12 rooms. The La-Zee Inn and Dora's Place each had eight rooms – they filled in alongside the Flamingo, sharing a common pool, a parking lot, and the same tired, salmon-pink exterior.

Driving south towards Alamosa, the first one the team encountered was the Flamingo.

The surly teenager behind the front desk barely looked up through his curtain of dark hair as he slid their keys across the counter.

"Three nights. Room 12, right on the end. The rules." He slid a pamphlet across the desk. "It's also on the back of the room door. Basically, no smoking in the room, no pets, no guests. There's food in the vending machines and gas 12 miles down the road. Have a good stay."

If there was an award for disinterest, he would have come last, because of his utter disinterest.

Eddie nodded his head, and Mathilda flashed a cheesy smile before they walked out the reception and down the length of the building to the room at the end. Odelia jumped out the back of the Ford and trotted over casually. They waited for her at the door before they closed it behind her and settled into the room.

Eddie pulled out his phone and made a call.

*

Things had not been going well for Jose Gusano. He had caught a cold three weeks ago and it had shifted into full-blown influenza. He was sweating and coughing all the time, he had bags under his eyes, and his nose constantly dripped. One week in, his girlfriend, Maria – the bitch – had walked out on him, and she took his fucking dog, and his stash. Now he couldn't find her, and he owed the Brujos for the stash. If he didn't pay by the end of the week, things would be bad for him. He saw what they did to guys.

He really fucking loved that dog too – Pepsi, a chihuahua. He was small, but he was feisty, and he loved to cuddle. It broke his heart to think that she would be pampering him and lying on the couch with him. They were *hermanos*, him and Pepsi.

Jose shifted in his seat as he drove past the Three Sisters motels.

A 1970s, old-style Ford pickup – cherry red and white with a vet sign on the side. That was it! It was the car of the vet! It was the guy they were told to keep a lookout for. He slowed down and looked back over his shoulder – it was definitely the one. He pulled over just out of sight of the motels, and reached for his phone.

*

"Boss?"

Shifting Sands opened his eyes.

Janet was calling him through the closed door. She had not entered. That would not have ended well for her.

She had been around for some time. Wasn't as fast or as powerful as Betty, but she was dependable and obedient. That mattered.

"Yes?"

"They've found him – he's at the Three Sisters."

The shaman sat up, instantly awake. "Janet," he called out. "Get everyone there now. And call the Diabolos – tell them where that damn mage is. And tell them I'm on the way. Stay outside the grounds until I get there. Nobody goes in thinking they're a damned Apache Aiaha, understand?"

Some scrabbling behind the door.

"Janet?" He raised his voice, rasping and leathery.

"Yes, boss, got it. On it. I'll let them know. Must I get Pepe to bring the car?"

"No." He stretched his arms out sideways like wings, a flicker of happy emotion slipping across his face. "I'll find my own way."

*

Room B at Dora's Place was full. It was a small room, and the two people in there had bags of gear spread out all over the floor.

Becca was dressed in black military pants and a shirt to match. Billy wore a buckskin jacket, a navy, button-up shirt, and a pair of black jeans. In his hand was Geronimo's tomahawk. Two black canvas tube bags were on the bed, divested of all their contents, which were laid out on the bedspread.

The family of mages had done this sort of thing before. Not this exact thing, but similar.

Deflection charms to diffuse bullets shot at them. A blur glamour to make them harder to hit. Headset and comms package. Bulletproof vests. Web balls of different colours.

Billy held three web balls – two blue and one red – and he was trying out his juggling skills.

"I'd be careful with those, if I were you."

Billy stopped. "But they're just balls of rubber bands?"

"Nope. That's where you're way wrong. They're actually plastic strands that expand on command. The blue ones are like sticky strands that entangle, and the red ones burn. Kind of like acid. Try not to drop them."

Billy placed one of each of the balls in his jacket pocket and placed the third on the bed. "Geez, you guys are pretty hardcore. What's the command for the balls?"

"You channel some power towards the ball and say '*Explodo*'."

Billy laughed. "Seriously? *Explodo*?"

"Yup. Colm, the mage who made them, has a funny sense of humour. Still, I'm glad he's on our side. He once used a credit card to kill a guy."

"Damn, man! With a credit card?"

"He's a plastic mage, so if it's plastic, he can do just about anything he wants to with it. He imbued the card with super strength and gave it a razor's edge, and used it to slit the guy's throat. The guy had accused him of cheating at cards and called him a card sharp, so Colm pulled out his credit card and spun it across the table and it sliced the guy's throat out. Colm said, 'Why don't you talk to me about being a card sharp now?' Then, giggling his ass off, he left the room. Like I said, funny sense of humour."

"So, he killed him over a game of cards? Just like that?"

Becca shrugged. "I'm sure there's more to the story, but that was just the part that Colm told me. He's not a bad guy, he's just… well, he has some troubles. Maybe he is a bit of a bad guy, but let's just say that society hasn't always treated him well." She shrugged. "He's family." As though that was enough. It probably was.

Billy picked up his tomahawk from the bed and slid it into his belt. With his other hand he opened an old box, not much bigger than a shoebox, and he pulled out a dusty, blue steel Colt Peacemaker.

He blew the dust off, and shined it on his sleeve. "This was my grandfather's. Colt Peacemaker, made in 1877. She still works!"

After a few moments, they were ready. Billy, armed with charms, an antique firearm, and an even older tomahawk. Becca was charmed to the hilt, a soft, purple glow around her right hand, with a loaded hand-crossbow in her left.

"Say, Billy, I've been thinking about something for a while now. Before we get into this big thing, can I ask you a serious question?"

Billy took pause for a few seconds. He raised an eyebrow to Becca as if gauging how serious she was being, and clearly decided that she was fine. He shrugged.

"Okay."

"So... I've seen you and Mathilda around each other... googly eyes, lots of texting, you know... what's going on between you two?"

He shrugged again and put his hands in his pockets.

"You like her?"

For once, the stony grimace that always seemed to be on his face dropped. Billy looked down to the floor sheepishly.

Becca nodded, all business-like, with a slight smile at the corner of her lips. "Thought so! So, listen up, lover boy – it's her first fight, and she's new to this, so you look out for her, okay? Eddie's going full bear, so he's going to have his hands full – that means that keeping her safe is going to fall on us. You good for it?

"I'm good," he responded, a bit louder than he'd have liked.

Becca reached across the bed with her fist, and they fist-bumped over the bags of gear.

She nodded to Billy and, face set with a determined look, she engaged her headpiece. "Team 1, Eyeballs, this is Team 2. We're all good, awaiting engagement." Becca spoke into the mouthpiece of her headset with a practiced ease.

Both of their headsets crackled to life.

"Team 1 locked and loaded," Mathilda's voice came back over the radio, crystal clear. "Ultimate Dog and Golden Bear are on the bed having a nap. Little Owl on watch, out."

Tod's laughter erupted over the channel. "Golden Bear would sleep now! Who chose 'Ultimate Dog'?"

"She did."

"Thought so. Damn, she's a funny dog! All clear here. It's looking like we have a couple of cars on either side of the motels. First there was just the one, that beat-up, old, yellow Pinto. It was joined by another one maybe 20 minutes later, then another 20 minutes on, another two closer on the near side to me. So that makes five, I suppose.

"I'm safe and sound here, dug in like a bug in a rug, cammo'd up and shielded – they'll never know I'm here. Macmillan loaded and god-killer ready for insertion. These fuckers will rue the day they took us on. I'm itching to see that old bastard so I can put a bullet right between his wrinkly, old, undead eyebrows. Okay, this is Tod, out. Sorry – Eyeballs."

*

Time wore on, as it does. The sun rose slowly into a blue sky punctuated with the occasional dark cloud. Despite the sun blazing directly overhead, it was pretty cold. These tense times, Tod found, were the most tiring. As time dragged on and there was no action, the waiting – but waiting under suspense – was very stressful.

When the action finally happened, it was a release – permission to unleash the dogs of war that permanently lived inside his chest. Permission to shoot unrestrained. Kill indiscriminately. In this case, there were many. So many different targets. Some almost 2000 yards away... what shooting he would have! There was nothing that made an accuracy mage's heart more full than this.

He sipped water from his bottle and, lying as he was beneath the sand-covered and bespelled tarpaulin, he went back to his sights.

There was a mix of bikes and cars that had begun to trickle in steadily over the past hour, and now he would guess maybe 70 bodies that seemed to fall into two clear groups. There were the Brujos –basic drug-running scum. He was sure they would have some mages amongst them, but in the main, he knew they would be armed with knives and guns, most of which seemed to be carried in plain sight. The other group – a lot smaller, maybe only a dozen or so that he could see – were the Diablos Cuchillos. The bikers were a tough-looking bunch of criminals for sure, and there were some that were tainted in some way with a heavy demonic hex that he could see easily, even from this far away. If they were anything like the possessed Diablos that had attacked Eddie and Odelia in the last attack, these guys would be tough to take down.

Except, of course, that this time, the accuracy mage was actually there. With a heavy-calibre rifle.

A small shape drifted into his field of vision. Out of the top right, slowly sinking down from the Sangre de Cristo Mountains, in whose foothills he lay ensconced. A large vulture, black wings outstretched, flew expertly out over the road and banked towards the three motels.

Lazily, the vulture drifted on the warmer air currents pushed out of the high mountains, heated by sun-warmed granite, and flew in a large loop above the motels, before angling into a slow, circling descent towards the far group of men. It was mesmerising – the ease of flight, the beauty and economy of motion. Given the chance, he'd loved to have taken a shot. But he was here for the undead mage, not some vulture familiar. He couldn't give the game away yet. Not before Shifting Sands showed.

The vulture landed near a group of Brujos and began walking towards them, the ripple in the fabric of things suddenly flaring as the bird turned into a man. So, Shifting Sands *was* there. As Tod adjusted his grip on the rifle, Shifting Sands walked into a throng of his people, sight of him covered by Brujos and vehicles.

Tod pulled away from the gun's sights to load the god-killer bullet. It was dense, far heavier than it looked – a thing of sleek, rune-covered beauty. The spells that impregnated every inch of the bullet almost sang to him. He just wanted to inhale it. He placed it as the last bullet in a box magazine of five. That meant it was right on top, and the first time he pulled the trigger, it would launch the most ensorcelled bullet on the planet speeding out at over 800 yards per second, or almost three times the speed of sound. He smiled to himself. The bullet would hit Shifting Sands before he heard the crack of it leaving the rifle.

Now loaded, Tod put his eye back to the scope to see the shaman, surrounded by dozens of his crew, walk in towards the motels. The two groups were walking to meet in front of the buildings, forming a loose semicircle facing in towards the parking lot. With more than 60 targets, there would be plenty of shooting today.

He spoke into the mouthpiece of his headset. "Team 1, Team 2. Heads up, I am live with the Ares bullet, and the big bird has landed. Repeat: the big bird has landed and he's walking towards the site, maybe a hundred yards out. About just over 60 bodies in all approaching."

"Got you." It was Eddie now, clearly up from his nap. From the gravel in his voice, Tod could tell he was running hot with stored juice to transform into his most powerful and enhanced bear form. Those poor bastards out there – they thought they had him trapped. Wait until they learnt the bad news.

"It looks like they're walking in from across the road and they'll hit the parking lot, then converge on the buildings. From then, I'd imagine he'd be able to pick you up, Golden Bear, so you better be ready to hop."

"We are." It was Mathilda.

"Likewise. Limping Bear and me are locked and loaded," Becca announced, before adding: "I can see them through the window. I reckon I could drop as many as half of them with the Great Dance. They're going down."

"That," agreed Tod, "they are."

The voices in his headset went silent.

The wind gusted gently around Tod, every now and then tugging at the tarpaulin covering him.

A calm settled on Tod. He watched Shifting Sands, the Brujos, and the Diablos merge and walk towards the parking lot. Guns were pointed at the buildings in general. Shifting Sands was still a difficult shot and, as good as Tod was, he needed the shaman to be clear of his people. There was only one Ares bullet.

The door to room 12 of the Flamingo opened. It swung outward slowly, heightening anticipation. Eddie Burma stood in the doorway, his hefty frame filling the space – but more than that, he seemed bigger than his physical frame belied. Larger than life, engorged with power. At a glance, one might get the fleeting impression of a bear, and on second glance, a big bear of a man. A casual observer might have to shake their head to clear the confusion.

Shifting Sands was not confused. He knew this mage that was in the doorway. Power poured out of Eddie, spilling gold into the lot, like a fountain in overflow. As Eddie walked out of the doorway, he seemed to grow larger with each slow, sauntering step. Shifting Sands had seen medicine like this before, but never this powerful. Whatever that mage was about to become, it was going to be something horrendous.

Tod had Eddie in his crosshairs. He transferred his sights across the parking lot to get a bead on Shifting Sands. The wrinkled and bent shaman was advancing slowly in front of his amassed crew. Tod settled into the rifle. He breathed out slowly, then breathed in again... and as he breathed in, he smelt it.

There was something in the air. It was faint, but he sniffed again, and this time it was more intense. The air tasted like burning garbage and sulphur and ash. And it was getting stronger. A pressure seemed to brush over Tod's mind, and he felt like a minnow that had just been swum over by a whale. His calm was shaken. Something was coming. Something was wrong. The growing reek of fire and sulphur assailed him, and he almost choked at the unexpectedly strong acrid tang at the back of his throat. A chill washed over him, and he shivered.

"Team 1 and 2 – guys, something's coming."

"What?" It was Becca. "What's coming?"

"I don't know, but it's bad. I've never felt anything like this before. It feels unreal, like it shouldn't even be here..."

"Where?"

"I don't–" Tod stopped, mid-sentence. A black smudge had appeared in the sky above the Three Sisters, like a low-hanging cloud. In fact, it was a cloud. A dark one, growing very quickly.

"Tod?"

"Look up."

"What?"

"Look up at the sky."

A black cloud was spreading over the motels. It was expanding rapidly, shifting to dark grey as it swelled. At the rate it was growing, it would cover the entire motel complex in another handful of seconds.

"Woa! I've never seen anything like that!" Pretty rich coming from Becca, who – despite her young age – had seen more than many mages, let alone regular folk.

The cloud continued expanding, soon stretching out past Tod's hiding place.

A light drizzle of warm rain began to fall. Warm rain did not fall in winter in Colorado.

Eddie, with magical power surging and building inside of him, felt it, and looked up. For almost a mile in any direction, a dark grey cloud hung over the land, with the motel at its epicentre. All of the Brujos and Diablos Cuchillos looked up. Shifting Sands, who knew when an epic event was unfolding, looked up. A fine dust began to fall with the rain, and the stench of sulphur, fire, and molten lava hung in the air. It was the smell of Hell, and the fine dust wasn't dust. It was ash.

Every person there – at least, those who could still feel – felt an immense pressure weigh upon them, like they were trapped under a heavy object and battling to breathe. Their brains became fuzzy and dumbstruck, as if struggling to understand what was going on.

Things became clearer as the clouds parted.

Afternoon sunlight streamed through the gap in the dark cloud and, with wings spread wide, floating gently down to earth like the most righteous of seraphim, came Bethshiel, Demon Lord of Hell.

He looked like a devil was meant to. Eight foot tall, with horns that curled out forwards and up another foot. Skin burnt amber and red. Powerful, muscled legs that ended in a set of goat's hooves. His right hand, tipped in long, sharp, clawed black nails, was out in front of him, fingers spread, palm down. His left arm was out to his side, gripping a giant, black trident, which flickered with flames off its tips every so often. Built like an image of God from a Leonardo da Vinci fresco, strapped with muscles, oozing a raw physical power that was palpable even to those who were still hundreds of yards beneath him. As he got closer to earth, his outspread, red bat wings blocked out the sunlight, creating an eerie silhouette.

A field of power spread out from the fallen angel, oppressing all those in its range. He may not have been one of the first fallen, but he was an ancient being, one of the deathless, and powerful beyond this realm. Even this form, impressive as it was, was but a shadow of him, at best. On this plane, it was a powerful shadow, but a shadow nonetheless.

As he descended, his aura touched the gathering of men and, as it did, they sunk to their knees. Some fell to their faces on the ground, grovelling as though compressed.

The field descended on Eddie, and he felt an immense compression. His knees swayed for a second, and then he stood firm. Eddie stayed standing. As did Shifting Sands.

Bethshiel's arms stretched out wide, and an inhuman cry of rage and anger echoed out for miles around, the sound loud and foreign to human ears, from a set of lungs not designed for this world.

On the ground beneath him, noses started to bleed, and several men bent over, vomiting. Some, whose fear had managed to trump the power of the demon's aura, began to crawl slowly away, fighting the otherworldly pressure.

It was a fear beyond self-preservation, of mere physical harm. It came back from another time. From a brain that remembered moving through the deeps. Dark, and cold, with massive shapes rising up from beneath. Shapes with teeth.

Becca's voice crackled out over the radio. She was frantic.

"No, no, no!"

Billy was shouting ancient chants in the background.

"Fight it!" screamed Mathilda over the radio, her voice shrill and desperate. "Don't give in to the fear!"

Odelia growled bravely – almost a whine, almost a whimper... but it was a growl nevertheless.

Outside, Jose Gusano had no way of comprehending what was happening to him. All of the Brujos except Shifting Sands and Janet were down. Most of the Diablos were standing, and this giant vet bear guy who walked out of the motel.

The demon descended. It was worse than anything out of Jose's worst nightmares, because it was real. Tears streaming down his faceJose crawled, blindly, scraping his way back out of the parking lot. He wasn't the only one.

Eddie roared in defiance. His hands reached out to his sides, as if in pain, and then, he grew. Golden fire spread out from inside of him, and he transformed even more, into the animal spirit he was meant to be. Eddie was becoming the Golden Bear. Giant, spirit-formed, and powerful. A pulse of force spread out from him, and those nearest to him stumbled.

"No!" Eddie roared. "We will not fear!"

And in his rage, Mathilda found a shield. Odelia found a rallying call. Becca heard defiance. Billy heard his battle cry.

The Brujos on the lot were pushed a step further away from Eddie, all except Shifting Sands. The ancient shaman also felt the effect of the demon lord's presence – the uneasiness, the unrealness – but his mind was strong. Drawing on inner reserves of strength, he shook off Bethshiel's aura, and began chanting under his breath, ready to cast his spell so that he could finish this white usurper mage in front of him.

All the while, Bethshiel sank ever closer to the earth.

As he neared the asphalt surface of the parking lot, men squirmed on the ground, trying to roll away as best they could, debilitated by the otherworldly compression and a fear that they could not comprehend. All except the Diablos who had received his taint. Gently, Bethshiel's hooves kissed the tarmac, which crunched beneath him as he alighted. He sank a few inches into the earth.

Shifting Sands, still chanting, lifted his foot and stepped forward, towards Eddie.

The headpieces hissed to life, and a voice rang in the group's ears. It was Tod. "Guys, I don't know what the hell is going on, or who the hell that is that's dropped from the sky, but I have Shifting Sands in my sights. I have a clear shot."

Looking out over the terror he had created, Bethshiel laughed – a guttural, ugly sound – and his laughter drove the fear to a crescendo.

"Shoot the demon!" It was Eddie, but his voice was distorted, consumed as he was by the spirit of bear.

"What?" Tod shouted back. "The plan was Shifting Sands!"

"Fuck the plan!" screamed Becca over the comm-set. "Kill the demon! Get him out of our heads!"

Eddie was growling, his body shifting and wrestling with becoming full bear. The muscles and bones began writhing beneath his skin. At the same time, Shifting Sands started to transform – his skin flickered a pale green.

"Kill him, Tod! Kill the demon, please!" Mathilda's voice shrieked in a tone Tod hadn't heard before.

"Take the shot, Tod! Kill the demon lord!" Eddie roared into the air, with the last vestiges of his human voice. "Take the shot!"

Bethshiel raised his arm, trident in hand in a powerful display of the force he controlled, revelling in the horror on the faces before him.

The scene outside the motels was poised for dramatic scene effects. If this had been a movie, classical music – maybe even Carmina Burana – would be playing loudly, with giant church organs belting out ominous chords evoking Latin, and chanting monks. All that was missing was an old English narrator. And, much in line with the dramatic panoply arrayed out on the ground before Tod, the drama was only about to intensify.

Tod pulled the trigger.

The Ares bullet shot like a red bolt of lightning, leaving streaks of yellow, burning air in its wake. The bullet punctured the field around Bethshiel. It carved its way through magically dense air. Through ensorcelled shields. Through forcefields. And, finally, through the armpit of Bethshiel himself.

It was a perfectly aimed heart-lung shot, the spells embedded within the bullet working to strip layers of defence and power away, until all that was left was a living target, receiving a killing bullet.

The bullet struck with the clap of a thunderbolt that rung out around the parking lot, and echoed over the fearful groans of those spread around the motel grounds.

Bethshiel shuddered. Panic rippled across his face. He dropped his trident, stumbled, and reached across his chest to clutch his side. Black gore and yellow-orange light spilled out of the hole in his flank.

In immense frustration, rage, and pain, he screamed a scream to end all screams. It was a scream louder than any present had ever heard, and it broke glass, dented doors, drove men crazy, burst eardrums, and touched hearts in a way they would only remember again as the source of their worst nightmares. Bethshiel bent his knees, turned, and launched into the air, three massive sweeps of his bat wings lifting him high beyond the anguished gathering, and he flew southwards, black gore and pus-yellow light spurting out of his side in a trail behind him.

In the absence of his influence, the parking lot sprang to life. As the demon lord fled, so did the terror and oppression that came with him. The mighty cloud above began to dissolve, and within seconds, gaps appeared, and light shone through. Gang members began to stand and shake their heads, looking around at each other in bewilderment. The members of the

Diablos had either collapsed on the floor in shock – some form of catatonia – or were stumbling, drunken-like, towards their bikes to chase Bethshiel.

Shifting Sands was still standing, transforming – elongating and changing colour. Eddie was now completely transformed. There was a brief second – maybe even less – where an ancient, undead predator faced a source of power for good. Their eyes locked across the gap, and now, without Bethshiel to contend with, they steeled their wills to do what they had come to do. This was the main event.

The Golden Bear lowered his weight to launch forward, and the ancient shaman lowered his in turn. They both sprang across a expanse that was too big for them to make in one leap, but they leapt nonetheless.

Shifting Sands launched like a spear from the hands of Zeus himself and, as he did so, his form changed further. His body thickened and elongated; his head flared into a triangle shape. A pattern of white diamonds appeared along the length of him, and a rattle grew from the end of his tail.

Shifting Sands had morphed into a giant western diamondback rattlesnake, the most dangerous snake on the continent. Except this one was over 15 feet long and as wide as a man at the waist. It was a column of venom and muscle, with fangs as long as a man's forearm, sharp as a stiletto and with enough venom to kill a monster beast.

In a thunderous clash, two titans surged across the tarmac and collided in a wrap of giant, shaggy arms and python-thick yards of muscle. The black and green of Shifting Sands's magic spilled against the gold of Eddie's, and the behemoth of a rattler and the 9-foot bear bundled to the floor in a truss of fur and scale.

Eddie's growling muffled as he sunk a mouthful of teeth into a chunk of rattler, his two front paws wrestling away the snake's head as it struggled to return the favour. It was a gargantuan battle between two intensely magically powered beings.

For those who were not naturally imbued with magic, or who had not been in close contact with those that were, it was a crazy and mind-bending sight. Finding out that all the stories were true – not only the good ones, but also the bad ones – was devastating to their sense of reality. The malleability of the human mind in seeking rationalisation is a phenomenon truly unmatched, even by the most skilled contortionist in the most extreme and exotic circus. Still, after seeing certain things, there is a point of no return, after which people become serious – if fearful and reluctant – believers.

Every single soul there that afternoon crossed that line. Illusions about the nature of reality, magic, gods, and devils were shattered like brittle piñatas amidst a brutal pack of ten-year-olds on a cocaine high, armed with spiked maces and pickaxes. Some would never recover and would forever remain catatonic. Others would believe, but would be permanently bruised in certain parts of their minds, until the day they died, with the lights on, praying that what they saw that day would never again come to pass.

Once the hangover of the demon's presence

lifted, the curiously spiced, sharp-edged, and dangerous fragrance of magic tickled the senses.

Jose woke up on the edge of a pile of bodies along the roadside of the Three Sisters' parking lot. Each person there was rousing to life, unsure whether they had just had the craziest nightmare possible, or whether an indescribably terrifying demon lord had just descended from the sky, been shot, and then flown off again.

What was more, now Shifting Sands – the boss – had turned into a colossal green rattlesnake, and was wrestling with a glowing golden bear.

Of course, Jose knew the Brujos did magic. A curse to give you bad luck. A hex to cause you fear. A charm to help you see in the dark. But not a giant, venom-pouring snake and a glowing golden bear. He had to get out of there and live, so he could get his life back together, and get the hell to church on Sunday. He would go and get Pepsi back.

Janet, ever the dependable captain, roused from the demon fugue as if waking up after a heavy night out. She knew something had gone down, but still couldn't bring herself to believe exactly what. But she could believe that Shifting Sands was taking on the mage vet, and that was what they were there to do. She raised herself up tall, and lifted her arms.

"*Hermanos*, on me!" Her voice was louder than should have been physically possible, powered by a craft her grandmother had taught her. Her call had been heard over the growling, roaring, and hissing of the supernatural fight raging behind her. It was impossible for her to get involved in that bunfight, but she knew the mage had friends, and they were here. She would make sure they got them.

In what, observed from a distance, looked like parody of zombies rising from their graves, a groggy and recovering group of Brujos pulled themselves to their feet, some gathering weapons, all turning to look for leadership. Their leader had turned into a giant, green rattlesnake and was preoccupied with wrestling a giant golden bear. Everyone backed away from that as fast as they could, but one unfortunate had been caught in the tussle, slammed across the back by a flailing tail, and been flung halfway across the lot, landing with a crunch on a broken leg.

Janet was a beacon. She called, and the Brujos listened. One or two remained stupefied, unable to move, but almost all did move. Most ran towards her, fumbling for weapons. One or two ran away.

Notwithstanding the supernatural fight ensuing behind them – a fight beyond the reach or capabilities of mere mortals – they had a job to do. They had to vindicate themselves; to show that they were still tough, still brave, still real gangsters. Hard to do when the tears and snot of childlike fear were drying on their cheeks, but emotions were high, and they had something to prove. Guns were cocked and blades were bared. Screams and shouts of support roared out from the 40-odd Brujos. They were ready, and, led by Janet, started to move towards the buildings of the Three Sisters.

A door on the far right burst open, bounced off

the wall, and started to swing back in again – until it was swatted out of the way by a pair of figures charging through. Becca, followed by Billy.

Hand-crossbow raised, and two steps out of the door, Becca used her other hand to toss something into the cluster of thugs. A massive overhand hurl, like a grenade tossed into a Nazi bunker on D-day.

It was a cellphone in a chunky, rubber case, and it clattered to the ground amidst a nervous group of Brujos. As it landed on the tar and skidded to a halt, a nervous titter spread out from those around the point of impact. Thanks to Mother Mary, it was not a grenade! The Brujos ignored it, and raised their guns at the two figures who had run out the door.

The first sound whispered out of the cellphone lying on the tarmac. Becca spoke a word of command, discharging the power she had been building for days: "*Dannsa na Cuirm Mhòir.*" She released the Dance of the Great Feast, a spell from times ancient.

The volume on the cellphone increased instantly and dramatically, as if someone had moved giant speakers to the middle of the parking lot. An intro with a Spanish beat drifted out across the crowded mob. It was the first few bars of "La Macarena".

Those closest to the cellphone felt themselves moving uncontrollably. Shoulders shifted. Hands dropped down to their sides. A ripple spread out from the phone, through the crowd, and weapons clattered to the floor. The Macarena blared out from the ensorcelled phone and those nearest started to swing their hips from side to side and bob their heads.

Like a scene from a Michael Jackson music video, the Brujos started to move in sync, shaking shoulders and hips, wiggling backsides and shuffling their feet in time to the beat. At the raucous call of "Heeey, Macarena!", a dozen Brujos jumped in the air, changing direction with both hands on their behinds. The spell was spreading. In an ever-increasing circle, Brujos were starting to move and dance.

Realising that there was some spell emanating from the cellphone, other Brujos began to scramble away from it. One charged in to destroy it, but as he neared the source, he stopped charging, and – like a marionette – began jerking and moving his body to some hidden set of strings. Within seconds, he had dropped his pistol to the floor, and was shimmying across the parking lot, flipping his hands in time to the music pouring from the bespelled cellphone.

Janet pulled in her power and probed the spell that held the bulk of her men in its grip. The spell was like none she had ever encountered – it was complex and rich and deep, intricate and colourful, and it smelled like... like cinnamon and oranges and cloves and a fireplace and warm hot chocolate. It made her think of autumn. This was why she had gotten into magic: it was this intricate richness, this challenge of craft and science and power and emotion – this rich blend of reality's greatest offerings that had always drawn her to it. This was power. It was a gift from the universe that at least she had gotten to see an ancient spell of grace and beauty before she died.

Janet could not break the spell, so she turned to the source: Becca and Billy. She pointed towards the two. "Them!"

A group of five Brujos out of range of the dancing spell ran toward the pair of mages, guns pointed and shooting. It was a poor effort. The first one died as the top of his head exploded in a fine mist, vapourised by a bullet from Tod's Tac M50. The next one died two steps later as two slugs from Billy's Colt caught him in the chest. The third died clutching the poisoned bolt from Becca's crossbow in her throat.

Two more kept pumping shells and ran in to close the distance. One of them took his last step as Tod fired again, and showed why every major government in the world loved an accuracy mage with a sniper rifle. The last Bruja unsuccessfully attempted to dive out of the way of a purple shaft of plasma that flew from Becca's hand and sunk into her side, spreading across her body in an electric web that left her paralysed. She fell to the floor heavily, unconscious and unable to move. At least she would live.

Janet began casting Fenwick's Cutting Air, a deadly spell that sent shards of hardened air into an opponent, like a flechette rifle on full automatic. "And now," she called out, hands raised and aglow with blue energy, "prepare to–"

At that moment, a 500-pound freight-train behemoth of a dog in wereform slammed into Janet, grabbing her shoulder and upper back in massive jaws that crunched bone into fragments, and flinging her body into the air. Fortunately for Janet, her broken neck – damaged on impact by the rush of the spirit-powered werebulldog – meant that she didn't feel her shoulder being ground into smithereens, nor the collision as she hit the ground like a crumpled beer can.

Almost two dozen Brujos were left alive and still unaffected by the Dance of the Great Feast. They gawped at Janet lying on the floor, Becca and Billy crouched low and now taking cover behind a parked car with weapons pointing at them, and then over at Mathilda coming out of her room, hands aglow.

In the centre of the lot, in a contest that echoed the efforts of the titans who formed the world, manhandling the elements, Eddie and Shifting Sands wrestled, immense snake fangs sinking into oversized bear paws. The snake was wrapped around the rolling bear, its bottom third shredded by 6-inch-long rear claws, its upper third fighting for purchase and power, attempting to sink its teeth into the mage.

A flared head raised back to gather force, and then pierced forward in an attack that would have shattered bone and driven short-sword-length fangs through armoured plate and injected enough hemotoxin to kill a tyrannosaurus. The head came down like a hammer strike, blindingly fast and lethal – halted in a dead stop by a pair of front paws larger than banquet platters, and powered by magic and spirit and muscle.

The rattler squeezed its middle around the bear's torso, driving breath from its lungs, the bear sinking its teeth into the snake's side, ripping out chunks, while its rear claws dug into sheets of scale and muscle. Hissing and roaring escaped from their mouths, spittle flying with blood and gore. The bear shredded another piece of snake, giving him a second's pause to shift his grip – one clawed paw gripping a top fang and the other gripping the bottom, using them like handles to turn the snake's face aside. Jerking its head and bucking like a fish out of water, the snake twisted and skidded in the grip of the powered bear paws, the pair of them rolling in a deadly embrace around the lot. They crashed into cars and lamp poles. By this time, all those who could clear the area had done so. Those who couldn't, would probably not be going anywhere ever again.

With Janet down and Shifting Sands busy, the Brujos were leaderless. Each team looked to their captain for direction. They knew that they had to fight, or it was prison for them. Maybe even death. Three captains decided that two of them and their teams would take on Billy and Becca, the other team of seven would take on Odelia and Mathilda.

The Brujos split into two groups, the smaller set breaking off around the swirling maelstrom of Jurassic-sized spirit creatures battling in the middle of the parking lot. The larger set headed towards the family sedan that shielded Becca and Billy, who were each cautiously peering over the front and rear of the car.

The other seven came in towards the girl and the dog, guns blazing, bullets flying and chunking into the tar around them. The deflection charms on both Mathilda and Odelia were buzzing hard, and the blur charms, freshly powered by Becca only a day ago, were starting to smoke, constantly seeking to displace their images amidst a hail of projectiles.

Odelia bounded towards the Brujos in a couple

of great leaps, and then she was amongst them. The Brujos that closed in on her only realised how fast and powerful she was as she neared. She hadn't seemed so fast from a distance, her bulk belying her speed. They would only make that mistake once.

The other gunmen charged in towards Mathilda. She raised her hands, and even though her heart was pounding like a machine gun, she closed her eyes, and slowed her heart and mind, gathered her power, and cast her spell. Her one offensive spell. That she had only started learning five days ago, and got right two days ago. Well, sort of.

With both her hands outstretched in front of her, she abruptly pulled them back and clenched her fingers as through grabbing fistfuls of clothing, and giving them a tug. The spell was Soul Tug, a cantrip designed to pull on a person's soul, destabilising them, leaving them disorientated and, in some cases, dropping them unconscious. She felt her spell hook on the four Brujos coming in, and pulled.

Seeing things in the realm of the spirit, for the split-second the spell was cast, allowed her to see fine threads stringing from her fingers to the pale, shimmering souls flickering within the physical bodies of the Colorado drug-runners.

In an instant, she felt the threads latch on, and she pulled. Tugged, actually, in the signature movement that gave the spell its name. The threads loosened off the Brujos and slid back towards her empty hands. She had failed!

The Brujos shook their heads, clearing the haze

that had, briefly, threatened to overcome them and then had suddenly gone disappeared.

With the intensity of four falcons that had simultaneously spied a well-fed, slow-flying dove, the Brujos focused their gaze on Mathilda. Under the weight of their combined scrutiny, she began to backpedal. They moved forward. They sped up, rushing towards her, and she turned and ran.

Three weeks into magic, and the thought of tussling with four armed gangsters with a spell that the paint still hadn't dried on yet, was a scary one. Scarier still, she had leftover demon fugue hanging over her, she stood alongside a brawl of mammoth magical forces and, across the parking lot, an ancient spell of Fey forced over 20 Brujos into a crazy parody of dance. It had been one unbelievably crazy day.

The sound of Odelia ripping into the three Brujos was sickening, punctuated with splatters of blood as she gouged chunks out of the hapless drug dealers. Although Odelia was one of her own, and crunching noises generally meant things were going her way, the sounds still made Mathilda feel sick. She felt bile rise in her throat as she ran – not sure where to, but she had to go somewhere. As she ran, heart pounding, a bullet hit her in the upper back. Her vest caught it, but the impact knocked her to the ground, her hands scraping on the tar and her head jarring as she fell.

Panic and chaos raging through her head, Mathilda rolled over and saw the Brujos, guns firing wildly, charging towards her. Panicking, she skittered backwards along the floor, the gangsters' bullets splattering into the tar like hard raindrops. A bullet caught her in the arm near her shoulder, and she screamed. It was more painful than she had ever thought possible, and just as she was comprehending what the hell was going on, a second slug punctured her upper thigh, and more thudded into her vest. Mathilda panicked. She screamed. She cried. Tears of pure terror ran down her face. She was going to die here, today, her screams unheard by her friends, each one deep in their own life-and-death struggle.

Nearer the entrance to the road, a gang of Brujos was tirelessly dancing the Macarena. Eddie and Shifting Sands were rolling around the middle of the lot, slashing pieces out of each other, and she had no way of knowing who was winning. On the far side of the parking lot, seven Brujos were left alive behind a pair of cars in a shootout with Becca and Billy, and every time one of them stuck their head up, Tod put a bullet through it. Two more were stuck immobile on the floor in giant blue webbing balls.

Mathilda screamed some more, as the four Brujos approached her. She raised her hands and cast the Soul Tug. She cast it with everything she had. Two thick strands of light flew from her hands and wrapped around the two nearest Brujos, and instinctively, desperately, she pulled. She screamed, and tugged at the threads as hard and as fast as she could, shaking the souls of the Brujos. She felt them stumble and begin to fall, and she poured her life, heart, and soul into it. She screamed again, desperation making her throat hoarse. The Brujos fell to the ground, inert. Their compadres gaped at the bodies, and then at each other, their attention momentarily wrested from Mathilda.

Blood still pumped out of her leg and her arm, spilling across her abdomen, and she could barely breathe. Something had broken inside her chest, or her side – she couldn't be sure where; it all hurt. She curled over as much as her vest would allow, and slumped onto the tarmac.

Across the lot, Billy looked up over his cover behind a bullet-ridden family car, and he saw Mathilda on the ground.

He panicked. The Navajo shaman raised his tomahawk above his head, chanted as loud as he could, screaming war cries, his Colt still firing towards the Brujos shooting at him as he ran across the asphalt. He sang for speed and he sang for strength and power. He did not register when his Colt stopped thundering and began clicking. He ran on ensorcelled legs, thighs pushing powerfully, propelling him across the parking lot faster than the blink of an eye. But not faster than a speeding bullet.

A bullet caught him in the back, above his vest, near the base of his neck. Billy faltered , and his head spun as another bullet caught the side of his skull. He staggered, momentum moving him forward, towards Mathilda, blood shooting out around him in a dark circle. Both the Brujos near Mathilda had turned to face the charging Navajo shaman, and unloaded their guns at him at short range. Bullets tore into Billy, but they didn't slow his course. He got within yards of the flustered Brujos, who couldn't pour bullets into him fast enough. The closest ran out of shells, and pulled a cheap survival knife out of his belt. He was going to put this Indian down. Billy hurled his tomahawk, the weapon of Geronimo himself, which flew out of his hand and careered through the air, into the face of the Brujo, who fell, instantly dead, his smug expression split in two. The survival knife let out a high-pitched cracking sound as it fell to the tar and broke.

Billy lurched forward with one more surge of strength, and landed on top of the blood-covered Mathilda, falling unconscious as he lay protectively across her, shielding her. Two bodies, lying still and unmoving in a messy, bloody pile on the floor.

*

We all have memories that shape us. Some of these are positive, and these become the markers of joy that we hold up to measure the standard of our happiness. Sadly, some of these are negative, and they shape the wounds that we need to overcome – or, in some cases, succumb to.

At the edge of his awareness, Eddie saw Billy and Mathilda collapse to the floor. The Golden Bear felt instant shock, and desperation, and something else... Beneath the pain at realising that Mathilda and Billy were down in a bullet-ridden pile, covered in their own blood, was another pain, far older.

This older pain was larger than the smart of recent hurt. It was not the sharp sting of fresh grief, but rather, it was a timeworn ache from deep within. It was a long-buried hurt – the pain of loss. It was the loss of his first apprentice – his wife, his love. And his failure to protect her. Within the giant, golden bear, Eddie surfaced, a lone man rising from some deep, Jungian depths.

Eddie didn't understand what was happening to him. In his last fight with the Brujos in the general store, he had felt a depth of love and care that he normally shied away from. His relationship with Mathilda was taking on seriously caring overtones. And now, in the midst of a magical battle the likes of which hadn't been seen in many years, he felt repressed emotions rising.

It was ten years ago that Christy had died. His apprentice, then lover, then wife. He had dealt with the trauma in the time-tested way of the men in his family, and the true way of action heroes – by burying it deep, and ignoring it as long as they could, until they had a heart attack or a stroke, and then died.

But now it was surfacing. In real time, something horrific and momentous was happening, and nobody around the devastated, body-strewn, spell-ridden parking lot outside the Three Sisters motels could stop themselves from looking at it. Remarkably, the golden bear began to grow even bigger. The immense form pulsed a deeper gold, and, unbelievably, Eddie grew even larger. Power, born of heartache and rage, coursed through him, and the golden bear grew from titanic to behemoth. He grew another two feet taller, and another two feet wider, his torso thickening, his legs bulging with dense muscle and his arms swelling into dark-furred, colossal appendages. His claws too, thickened, lengthened, and sharpened.

Eddie roared in fury, a roar of unmistakable power. It wasn't as fearsome as the demon fugue, but it was a magical call that invigorated his allies and caused fear in his enemies.

Mathilda suddenly opened her eyes and weakly breathed in, air wheezing slowly into her lungs. Billy did not. The remaining Brujo facing them dropped his gun and bolted from the parking lot. Things had not gone anywhere near how the Alamosa desperados had hoped. Their entire gang was either wiped out or ensorcelled, and their boss was still stuck in a one-on-one wrangle with a magical, giant, glowing bear – and it looked like that was about to end soon, and badly.

Across the lot from Mathilda, the Brujos behind the car looked at each other, and they knew it was time. They did not want to die here today. Not from fear of the falling demon, nor from the bullets that disintegrated heads out of nowhere, nor the giant, carnivorous weredog or any other kind of crazy magic shit that was going on. They were at the point where a handcuffed ride in a nice van with blue and white flashing lights seemed like Twinkies to a starving man. The captain dropped his gun and raised his hands.

"We see you," Becca shouted over the gap. "Hang on, Tod!" she spoke over the comms, breaking the radio silence. "It looks like they're giving up – hold your fire!"

"Roger."

Becca focused her voice towards the Brujos. "Drop your weapons, hands in the air. You won't be harmed. I've spoken to the sniper."

They were hesitant at first, but the captain – hands still in the air, above his head – stood up. He looked around, and for them, the fight was over. Apart from the clash of titans going on in the lot on his left.

"You won't be harmed, you have our word," Becca called out.

Weapons fell and hands rose. The remaining Brujos stood up from behind their cover. It was over now, and they knew it.

Becca released the Great Dance spell and the rest of the Brujos finally stopped. They stood around, unsure of their freedom. Some examined their arms and legs, now back under their own control. Then they, too, put their hands in the air.

With renewed power and rage, the golden bear hurled the head of the prehistoric-sized rattler away from his face, and contemptuously kicked its lower coils off his legs. The foot-thick column of solid snake muscle that only seconds earlier had been wrapped tightly around the legs of the behemoth bear flew off easily. Shifting Sands coiled and sprang forward with blinding speed, gore- and venom-covered fangs bared to sink into the bear mage in front of him.

The golden bear swatted the snake aside as it struck, the seemingly clumsy manner belying the supernatural speed and unearthly power that he struck with. A paw bigger than a tennis racket thundered into a snake head built like a venom-spewing T-rex, and the smash of shattering bones reached sickeningly to either end of the lot.

The giant snake flickered and twitched as it landed, body sliding like quicksilver to turn and launch another deadly attack. Incomprehensibly, the golden bear was faster, and he reached down and gripped the tail of the rattler in one clawed hand, and then another. With a bestial roar, powered by every ounce of emotion that he had, Eddie – the golden bear, more so now than he had ever been – raised the tail above his head and, with a mighty heave, swung the snake to his left, then he pulled again in the opposite direction and lobbed the snake across the lot with unbelievable power, hurtling it into the side of a car that crumpled at the impact, like it was made of tin foil.

The snake shot towards the bear again, but this time it got dragged by its tail, and hurled overhead to crash down into the surface of the lot, sending up a spray of broken tar. The bear pulled on the snake's tail and swung it around his head like a vengeful child with his rattle, before ramming it face-first into the white car which was providing cover to the surrendered Brujos. The four who were in range screamed as the car flipped over and crushed their legs and lower bodies. The remaining Brujos ran as fast as they could.

With one more flick of his powerful paw, the golden bear tossed the giant rattler almost indifferently into the middle of the parking lot, and for a second watched it twitch.

*

Mathilda was still breathing, but painfully. Billy lay heavy across her, his body a human shield against the gunshots of the Brujo desperados. Odelia bounded over with her face painted in gore, and chomped off the head of one of the unconscious gangsters, before moving on to check on Mathilda.

A bloody nose nuzzled against Mathilda's side. She reached up and rested a hand on Odelia's great, furrowed head and gently, Odelia nudged at Billy, rolling his inert body off Mathilda.

By now, the parking lot was a ragged mess of tar, bodies, and deeply-grooved gravel – a demented carnival scene of magic and mayhem. All those that were left standing stared at the battered and torn snake.

As for Eddie, he had taken some hits – venom that had spewed from the fangs of the rattler poured down his arms but, despite the volume, and the fact that it hissed and spattered when it hit the ground, corroding at the tar's top layer – he seemed none the worse for wear.

Becca's face shimmered slightly and both her hands took on a purple glow. She ran across to the blood-covered Billy and Mathilda, tears already streaming down her face at the thought of losing either of them. Odelia pawed the ground, raring to rip up the giant rattler.

Shifting Sands lurched backwards, the vestiges of his power rippling his massive snake form out of existence. Green-tinged skin, sharp, reptilian features –

magic poured off him as the spell finally ended and the ancient Navajo sunk back into the body of a human. An ancient, broken body, horrendously ripped.

There was a moment of stillness as the two adversaries glared at each other across the gap between them. The bear still glowed a strong, pulsing gold. After a fight like that, Eddie somehow still seemed able to go on. He was a seriously powerful mage. Shifting Sands's shape seemed distorted, his body pale and waning. He was dying. He had been slowly losing the fight, inch by painstaking inch, b in the end, that sudden burst of rage and power by the bear had been too much for him. He had been handled like a powerless child – this bear mage was the most powerful human he had ever encountered.

This giant bear had power from the old tales. He reminded Shifting Sands of another bear, another time. A bear, hundreds of years in his past, from his childhood.

It had been said by the people of his tribe that the great bear of the Shadow Valley was powerful beyond man, and was a cousin to great bear Nyah Gwaheh himself. His name was Chahatheet Shash – the Dark Bear.

As a child, he had seen Dark Bear one night as it passed the edges of their camp. Just as the moon had shone on a gap beneath the trees, a shadow bigger than anything he had ever seen shifted: a great bear, massive in frame, layered in fat and robed in thick slabs of muscle. Deep, black fur stirred beneath the moonlight, a shadow moving amongst shadows.

He was a child, young, riveted to the spot in fear. As his eyes fixed on the immense figure slipping silently through the night, it stopped. With that sense that he later understood to be the source of his power, he knew that the bear had felt his stare. Slowly, with the speed that honey drips from trees, and just as noiselessly, Dark Bear turned his great head, whilst the rest of his body held perfectly still.

A moment passed between them – a moment that the child would never forget, even 300 years later. The bear looked right at him, directly into his eyes, and nodded. A shocked and stupefied child, with his mouth hanging open, was stunned. He nodded back. The bear paused, as if in acknowledgement of the power that he had seen in the child, then turned his head forward again and, as silently as he had arrived, slipped off into the night.

Shifting Sands had not visited that memory in almost 300 years. He smiled as he recalled his childhood of many lifetimes ago. That black night, all that time ago with the cousin of Great Bear, something had awakened in him. He had known then that he had a power within him. It had all begun with a bear, and now it all ended with a bear.

It was just a shame that after all these years of malevolence, he had caused a separation between himself and the Great Spirits. He was evil, and he knew it. He had done too many terrible things, and he would pay for that. He would be doomed to wander and would never make it into the Land of Eternal Summer. Heaven would not be his and he would never see those he had once loved.

Shifting Sands, wrinkled and bent old man that he was, dropped to his knees. The bear shuffled over and placed a paw, bigger than his entire head, alongside his face.

The medicine man knew this was his time, and stared forward, accepting.

He glanced at the group around him. The glamoured woman knelt next to the young female mage, her glowing, purple hands pouring healing into her. It might not be enough. Alongside her, on his back, riddled with bullet holes, lay the young Navajo shaman. The giant dog – the size of a plains pony – stood next to both of them, staring at him with glaring eyes, daring him to move.

But with the bear standing over him, he would not resist any longer. His death was inevitable. The least he could do would be to die well and go to whatever fate awaited him. An afterlife as a spirit roving the dunes, rootless, tormented and unfulfilled. He sniffed. He deserved that. He expected it.

A small, white rented car screamed down the road and pulled quickly into the parking lot, kicking up dust and gravel as it skidded to a halt in front of the motels. A short, lean man got out of the driver's seat, and pulled out a long and heavy rifle. Aah – the sniper. He had come to see the death of the old shaman.

With the rifle expertly cradled in his arm, the sniper walked over to where Billy Limping Bear lay, retrieved his tomahawk from the dead Brujo's head, and placed it in the young man's hand.

Shifting Sands smiled at this, and suddenly everything went dark. He never even felt it when the bear snapped his neck.

"Look." Becca pointed towards the body of Shifting Sands lying face-upon the floor. "Use your mage sight."

Mathilda looked up through puffy, tear-swollen eyes, unable to sit by herself, leaning on Odelia. She could feel that she was not healed, and something inside was still broken – Becca had just bought her some time.

Tod and Eddie also switched to mage sight.

The soul of Shifting Sands stood before them. His limbs were already beginning to stretch like a gaunt, withered, undead thing. Shadows clung to him as though he was hiding amongst them, one of their own.

Around him was only darkness. He looked around, confused at first, with a hunted expression. Twitchy, as though he could hear the hounds of his tormentors, but he was the only one that could.

The area gradually became a little lighter. Billy's soul rose up out of his body, a light around him, and he seemed at peace. The light that came from Geronimo's tomahawk, still clutched in his spirit hands, shone like a torch out before him. The spirit of Billy Limping Bear walked over to the already-transforming shape of the ancient shaman's spirit, and tentatively extended his hand out to Shifting Sands.

The bent spirit looked up at Billy, shocked, almost waiting for the hand to be pulled away – but it was not. Instead, Billy gently gripped the hand of the ancient shaman, raised the tomahawk above his head, like a torch to light the way, and began to walk up a sunbeam path that led upward. Eddie and Mathilda had seen this before – it was the path to Heaven, the Land of Eternal Summer.

Billy, his face a picture of mercy, sang his final song in this world. A song in his spirit, that all Navajo knew. It was the song to guide the way home. The sunlit path thickened and Billy led Shifting Sands upwards, nearing the Land of Eternal Summer. A slice in reality opened, and spread into a golden disc that grew in size until it was big enough for two men to walk through. As they neared, Shifting Sands began to look more human. He stood taller and prouder, his skin firmer. They stopped at the threshold, and Billy touched the disc. It opened before him.

"Come, brother," he said. "It's time."

Shifting Sands, beaming, now with the face and body of a young man, nimbly hopped through. He looked back a with an innocent smile – the kind that hadn't visited his face in over two hundred and fifty years.

Billy turned from the shaman, who ran into the sunlight of Heaven, towards the scene arrayed beneath him in the motel's parking lot. He was at peace. He accepted his fate, but when he looked out over his friends, and Mathilda, his spirit stirred. They had helped him free the stikini, had pulled him from his hiding place when his house had been riddled with bullets by the Brujos, and had accepted him like no other group ever had, not even his own people. Mathilda cared for him, and in truth, he had cared for her. He had cared enough that he had charged across a war zone and died to save her.

Billy's eyes locked on Mathilda, and tears began to well in his dark spirit eyes. They ran down his spectral cheeks, and he raised his hand to wave goodbye. Yes, it was his time and Heaven was in front of him, but it felt so soon – like he needed to know if they could love each other, if they could at least date, maybe build a life. He could fix his place and drink less... and, hell, it sounded like a cliché, but that girl made him want to be a better man.

Tears streamed freely down his incorporeal face, and Billy sobbed openly. He did not want to go, and he did not want to say goodbye, but he was already dead – what could he do? Billy turned away from his friends – from Mathilda – and faced the entrance to the Land of Eternal Summer.

"No!" It was Mathilda. "Not now!" she screamed. Still sitting, she raised both her hands, and with the last of her life she had left, cast a Soul Tug. Mathilda would not let Billy die.

All were watching, and all could see. Two gossamer-thin threads shot from her hands and latched onto Billy. They stuck onto him fast, and as Mathilda threw her magic and her life energy into the spell, the two thin, white strands thickened and became slender ropes, then shining cables, growing increasingly bright, blindingly white.

Mathilda started to falter, as her exertions undid

the healing that Becca had given her. Becca desperately grabbed her in both hands and yet again poured everything she had into Mathilda.

Mathilda tugged and pulled with every ounce of her being. Fear, love, hurt, regret. Friendship, care, love lost, love found. She tugged at Billy's soul with her one real spell, and she pulled it down, and back to earth, with every last thing she had. His face dropped, and his soul flew – tugged with surprisingly powerful magic – back into his body.

The gate to Heaven disappeared, the golden bridge closed, and suddenly, there was nothing to see with mage sight anymore.

Mathilda became deathly pale – she had pulled too hard – and her body fell to the side, onto the tarmac.

Everybody ran towards the bodies of Billy and Mathilda, leaving the dead body of Shifting Sands behind them, ignored.

As they did, the smiling, beaten and bloodied body of Shifting Sands transformed, turning into a man-shaped pile of sand. He had become true to his name. After a silent minute, the ancient shaman was gone, the sand was swept by the wind and scattered across the parking lot.

*

San Luis Valley Hospital, Alamosa, Colorado, USA

The beep of the heart monitor cut through the silence of the room. Eddie lay asleep in a chair next to Mathilda's bed, his face a mass of cuts and swelling. Becca, eyes swollen from tears, leant against the wall alongside the door into the hospital room, as Tod entered with a tray of coffees and a plastic bag of assorted vending machine delights.

In the bed furthest from the door, Billy lay fast asleep.

As Tod came in, Odelia – who had been snuck in by Eddie – raised her head, and got up from where she slept beneath Eddie's chair. She sauntered over to Tod. After all, he had the snacks.

Tod walked over to Mathilda, and he gently shook her awake. He motioned with his head to the coffee and pack of biscuits he had just put next to her bed. Becca shook Eddie up, and he came out of a deep, fatigue-driven sleep, mollified by an extra-large black coffee and a peanut butter Snickers. The first thing Eddie did was check on Mathilda. She looked at him and smiled, and he reached over and put his hand on her arm.

Becca was still coming to terms with this emotionally demonstrative Eddie over the last couple of days. It was a new change and Becca supposed it was a welcome one – but a change to Eddie was like a change in the firmament. She had been a part of the family since the age of 15, and Eddie was this glacial presence, this immovable bear of a man. He was constant and unchanging – he was this guardian that stood over them, and woe betide any who threatened what he loved. Except now he was movable – he was emotional, and Becca still had to figure out how she felt about that.

Now everyone was awake, with a hot coffee and a sugary snack in their hands. All except Billy, who was medicated enough to sleep for the next week, and he probably would.

After Mathilda and Billy had been rushed to the hospital in Tod's cheap rental, Mathilda had spent the past two days and nights in hospital. The bullet wounds in her arm and leg were the least of her concerns – it was the shotgun shells that had broken ribs, which had pierced her lung, that was the real danger. But it had turned out to be a simple traumatic pneumothorax, and after the lung had expanded on the first day, it was simply a case of allowing her body to heal from the collective trauma of the punctured lung, the gunshots, and the heavy use of magic – as well as the distress of literally seeing Billy die and pulling his spirit back into his body again.

Mathilda was well out of danger – no doubt the daily healing from Becca aiding greatly. Becca was no Elle, but what she did helped. As soon as the doctor was happy that Tilda was beyond the chance of infection, he'd let her out.

Billy, on the other hand, was another story entirely. He had taken numerous shots to the body, head, arms, and legs. The vest had helped, but between a bullet to the side of his head and the substantial blood loss, he should have been dead. The doctors couldn't explain how Billy was still alive, given the extent of his injuries, but, of course, they didn't realise that his soul had been pulled directly back into his body, and that he had been receiving healing from Becca as often as she could give it. In truth, his only chance of getting out of that hospital bed on his own steam was a miracle.

Tod pulled his laptop out of a bag and dialled Sko, then put it at the foot of Matilda's bed, facing her. The others all moved their chairs around to the sides of her bed so they could see the screen. The blue glare shining backwards and upwards lit the dim room. Time for another family conference.

"So," Sko started with a beaming smile. "Hi, everyone. I have some great news! Sorry for just blurting it out like this, but I think it's something we're all going to love... I've asked Elle to come down and have a look at Billy, and she said yes! She's flying in as we speak – and you know how she hates flying..."

"Unless she's on her broom!" Eddie butted in with a grin, his spirits suddenly buoyed by the news.

Becca clapped her hands together excitedly. Billy needed a miracle, and a healer like Elle was as good a miracle as they could get. This was great news!

"Do you think... Do you really think Elle could help?" Mathilda asked in a soft voice, uncertain.

"Hell, yeah!" Tod rejoined. "She's old school. Eye-of-toad and wing-of-newt kinda old school. She knows how to fix plagues that haven't even come out yet! Seriously, she is a great healer, and has studied in one of the most powerful magical healing traditions out of Europe. She really is one of the best in the business."

Sko continued: "Mathilda – Elle is a fantastic healer. I've told her what happened, and she genuinely feels there is a chance she can help. A good chance. If she didn't feel she could make a difference, she wouldn't have gotten on a plane. Have some faith in us, and tonight, when Elle gets there, you'll see."

Mathilda nodded, awash with emotion. She wanted to hope, she really did, but she knew the cost of misplaced hope, even at her young age.

"So, there's more," Sko went on. "I've got some leads on the demon and his Diablos in New Mexico. I think Tod should go down and check it out – he's the best manhunter amongst us. Colm is on his way, to support Tod with backup. We can keep an eye on their movements, and when we have them tracked to a suitable location, we'll send this demon back to where he belongs, once and for all."

Tod whooped. "Here we go, baby!"

"So, Tod," Sko continued after the outburst, "You and Colm, just find him and monitor. The rest of us will come down in a few weeks, after we take on our next piece of work."

Sko turned his head onscreen. "And you, old man?" He was looking at Eddie. "You're looking pretty beat up over there. How you holding up?"

Eddie smiled a wry grin, and took a bite of Snickers. "I'm tired, Sko. That was one helluva fight, and I don't think I've ever channeled as much bear as that. It was…" He shrugged. "I dunno. It was intense."

"I'm sorry, my friend. But if ever we needed a

man in that fight, you know I'd back you ten times out of ten. I don't know many other mages out there who could have gone toe-to-toe with Shifting Sands. We needed you."

Eddie nodded wearily.

"You've got a few days to rest up. I'll make sure Elle has something in her bag of tricks for you." His tone lightened. "Some good news for you, too… I'm sure a week or two kicking your feet up in Nua Dannon will help ease things for you."

Eddie perked up. "The queen?"

"Yup. Queen Danithel needs us. It's a great gig. No demon lords, no undead shamans, no crazy missions – it's a bit of elven babysitting. We're going to iron out the details over the next few days, but, basically, it's a milk run."

Eddie burst out laughing, almost choking on his coffee. He'd heard that before. "Sko, why the hell do you have to go and say that? You know there's no such thing as a milk run!"

"But there will be, Eddie," Sko was laughing. "… one day! There has to be! Not every job we do has to be a hard one!"

"Sure, Sko," Eddie sighed with a cynical smirk. "A milk run… maybe. Maybe this one time is it, hey? A milk run in the Elven Kingdom."

"Right," Sko said. "I need to tend to the demon lord's mystery hacker, prep for the queen, loads to do. So I'm going to sign out. We'll speak soon, hey?"

They all said goodbye, and the screen went blank. Tod shut the laptop and slid it into his bag, then slung it over his shoulder. He looked meaningfully at Becca. She gently inclined her head, and Tod and Becca walked out, giving Mathilda a small squeeze on the way.

Eddie and Mathilda were left facing each other, alone in the room (except for Odelia lying on the floor, and Billy asleep by the window). Mathilda lay back in her hospital bed, and Eddie was standing up alongside her.

There was a tender moment when they looked at each other, and Eddie leaned in and wrapped her up in his bulky arms. He breathed out, just holding his young apprentice. She buried her head deep into his neck, his meaty shoulder pressing up against her face. After a few seconds, she let out a sigh, and shuddered as tears ran down her cheeks, into Eddie's coat.

"It'll be okay, Mathilda, I promise." Eddie placed a caring hand gently on her head. "We got this."

Chapter 13: That post-credits scene that we all love

London, England, May 1314

It was a cold and miserable morning. Why the hell Samael chose these dirty, sewer-ridden cities, Miriam had no idea.

He had seen the glories of Heaven, and had basked in the light of nature's dawning and earth's early sun, when the skies were as blue as mountain pools. Why mankind's dirtiest industrial capitals? It was probably the whores. Actually, she knew. It was definitely the whores.

London had her fair share of whores, some going so far as using scripture to call London a whore of Babylon herself, being the hub of commerce and industry that she was. Miriam always got indignant about men using the scriptures to justify their crazy hangups. Especially because she had been around for a big chunk of it. Well, the early parts, at the very least.

Leaving the docks, Miriam turned north towards Cokkes Lane, near Newgate. The streets were not crowded yet – it was still too early, yet the close-knit streets of London always made her feel claustrophobic.

She passed the White Tower as she made her way north, watching as she always did for followers. It didn't have to be ancient secret societies, or even new secret ones, that followed her. A handsome woman alone, on a street of London, in the worst areas of the city – particularly for women – well, there were even more threats from the mundane than from the occult.

Although the city smelled, she loved the walk. She had always loved walking, but as times had progressed, so had the industry of man... and the development of shoes. It wasn't that mankind had not had shoes before, but early shoes were crude affairs, generally not as effective or comfortable as shoes were in these more modern times. Today, she wore chestnut, wooden-heeled, polished leather knee-high boots with ebony buttons, lined with lamb's wool. They were warm and divinely comfortable, and great for the muck that mired streets alongside the London docks.

A few short minutes later, she approached The Stews, the section of the city where the streets were lined with Roman-style baths (in name only, of course). The similarity they had to actual Roman baths was like comparing a rural cattle wash in the farms of Champagne to the salons of Paris. In short, she headed for the street with the most brothels, and on that street, she headed for the crown jewel amongst those brothels: La Reins Zezette – The Queen's Quim.

The double-story building had a facade facing the street, painted in gaudy reds and whites with edges in beaten copper, shone to look like gold. It was bright and tawdry, far better kept than its neighbours, and, typically, with a far better clientele.

She snuck down a darkened alleyway along the side of the house, via the stables, and entered through the back door. After taking her hood down, was shown up to Samael promptly.

Throughout the ground floor, only awakening now after a busy night, select guests were being treated to breakfasts and more alcohol. Up to the first floor, through a warren of small rooms, each just large enough for a bed – in some cases, a large bed. Up through to the roof garden, where Samael spent much of his time.

She came out onto the roof, beneath the grey, cloud-covered London sky. Standing naked in the wan morning sunlight with his back to the doorway, with giant, white wings spread out, arms reaching up and slightly backwards in morning stretch, Samael was an absolutely perfect physical specimen.

Samael: seventh archangel of Heaven, father of the succubus and husband to Lillith, once the avenging angel, known in some texts as the lord of Satan. And he truly was more or less all of that. It was rather complicated. But to Miriam, it was simpler.

"Hello, Father," she called to him. "We have a new group of mages who I think are competition for the Tufaahatan."

He turned a glance over his shoulder and raised an eyebrow in query.

"It seems to be a powerful group of mages," Miriam continued. "They're really organised, and carry some influence in Rome – but more clandestine than the usual ones. They look to be made up of oddly dressed gentlemen."

END OF BOOK 1, THE RULES OF
MAGIC: BAD MEDICINE.

Lookout for book 2, Court of
Fey, coming out shortly.

Make sure you read the prologue for Court
of Fey, attached as Bonus content.

BONUS CONTENT

In book 2, Court of Fey; Eddie and the Family get drawn into an ancient elven forum fraught with peril at every step, chase Bethshiel - the wounded Demon lord - across Central America and finally end up in a showdown that is more dangerous than anything they have ever faced before.

Turnover to deepen your journey with Eddie and the Family...

COURT OF FEY

The rules of magic, vol 2

Prologue: Fox in shadow

A shadow slipped between shadows and noiselessly moved closer to the palace. A figure lay still on the floor, its feet almost reaching the edge of the shade cast by the tall trees, as if reaching for the light, but it would never walk again.

Another figure walked out of a grove of trees onto an open lawn between the palace and the perimeter wall. As this figure paused to investigate a copse of bushes, a small steel spike whipped through the air and thudded into his neck. His eyes went wide, right hand reaching for the sting, and came away covered in red. His eyes went wider still, and he sunk to his knees, and then to the ground, wondering what exactly had happened. Sadly for him, he would die never knowing. Now another body lay still on the ground, forevermore in the shadows.

A shape – blurred at the edges, a black shadow, low to the ground – scurried out from the darkness, grabbed this body, and quickly dragged it deeper into the bushes. If there had been a guard still alive to look directly at the figure, his head would have begun to ache, and he may have squinted, as though staring at the sun. He might have rubbed his face with his hands, and looked up, and away, not too sure what he'd seen in the first place. If asked later what it was, his mind would have volunteered all sorts of memories – a raven, a dog, a shadow, a black plastic bag, a tumbleweed. But not a fox. Specifically, not a large, pitch-black fox with seven tails. A nogitsune. No, definitely not a fox.

The not-fox shape moved across the garden in the waning afternoon light. It had needed the light to get into the land of Queen Danithel – her autumn magic, dark and rich, loved the night. He would never have been able to get into the kingdom at nighttime. But now, once in, when the night did settle, he would strike in the darkness, a blade in the night, a whisp of blackened mystery, leaving his targets to die quickly, and then he would leave.

Kuroi Nogitsune Hai – The Black Ash Fox, assassin supreme, malevolent entity from deep in Japanese mythology – found the window that had been left open, slid up the wall like a shadow growing long in the late afternoon sun, and hopped in through the opening.

He had, in all his long years, never seen wards as complex and powerful as this. They were almost interesting., But to a spirit of mist and shadow, a fox of the field, these wards were nothing more than intriguing. He smelt the wards the scents of autumn and the power of the immortal queen that cast them. Damp leaves and roots, lukewarm sunshine, loamy soil. A hint of ancient shores, green moss and giant stones that had been in place so long they were like exposed bones of the earth. Frankly, he loved the smell. He was a creature of burrows, dark and rich with the fragrance of soil that nourished life, with thick gnarled roots running like boughs along the ceiling. Her power smelt like a place he could stay in, for a while.

Despite their power, it was easy for him to walk between the lines of wards in mist form, nimbly hopping over faintly glowing beams and between wards in the shapes of ancient glyphs and even older runes, all joined by swirling lines like tree roots reaching out with intertwining tips beneath the soil. It tasted very intimate on the tip of his tongue and teased at his nose and whiskers.

He licked the air, a black-furred fox with seven bushy-ended, sashaying tails in a mist form that allowed him to walk through wards that others couldn't even see. He smelt magic and tasted enchantment. He was almost a thousand years old and had trained to kill at the hands of Furui Yama no Senshi, the most ancient of tengu – a truly horrendous and dangerous old man who drank far too much sake and remained unwholesomely hard to kill.

Hai cleared the wards and landed noiselessly in a wooden passageway. It was simple and gorgeous. The floor was polished to a pale gold; the walls and roof a paler hue in long, wide horizontal strips. These halls were not fancy and, apart from the occasional tapestry, the wealth was in the age, and type of the wood. The magical charms that overlaid them – and the power that coursed through them – was, in some sense, beyond price. The enchantments they carried were an extension of the queen herself, and were a part of the larger surrounding Elven Kingdom.

She would know any being that set foot in these halls. Unless, of course, they were an ancient fox spirit. He was impressed at how sensitive the wards were, and how the wood seemed to pulse with life – an ancient and glorious life, imperious. The floor felt warm beneath his paws, and – field fox that he was – he enjoyed the feeling.

His ears pricked up as he neared a turn. Footsteps. Three sets. He shifted along the wall, between a set of warm, yellow sconces, seeking the patch of deepest shadow. Shadows worked for field foxes. Truth be told, these were pale shades, and shone through with soft golden light. They were truly not good enough for hiding in.

Remaining in mist form, he sunk to the floor and tensed himself to transform for action. Just in case. Most likely, they wouldn't see him, but these were magical halls, and well lit with magical light. And the people coming around the corner would most likely be elves. Which meant they would be, to some extent, magical. Exactly how magical would make all the difference.

He crouched in mist form, keeping his eyes to the passage end, probably fifteen feet away. Both his ears pointed forward. He held his breath, his muscles loaded, ready to launch.

The three elves rounded the corner with slow, casual gaits, smiles all round, in the relaxed and easy way that close friends had in each other's company. They were long-limbed and slender; auburn-haired – well, except the one at the back, slightly older with a rounding middle. His hair was strawberry blonde. They were wearing T-shirts, jeans, and sneakers. The front pair were wearing band tees – a black Led Zeppelin and a bright yellow Fleetwood Mac. The fatter one at the back wore a navy-blue tee, the front covered in gravy stains.

It smelt like pork to Nogitsune the fox.

It was the older one who responded first. His smile dropped for a second as he rounded the corner. His eyes flickered around the passage, down to where The Black Ash Fox – Nogitsune Hai – hid in mist form.

For a split-second, his eyes paused, and then looked up again. The pause was the giveaway, and all the trigger the black fox needed.

He leapt, materialising in the air as he did so: transforming from a fox into a short, elderly Japanese man. He was barefoot, in loose, black clothing. An aged, perfectly manicured foot lashed out at speed as he rocketed towards the elves almost too fast for the eye to see, and smashed the smile off the face of the elf wearing the Fleetwood Mac tee. Faster than the blink of an eye, a short and sharp whipping sound cracked through the air, leaving a thin silver blur in its wake. Led Zeppelin died, as the top half of his head fell off, sliced diagonally from left temple to right jawline.

Crouched low in front of the dead and unconscious elves, staring at the stunned, fat, old elf, was a wizened, bald man with a katana sharper than a glint of sunlight. In that split-second, as both elves fell to the floor, the man's scraggly white beard split into a feral grin. Like a fox in a henhouse.

The older elf raised his hands, and air began to swirl around his fingers. This was happening at the speed of thought, but it still wasn't fast enough to stop another cut with the short, black-handled katana. Or two. The first cut sliced upwards, removing both the elf's hands; the second returned down to end his life before the blood could even spurt from the severed stumps. Before the aging elf realised his hands had been severed.

Nogistune Hai, The Black Ash Fox, jumped over the dead body of the old elf, and flickered into fox form in the air, like a freeze-frame special effect from an ageing celluloid movie. Then he disappeared into mist and vanished down the passageway, towards his real target.

*

Winter had already arrived, but in the Autumn Kingdom, winter could not hold sway. It was acknowledged, yes, but in a land where reality and time bent to suit powerful and ancient magics, Autumn was queen, and her name was Danithel. Her power was felt throughout her kingdom and in it, she lived eternally. Some price for immortality. The entire kingdom was her home, and because of that, her palace was a particularly un-ostentatious one. The fact that the full kingdom was to some extent a manifestation of her power, was a bigger flex than a sparkly palace and a clutch of pretty chandeliers.

All who entered knew where the power lay – it was vested in Danithel, the Autumn Queen, recently chosen as head of the Unseelie court. She was the first Autumn ruler of the Unseelie in over a thousand years. It heralded a time of great change and potential. And danger.

Danithel nodded her petite head gently and subtly, in the way of elves. Theirs was a reserved and refined culture. To one of her people, a simple nod of her head could mean life or death – or a thousand other things, depending on the situation. Today, it meant she was pleased, and the builder was to be rewarded for the mill that ran off the blue waters of the Byrthwraithe and helped feed her people.

As she turned from the solid stone structure, with its sturdy wooden bones and stone and mortar body, she felt that sense for the first time.

It was a sense of unease. It came, unwelcome and unexpected, like a sharp-knifed man in the dark. The queen stilled herself and felt out through a network of power that spread across the land through every living thing – every tree and person, every bough and every limb. She shut her eyes and communed for a moment with her kingdom. Her eyes opened, and she knew. There was an intruder in her domain. A killer on the loose. A snake in the roots of her garden.

Nogitsune had moved further through the palace. Two uniformed guards lay dead on the floor behind him – more casualties of the lethal assassin. Now that the alarm had been sounded, he heard the clatter of many feet slamming the floor in hurried run. He had little worry about getting down into the dungeons to carry out his mission. It was the getting out that concerned him. They would be on watch and waiting – aware. What's more, she would be there. Her kingdom wasn't that big, and she wasn't that far away.

The best option was to get in and out before she arrived, but the chance of that was receding by the second, as increasing numbers of elven warriors and mages made their way towards him. The noose was drawing ever tighter. He grimaced and stretched his neck, then rattled the lock of the dungeon door. The door swung open in front of him, opening into a black, shadow-strewn passageway – yawning and ominous, a dark path, downwards to hell. He stepped over the threshold, and into the dungeons of the elf queen.

*

Time was crashing towards him like a peregrine falcon, short-tipped wings tucked tight, plummeting to earth at reckless speeds, the wind of circumstance clutching at its finely clustered feathers, unable to slow its descent. Too fast to stop. Too fast to be tracked. He had never caught a peregrine falcon.

Sadly, Hai remarked to himself, the passageways through the dungeons had become a vision of carnage. It was his doing, true, but this was not his way. At least, not anymore. He was, in some ways, a changed fox. He was older, and wiser. There had been a time when he would have gloried in the slaughter of hens, their blood running warm and iron down his throat, in his fur and on his face, congealing dark and sticky and hard on his neck.

He would totter off into the woods afterwards and clean himself over days, the lingering scent of blood a trophy of the slaughter, a reminder of the speed of his bite and the sharpness of his fangs. His ability to feed himself and his mates and his pups.

He had matured since those times, now slaughtering only for sustenance. Time had asked some questions of him: what good is slaughter for its own sake? Where was the challenge, the artistry? Where was the skill, the deft touch, the sardonic repartee against a foe whose skill would haunt him and whose ability and persistence would be the rock on which he sharpened his blade? A foe of legend. Where was the vicious mastiff, or the sheepdog with unending endurance? Why is it that all he ever found were fat, soft hens?

He had taken the mission into the Elven Kingdom because they were known to have powerful magic, but to date all he had found were more clucking egg-layers, content to sit on a pile of hay and be fed. It occurred to him that maybe he needed to take on the queen herself, but that seemed somehow inappropriate. She was, after all, a queen, and he an impudent fox. A powerful, impudent fox; an assassin of legend, of course. But she was an immortal queen and killing her didn't seem right. Unless she had some guard, some warrior of mythical power, equipped with artefacts mighty and armour impenetrable and layered with spells unbeatable. After many battles, he would eventually overcome this foe, and then he would – mercifully and gently – end the life of this queen. Her blood would spill gracefully on the floor, and it would be a scene that artists would paint for eons to come.

A guard charged through a doorway behind him, and Hai ducked as a pillar of flame lanced out of a guard's hand. Then he straightened up, casually sliding his sword into the man's throat as though he were skewering an errant pea with a fork. He pulled out the blade and spun to his right, leaping, so that both feet hit the wall and flipped him over and forward, his spin landing just short of the pistol-wielding prison guard who was emptying shells at him.

He sliced the blonde elf's head neatly in two. Of course, it was easy when your sword was sharp enough to cut lustful thoughts from a drunken man's heart. The sword's name was Jundo – Purity – and he loved her dearly.

A footfall landed behind him and, almost too casually, Hai reached into his black, kimono-styled shirt and flicked an object behind him: a thin, black spike hurtling through the air at the speed of a bullet. The guard, a cautious veteran, was pulling his head back behind the doorway, but he was too slow and too late, as the steel spike sunk four inches into his eye.

Hai, the large black fox in the shape of a small, wizened man, walked deeper into the elven dungeon without looking back. The sound of the guard falling to the floor was all the confirmation he needed that he had hit his target – not that he needed confirmation anyway.

The elven prison was defended by many spells and countermeasures, beyond mere guards. He had already despatched a dozen of the defenders. He had overcome the magic that should befuddle the senses of intruders. He had found the doors that were hidden by a glamour which he had to admit had been hard to sniff out, but sniff it out he had.

And now, deep beneath the palace, amidst dark stones, curses, and enchantments, through winding passageways, dead ends and (now) a mess of dead bodies and blood-spattered grey walls, he stood in the chamber he was looking for, in reach of his quarry.

Hai faced a large, rectangular room, from a doorway situated directly in the middle of its length. The opposite wall was lined with black-barred prison cells. Cell after cell ran down the entire length of the room, twenty cells in total. All but two of them occupied.

This was the room where elven prisoners were kept.

Prisoners from the other elven realms. Prisoners of the Summer, Spring, and Winter courts, languishing in the dirt, grime, and dark beneath the palace of the Autumn Queen.

All of them were manacled, with rune-covered chains affixing them to thick, iron rings in the floor. Even from where he stood at the entrance to the room, Hai felt the power coursing through the bars of the cells.

The fact that he could even see the cells was testimony to his intrinsic magical nature. And whilst he had overcome many challenges – and, as a fox, inherently could sneak into many places – he would never be able to break into these cells. Fortunately, his employer had provided exactly what he had needed to gain access: some jail-breaking assistance.

He stepped gently and silently into the room. The elves in their cages looked up as he entered. All silent, but wary. Cautious and curious glances came his way, as the captive elves speculated what new torment the Queen of Autumn had in store for them. The Queen of Autumn was, after all, one of the Unseelie fey. In a world where good and evil ran up and down a sliding scale, she was more grey/black than white/grey. The face of an angel with the heart of an Inquisition torturer.

Not that Hai cared. He was an assassin, a born predator – morality was something for the birds and deer. It was a tool that lords and priests used to control their citizens. It was a lie. "Moral" citizens didn't rebel against their lieges, didn't think for themselves or act for themselves. Morality was used by those who had no true martial strength – because if one had no martial strength, one needed lies to control others. As far as Hai was concerned, morality was just another deception in the arsenal of civilisation.

He was under no illusion that the elves in the cells – royal hostages used as bargaining chips – had had an easy existence in the dungeons of the immortal queen. In some respects, their death would be a mercy.

Looking into the cells, he could clearly see the elves according to their types. The Summer elves, majestic. Five in all, golden-haired, blue-eyed and regal; some with skin still holding the kiss of the sun, even after all their time in the cells beneath the ground. The seven of Spring, youthful and pale, like the first plants that bud through the soil after winter. Their eyes were brown, hazel, green, and gold. Finally, the six of winter: pale, tall, sharp-boned. Eyes of piercing blue-grey. Physical manifestations of the chill of frost and the bite of snow.

Before today, he had never killed an elf. Now he had killed dozens, and after today, he would have made enemies of all four of the Houses of Fey. If they ever found out it was him.

Up against the wall, a few feet to the right of the door, was a stone column, waist high, with a brass dial atop. This was the control for the magical grid which manipulated the magic of those in the cells in two ways. First, the cell bars themselves dampened any other magic generated within them. Second, the manacles ran a permanent power drain that weakened one's ability to access the power of magic. It was, all in all, a well-designed prison, and Hai wandered if it could hold him. Elves were inherently more magical than regular humans. They were like... a sort of human variant. Like different breeds of chicken: even though they all bled the same, some tasted better than others.

Elves were, in effect, a nicer-looking breed of human. A combination between a magical creature, like himself, and a human. A better-looking, cleverer chicken.

Being elven royalty, all the unfortunates manacled in the cells were delightful to look at. Despite months of containment, torture, and deprivation, one could easily see how they could be undeniably gorgeous, in the totally unattainable way that fey and magical creatures were. In the way that men and women had lusted after since they had first gathered around fires to talk about the one that got away.

They were beautiful, and it would be a shame, in some respects, to kill them. He did admire beauty – he was a predator, not a savage, after all. However, the job was agreed, and a contract taken. And so, needs be done what will be done.

He reached into his jacket and pulled out a tiny black cube, not much smaller than a matchbox, on the end of a wooden beaded necklace much like a rosary, or a set of Buddhist beads.

He placed it on the brass dial and was about to press

its sides in the prescribed sequence when he smelt a presence nearing the door from the outside. His nose twitched, fox-like, and his whiskers bristled. A foe was on its way.

He pulled out his shortened katana and held it in his right hand, tip pointing to the to the floor. A figure walked through the door. He was tall, shoulders just broader than average, black hair tied in a ponytail – not in an aging computer programmer kind of way, but in the hip kind of way that the programmer had once believed he could be.

This figure was cool, the kind of cool that made black leather pants and grey, floor-length overcoats look cool. He sauntered in casually, chin held high and shoulders relaxed back, like an eighties action hero. As he walked into the room, he turned to look at Hai, and his grey eyes widened.

With great respect, he addressed the assassin. "I have heard of your kind, but have never met one. Well met, Kitsune."

Hai nodded. "Almost, elf. Kitsune are the white foxes. I am a black one – I am Nogitsune."

The elf nodded back. "I am pleased to meet you, Nogitsune. I have seen your handiwork so far – your cuts are clean. You have admirable skills. But you no longer face guardsmen and scholars. Now you face me: Gareth High-Oak, captain of the queen's personal guard, victor of battles, undefeated in a hundred years. You will not find me so easy a mark as some dungeon-dwelling, glorified security guard. I am the son of a line that saw the birth of civilizations. You will not win easily against me. If at all."

Hai smiled. If this elf fought as well as he talked, then maybe – just maybe – this was the challenge he had been looking for. Maybe this elf was the foil to his sabre, the buckler to his arming sword, the indomitable iron against which his own iron would be sharpened. Maybe he had found his nemesis.

Gareth High-Oak reached into his long, grey coat, arms crossing, each reaching towards the opposite hip. A steel shing rang through the air as he pulled out two short, light, straight-edged swords. Hai could easily see that they were gloriously made. Intricate runes ran along the swords' edges and the swords glowed faintly with a magical light. These were weapons of power.

They whipped sharply through the air as the elf captain flicked their points towards Hai. Gareth kept the left sword low and raised the right one above his head. He took a slight step back with his right foot, so that his left side was facing forwards, protected by the low sword, with the right above his head, ready to attack. He sunk lower and settled his weight lightly above bent knees.

A fine stance for two blades.

Hai's grin widened. He waited to see if his opponent could hold his poise, or if his mind was weak.

Hai stood open, with his katana at his side, waiting. Gareth stood, weight low, rear sword poised high, also waiting.

They stood for what seemed like an age, but was in reality just a few breaths. The longer Hai waited, the greater would be his chance of failure.

The elf captain inched across the room, shuffling his feet slowly, serenely, inoffensively forward. He was creeping for range, preparing to launch an offensive. If he was smart – and he seemed smart enough – he would wait for Hai to attack before launching his own. Presumably, he was unnaturally fast, because any other option would result in his immediate demise.

The fox settled his weight, sword out in his right hand. His single-bladed katana was shorter than usual. It was, in fact, a ninjato; the same as a standard katana in every respect, but about four inches shorter. A version of the katana that was perfect for speed.

Hai breathed out, and narrowed his eyes. He bent his knees slightly, feeling his weight on the floor beneath his bare feet, Purity, his ninjato, resting lightly in his hand.

Tension filled the gap between them, concentrating until it was as if nothing but the two of them existed: two points on either end of a strained wire, pulled taut with intent and deadly peril.

Gareth was waiting, clearly, because he knew that he

could. Hai admired that Gareth didn't gloat or talk to hide his nerves. This was good. The fox assassin was ready.

With blinding speed, Hai lunged forward on his right leg, Purity slicing up towards the front thigh of the elven captain. Instantly, years of training kicked in, and Gareth High-Oak dropped the tip of his lower blade and shifted it elegantly down and out to intercept the rising blade. As the blades kissed, barely touching, the sound of two metals sliding against each other chimed across the room like the opening notes of a symphony.

Still moving forward as a part of one continuous movement, Hai grabbed the handle of his ninjato – now held with both hands – and the moment it touched Gareth's defensive blade, he flicked it out, around, over his head, and down onto the head of the elven captain.

Again, the response was instantaneous. This time, the captain shifted his raised blade down and across the top of his head to intercept the onrushing katana. Before Gareth High-oak, captain of the queen's guard, could even settle his weight into the parry, the sharper-than-razors-katana of the legendary fox spirit flicked off the down-rushing blade and rebounded back up towards Hai's head, before it spun sideways to slicing diagonally down towards the right side of the elf.

Gareth shifted to his left, away from the incoming blade, and brought both of his rune-covered swords into the path of the blindingly fast strike, forming a perfect X, to wedge the ninjato between his two glittering elven short steels.

There was a pause.

Not enough time had passed for a thought to form, and already Gareth could have died three times with each flawless slice from the nogitsune. He had been up to every attempt.

The two men were locked still, blades crossed, weight pressed into their intertwined weapons. Hai began to shift, circling slowly to his left. Gareth shifted to his own left. The two men stared at each other across locked blades. The powerful captain strained against the small, potent fox spirit.

Hai smiled at the tall elf between the cross of their blades. This captain was good. Apart from Hai's sensei, there wasn't a being who had stopped three strikes from him in a hundred years. Maybe this was the one... the nemesis.

If magical weapons could talk (as indeed, some can), Purity would have been snarling at the two short elven swords. The elven blades would have been tossing insults back. It wouldn't have been a conversation that was safe for work.

Hai's smile grew, and his canines – sharp and fox-like – protruded further. Maybe, after all these years, he had found his adversary – a noble queen's captain; a tall, lean hero built for action pitted against the dark, bent, ancient assassin.

In an instant, Hai jumped away, his sword unlocking from the captain's blades. As he flew backward, his left hand reached into his coat and shot forward to propel a short, dense steel spike – a bo shuriken – across the gap, and towards the face of the captain.

Responding almost a second too late, Gareth flinched backwards and raised his right forearm to cover his face. The spike thudded with a dull impact against his grey coat and fell to the floor with a clink. Clearly, Hai noted, the coat was magically armoured. Despite looking like it had been made by Hugo boss in a tailored slim fit, it must have had significant armour to stop one of Hai's shuriken.

He sniffed indignantly. IF a fox was to wear a long, flowing charcoal coat, he supposed that one like this would be suitable. If he wanted to look like an anime villain, then perhaps he would get one. If...

The two adversaries summed each other up across the gap. A lone bead of sweat had sprung from Gareth's right temple.

Matching the speed of a nogitsune was difficult, but he had done it, so far – thanks to years of arduous training, battle against numerous foes, an armoured coat, and magical swords that enabled him to fight a foe faster than he'd ever faced.

It was time to see if this Japanese fox could get as good as he gave.

Gareth leapt forward into Hai, right sword batting at the katana in front of the assassin, left sword spearing forward in a deadly thrust. Hai let the tip of his katana be turned aside by the first strike, allowing the tip to circle around to point at the floor, while raising the handle above his head. He leapt aside, outside of the incoming thrust, and now with his hands above his head, he was poised to bring Jundo – Purity – down in one strike to carve through his adversary's head, like a spoon through jelly.

There was a moment. In that moment lay the seed of a thousand different moments. Parry, riposte, cut thrust, turn, jump. Comment, laugh, shout, battle cry. The seeds of all these lay in that moment. Hai, ever efficient, said nothing. He simply brought his blade down. Of course, it was not a simple bringing down of a blade; that would be far too mundane. It was an ancient creature of nightmare, a master assassin, bringing down a magically sharpened ninja sword faster than the speed of thought. Too fast, even, for some to see.

In response, Gareth – seeing the trajectory of his opponent's cut – dived to his right in a roll, allowing him to drop beneath the approaching blade, giving him time to change his angle and distance for the next clash.

Except he had never fought anyone as fast as the black ash fox. It would have been a perfectly executed move against almost any other swordsman.

His trailing left foot was less than a millisecond behind

the rest of his body. It was all the time Hai needed to carry his slice further down – to sink it through Gareth's leg, which was already moving at an implausible speed. But not quite implausible enough.

So the seed, in this instance, turned out to be one of despair.

Gareth finished his roll and righted himself, only to find that he no longer had a left foot to land on. It had been severed mid-shin and, apart from the surprise of having suddenly lost part of his body, he was shocked at how painless it felt. He fell backwards against the wall, left leg now stretched in front of him, pouring out blood at a rate that spelled a quick and inevitable death.

He drew in a breath to cast a spell that would arrest the bleeding – he knew dozens – but sadly, it was the last breath he would ever take.

A fox didn't live 900 years by leaving wounded foes behind. Even ones as worthy as the good captain.

Gareth High-Oak died with a length of steel through his heart. He closed his eyes, and his head fell to his chest, a trickle of blood running out the left corner of his mouth and down his chin. Against the grey coat, and the white shirt beneath, the dark red was rather fetching, Hai thought.

His body slumped against the wall and the famous elvish short swords clanged like dropped cutlery to the floor.

Hai sighed. He pulled Jundo out of the captain's chest and wiped the blade against the fine grey overcoat. He sheathed his katana, and picked up the two elven short swords, which truly were of the finest quality. They slipped into a pocket inside his jacket, that gave the impression of being able to hold much more than it should be able to.

He looked back at the dead body of the captain. Another let down. Another foe not worthy of the title. His shoulders sagged almost imperceptibly. Life would always contain disappointments.

The small fox spirit in the shape of a Japanese elder turned towards the plinth, where the small black cube still rested. He pressed its sides in the sequence instructed. It let off a short ping, and a wave of power spread from the cube into the plinth on which it rested. There was a spark, like a light bulb blowing, and the stream of power that ran along the bars of the cages fizzled out. That easily, the containment was overcome. Now, to the killing.

He walked over to the first cage, manipulated the lock – bypassing the rudimentary spell that sealed it – and swung the door open.

The woman inside had waist-length, golden hair that shone lustrous even in the dim light. She was on her knees, her hands chained and affixed to the floor, and she looked up at the incoming assassin with wide, deep blue eyes, her expression a mixture of defiance and fear.

She was the most gorgeous woman he had ever seen, and he had seen many. Incidentally, nogitsune could mate with humans, and if there was one thing he could appreciate, it was beauty. It would be a waste for her to die… but still, there was beauty in a quick and sudden death.

The assassin's hand flashed out and flung another piece of steel. In the blink of an eye, it had crossed the space of the cell, and the beautiful Summer elf died with a black steel shard in her throat.

She died with her beautiful blue eyes open.

Nogitsune Hai backed out and made his way to the next cell. The elf in this one was also of the Summer court, but he was younger, and gentler in spirit. He opened his mouth to plead, but the bullet-like shuriken embedded in his temple, and he fell to the floor, still manacled, a small, crumpled pile. It was pitiful, really.

Two down, sixteen to go.

Hai moved on to the next cell in workmanlike fashion – he had to be done before the queen arrived.

ABOUT THE AUTHOR

Lance Horsman

When I'm not writing up a storm, I train and teach martial arts, attempt to overthrow the tyranny of the four legged, furry dictators in my home and occasionally, roleplay. I have a blog on my website at www.lancehorsman.com

Jump in and drop me a note, see some of my other work and keep up with the latest developments!